The Quest of the Land of the Eagle Feathers

The Book of Spring

By

Joe G. Morin & Jo Ann Bullard

Edited by Jann Kaufman

Copyright© 2018

Published by

Lyrics and Books from the Heart Publishing Company, Inc.

2018

Preface

Everything on the earth has a purpose. Every disease an herb to cure it and every person a mission. This is the Indian Theory of Existence.

Morning Star Salish

Seven people from different cultures are chosen to save The Land of the Eagle Feathers. Each character must overcome their own demons for the group to survive. The group's mission is full of mysticism, spirituality, danger, love, hate, spirits and good and evil forces.

The Land of the Eagle Feathers is in danger from outside forces. This land contains the knowledge and power to fight evil forces that try to control all things. On this mission, the characters must learn to trust each other and work together. They must find the knowledge that is contained in four books to save this sacred land for mankind. If they do not, The Land of the Eagle Feathers will be lost and the world as we know it.

In this quest to find the first book, nothing is what it seems. All of the characters have their own special skills and powers. Is each individual strong enough to survive the journey? Will they be able to work together with nobody being whom they seem to be? Will they be able to conquer everybody's worst enemy-themselves? Many have tried to save this land but failed. Will this group survive? If they survive, they will become known as The Keepers of the Yawi.

Table of Contents

Chapter I
By Invitation Only:
Why Was I Chosen?

They knew they were in trouble the second they heard the loud clang. A large boulder hit the side of their old red faded train's passenger car, shifting them sideways. The black rusty steam locomotive had been struggling to make it up the steep mountain grade. Their outdated passenger car started leaning and moving back and forth. The half sleeping passengers jumped out of their seats confused. Someone yelled, "What happened?" A voice near the back of the car answered, "It looks like a boulder has hit us. If another comes down this old track, we could be knocked off this mountain to the valley below." As if to answer the man's prediction, another boulder hit the left front of the passenger car. The force of it knocked the passenger car off its tracks.

Luckily, the caboose behind them had become disconnected from the train and rolled back down the tracks. That didn't help them much. Their car was halfway over the edge of the cliff beside the tracks. Slowly, they could feel the car being pulled off the side of the mountain. The passenger car was moving ever so close to the edge of the cliff where a thousand feet below a green mountain valley was waiting for them. The back end of the car was starting to slide over, causing the back of the passenger car to dip downward.

Everything in the passenger car started sliding down toward the end of the car. Rose had been sitting in the left side passenger seat. Grabbing the seat in front of her, she held on to it. An Italian looking man pointed at an exit door and yelled for everyone to go for it. Rose stood up and turned her body toward the left side exit door. While doing this, the grip of her hand on the seat in front of her loosened, causing her to slide sideways toward the end of the car. She tried to grab the back of her seat, but she was slipping too fast. Looking at the back of the car, she could see that the back door of the car was open. Nothing was there but open space. Suddenly, she felt a strong hand grab her arm and tell her to hold on. The next thing she knew was she was being pulled out of the car by a young blond man. She did note that he was a handsome young man at that.

There were still other people in the car. The passenger car was still slipping. What she saw next was amazing. Apparently, the remaining passengers had formed their own ladder. They were working together. The farthest passenger on the end of the human ladder would pull themselves up, using the person in front of them. One by one, a passenger rolled out of the exit. With help from Rose beside him, the blond man assisted each one to the ground. Finally, just as the passenger car decoupled from the train, a strong black gentleman jumped free to safety. Rose counted that there were six passengers besides her standing on the tracks: three women and three men. All Rose could say with her Cajun accent was, "Nice to meet you. My name is Rose." All that the others could do was laugh.

A dark, angry cloud suddenly came over the mountain top towards them. Heavy snow from it was making everything white beneath it. Soon the passengers couldn't see a thing in front of them or behind them. It was what you call "white out conditions." The passengers didn't dare move due to the steep cliffs located only feet from them on both sides of the tracks. In a couple of minutes, the cloud disappeared. The passengers were covered by the white snow. Their clothes were wet and cold. A cold wind from the north had started blowing. The snow had stopped but still covered the ground and rocks with a white blanket.

"Why are you standing out here? You need to get back on this passenger car. We are losing time. We only stopped to move a small boulder in front of the locomotive," said the conductor in a loud somewhat irritated voice. The group was puzzled by what the conductor said. Then they realized that the conductor was in the passenger car that they had just escaped from, but the passenger car was standing on the tracks upright and attached to the caboose. It didn't have a dent or even a deep scratch on it. It was as if nothing had happened. Instead of saying anything, Rose could only whistle.

"You all look like you have seen a ghost or something," said the old fat conductor in his black suit. "Well, get on," yelled the conductor. "Haven't you seen a passenger car before?" One of the passengers yelled, "I don't know if we want to get on that train." The gray headed conductor said back, "If you don't, you will freeze in those wet clothes in minutes. That old north wind is very cold this high up. I don't think you have any choice but to get on this here train right now."

Rose said, as she brushed the wet snow off her blouse, "I don't know about you, but I ain't standing out here freezing to death when I can get in a warm passenger car. Those drinks that the conductor served us must have had a powerful effect on us. I guess we better get back on, but I am taking the seat next to the exit door." The rest of the nervous group watched her get on the train. The group reluctantly and cautiously followed her. They knew that they didn't have any choice but to do so. The last one to get on was the handsome Italian man. His cool and calm facial expression gave the impression that he knew more about this than he let on.

The old steam locomotive's engine shuddered as it started to move the train back up the mountain. The small group of strangers all sat close together. Nobody dared to say a word. They didn't know what to say. Finally, Rose said, "I know that you experienced the same thing I did." Everyone nodded their heads. She didn't have to say anything more. Everyone was thinking the same things. What have I got myself into by coming here? What is waiting for us on the top of this mountain?

There was something more that nobody was talking about. Each one of them had a reason for being here. Each one was searching for something missing. Maybe, they wanted a purpose or a philosophy to guide them. After this incident, each knew their decision to come probably was the best decision or the worst they would ever make. They knew that only a few people ever returned from where they were going; at least, that was according to the legends about the place. They would keep this fact to themselves, especially since nobody knew each other. There could be many different reasons why these people were here. Not all of them were good.

The old train lumbered in from traveling the steep grade into the train station. A tall thin Asian woman with long black hair named Lo Ming had been observing the other members of this group. She had been on adventures all over the world. She had never had one start like this.

Her knowledge about Chinese and Far Eastern myths and legends was quite extensive. She was incredibly surprised that one day several months ago she received an invitation to take a wilderness trip to a place called The Land of the Eagle Feathers. The invitation was too good to pass up. She had almost forgotten about such a place. But why did she receive such an invitation? Was it just one of those things that happened by chance, or was it fate? This was not the first time she had heard about this land. Her mother and father had told her about this land. They had told her bedtime stories about a land of myths and spirits, a beautiful, almost virgin land, full of beauty and of dangers. The dangers came from evil people who wanted this land for themselves and would not stop until they obtained it. They wanted the land for its riches and secrets. Lo Ming had shrugged these stories off as just fairy tales.

She would have to see for herself what this journey would bring. Maybe, she would find answers to questions about herself that she needed answered in this mysterious land. She could sense that several of the others in the group had similar feelings. If this journey was going to be anything like what they had just experienced, it would a journey of a lifetime.

A young Native American lady named June was seated next to Lo Ming. Her skin was the color of light copper. Her hair was a very dark brown, almost black, long and in braids. She looked like she had just graduated from graduate school except for her dress and her dark brown eyes. She dressed to blend in. She didn't want to stand out. Her eyes seemed to be studying and searching, almost researching what she was observing. There was something about her eyes. They were full of loneliness. Maybe, this trip was what she needed. Her grandfather, a great medicine man in her tribe, had told her that she needed to go on a quest. This trip was to be her quest for the truth of why she existed. When her grandfather saw the invitation, he told her that she had no choice but to go. The great spirits of The Land of the Eagle Feathers were commanding her to come. She had a destiny to fulfill.

The train's brakes made a grinding sound as the train slowly came to a stop by the old rail station in the middle of town. This was a small town nestled in the mountains. The passengers could see a roll of old wooden houses and businesses, lining both sides of the train tracks. There

8

were several local citizens dressed in period clothing from the late 18th century.

The small group of passengers stepped down from the old faded red passenger car onto the wooden platform near the old rail station, seemingly looking for someone. "We are looking for our guide. His name is John," said the dark gentleman to the conductor. The conductor pointed toward a large oak tree about 150 feet away. "He will be over there. I hope you have a better time than the last ones who took a trip with him. Be careful, not everyone comes back from his field trips," the conductor shook his head as he smiled back.

The conductor told everyone to go inside the train station. It would take him about 30 minutes to get their belongings from the baggage car. "There's hot coffee, Earl Grey Tea, and other beverages with some snacks in the main lobby. John is due to be here around noon. There are rocking chairs out front to sit on while you wait."

Lo Ming and the dark gentleman were glad there was some tea that they were familiar with. They wondered why he said Earl Grey. It's like he knew that it was their favorite tea. Everyone went into the station's lobby. A white cloth covered table with fine china settings awaited them. Lo Ming recognized the fine old set of china at once. This wasn't just any ordinary set of china. It was unbelievably valuable. A set like this would cost many thousands of dollars. There were at least two sets of this china: one with Earl Grey Tea and one for coffee. Several tables had place settings for people to sit, with place cards by each. There were fancy cakes and pastries on each table. This was certainly a pleasant surprise for everyone. It didn't take long for everyone to get their coffee or tea and be seated at their place setting.

Lo Ming started to reach for the teapot of Earl Grey Tea when the dark gentleman said to her, "Let me pour that for you." Lo Ming knew that accent. It had to be Australian. "Let me introduce myself. My name is Moses," he said with a smile. "I see that you like the same tea as I do." Lo Ming replied, "My name is Lo Ming. Glad to meet you," introducing herself.

Lo Ming noticed that their place settings were next to each other. Moses was dressed like a guide from the Outback of Australia. He had on a dark brown heavy work shirt that had the top buttons open with a leather vest that was made from crocodile skin. A large knife was attached to his leather belt with a black leather whip tied to the right leg of his leather chaps. His hat was an Australian bush hat. He was of mixed blood; she could tell he had some Asian blood in him. One thing for sure, he was a handsome man. "This could be an interesting trip," Lo Ming thought, as they sat down together.

Moses was instantly attracted to Lo Ming's striking beauty. She was exotic and sensual in her tight red silk dress with black dragon designs. He loved the way she carried herself. He could sense that she was an independent woman who could take care of herself.

Moses couldn't help himself. He knew it wasn't always the correct thing to do, but he did it anyway. He looked directly into her eyes. He would use his gift to try to understand more about her.

He was fascinated that she stared back into his. He could feel her mind searching inside his mind for answers. At first, he was surprised. He remembered what his Chinese mother had told him: one day he would meet a beautiful Asian woman who would be the love of his life. This must be the one. He laughed. Lo Ming asked him, "What was so funny?" Moses answered her by saying, "I just remembered something my mother had said." Lo Ming replied to him, "Your mother must be a wise woman." Moses stared back at Lo Ming and said, "More than you will ever know." Lo Ming replied, "A son must do as his mother tells him." Moses laughed saying, "Yes, I know. I will definitely do what she told me."

Moses decided to tell Lo Ming how he got here. He had received an invitation about twelve months ago. He had been working in his gold mines and opal mines for several months when a messenger brought him a letter in the Outback of Australia. How did the messenger find him? Nobody knew where his mines were located. This upset him so much that he decided to sell them to his partner for a few million dollars. Besides, he wasn't cut out for mining. He loved the outdoors and wild animals too much to be a miner.

Lo Ming listened to Moses' story with interest. She had heard of a bi-racial man from Australia that could talk to animals. He was part native and part Chinese. She liked the way he had kept himself in shape. His muscular arms told her a lot about him. Even though he was average in height and stocky, he moved with grace and a light foot much like a wild animal stalking his prey. His heroic exploits were legendary in the Far East, where she spent time collecting and selling ancient artifacts. Perhaps, that is why he is here. A man like this lived for adventure. Maybe…it was just destiny that he was here. Maybe… his mother was right.

Rose sat down beside the tan, blond young man who had saved her in the passenger car. His tie-dyed T-shirt and shorts with sandals made him look like a "surfer dude." Rose could sense that he was more than he seemed. He told her that his name was Nick, and that he loved the outdoors.

There was sadness in his voice. It was his eyes that told the story. He had what warriors called the "Thousand Mile

Stare." He didn't know why, but he told Rose that he had heard voices and saw visions that told him to go on a journey to a far away land. When he received his invitation to come on this journey, he felt it was his destiny. His grandfather told him that he must go, but to be careful. His grandfather knew of this place and of the man called John.

What Nick didn't tell her was that he had spent several months in a mental hospital. This trip was more for him than a wilderness trip. Rose noted that Nick had a way of not talking too much about himself. He had a past, but that was what made him so much more interesting. She introduced herself to him as Rose.

Nick looked at Rose. She had a sensual charm about her. She had to be in her late 30's. She was very pretty. He loved her white low-cut blouse with stars and planets in purple with a flowing solid purple skirt. Her dress and smooth dark brown skin reminded him of a fortune teller who he once saw in a circus. She wore a lot of jewelry on her arms and neck. The necklace on her neck hung down between her full breasts. It had a large crystal attached to it. She was short and had curves of a grown woman. Her shoulder length black hair was accented with a white ribbon. Her eyes were dark and brooding with a flash of mischief in them. Now this was a real woman.

Rose started to get up to get her another cup of coffee. Nick reached out his hand and said he would get it for her. As she handed the coffee cup to him, his hand touched hers for a brief second. That's all it took for him to know that she was here for a purpose. He could feel her pain. The pain of losing someone who she had loved very much. Little did Nick know that Rose, in that brief instant of touching, had found out more about him than he would want anyone to ever know. The visions of what she saw in his mind frightened her.

If there was anyone that was the life of a party, it was the Italian man. He was busy talking to everyone. He had long since introduced himself as Antonio. Every woman here recognized the type of man he was. He was a playboy. He was charming and very handsome. His dark Italian features gave him an air of mystery.

The group wondered why a man such as Antonio would be invited on this trip. Antonio had told everyone that he had the ability to decipher ancient writings and text. He bragged about knowing hundreds of languages. Not only could he translate them, he could speak and translate them into other languages. This ability led him to work for the Vatican many years ago. He left them because their values conflicted with his lifestyle. He had decided to free-lance. He couldn't pass up this opportunity to come here. It would only assist him in getting more jobs. The members of the group had wondered why he was here. He still didn't look like anyone who would go on a wilderness expedition.

Antonio was talking to a woman in her mid-thirties with shoulder length light brown hair. She had told everyone that her name was Mary. It seems that she loved going on wilderness expeditions. Her specialty was ancient medicines and legends. She had spent time in the southwest desert of North America, as well as South American jungles, studying and collecting native cures and medicine plants. She couldn't pass up this trip when she got an invitation in the mail to come. It would make a good topic for her next publication in medical journals. Besides being a medical doctor, she was a college professor.

June sat down beside Antonio and Mary. Antonio asked her what her name was. She told him it was June. Antonio asked her if she had introduced herself to everyone. He had noticed she appeared to be shy. She had been staying somewhat to herself. He decided to introduce her to the other members of the group. "Let me introduce this young lady to you," he said as he stood up. "Her name is June. Judging by her heritage, which is Native American, her Indian name is Dehaluyi. Dehaluyi is the name for the Cherokee moon or month of June. This month means the start of the growing season of corn and other plants. I do know of a legend of a beautiful Indian maiden named Dehaluyi that was a Meda or Priestess. It was said that she would go on many journeys or quests to save many people. Perhaps, June is the one." June looked stunned. She stood up and said to the group, "Antonio was right about my Native American name. I find the name June more convenient for me for many reasons. It is much easier for people to pronounce. You probably know the other reasons. I don't know about the Meda part of Antonio's statement. It is a nice legend. I must say, Antonio, your linguist skills are remarkable to know the translation of my name."

As June sat down, she could feel what the others were thinking. This demonstration by Antonio of his language skills and knowledge of legends backed up his story of being a very knowledgeable linguist. June was amazed that Antonio knew about the legend. It would almost be impossible for anyone to know about this legend, especially a white man. How did he know that I was Cherokee? Antonio either had made a lucky guess or knew more than what he should know. There was another thing about him. Antonio had been too eager to show his skills to the others. She could feel that he was not just a linguist. He was something else.

I sent word to the group in the station that I had arrived at the corral. As the group walked out of the train station toward me, they stopped and looked around. The old buildings were boarded up. Only the smell of coal smoke was all that was left of the train. It looked as if the train had already pulled out of the station. Nobody was on the streets or in the buildings except an old man, sitting in a rocking chair with his dog. This old man was dressed in faded old bib overalls with an old worn red flannel shirt. He had an old gray striped railroad cap on top of his almost bald head. His white beard had signs of years of chewing tobacco. He had a pocketknife, using it to whittle on a stick of wood.

Antonio asked the old man where everyone was. The old man spat some tobacco juice into a rusty coffee can on the wooden porch floor and replied, "What do you mean by that? There's not been anyone living here for over a hundred years. Why, the last train to stop here was in the spring about twenty years ago. Now, that last group of people that I saw here were like you. They said that had come on an old steam locomotive train. They said something like they were going into the mountains on an expedition with John. He's a guide of some sorts. If you are going with him, I wish you luck." Antonio asked, "Why he said that to them?" The Old man shook his head and said, "Because nobody came back with him the last time." Nick pointed toward a man, sitting by a large oak tree with a corral full of horses. "That must be John," Nick said. Antonio turned back to say something to the old man, but he was gone and so was his dog.

"Why doesn't that surprise me?" said Antonio of the disappearing old man and his dog to the members of the group. Rose replied to him, "Don't let anything about this place surprise you. This land is anything but normal. Isn't it why we all came? This land has its secrets like many of you do. Come on, let's go meet this John down there by the oak tree. What do you have to lose?" Moses muttered something under his breath that sounded like, "Only our lives."

I could see for the first time that everyone I had invited on my wilderness expedition had arrived. At least, they had made it. Many others had not survived to get this far through the years. That train ride up from the valley below was always dangerous. I could tell that they were wondering about this place. They must have thought they had traveled back in time. The whole station was out of place for modern times. This old train station was called "Eagle Station." Over the years, I would pick up several tourists and take them on expeditions into the mountains. An old 1880's steam locomotive train would stop and leave some passengers off. Some people called it a ghost train because it was only seen briefly every twenty years or so.

While I had been waiting for them to finish their tea and coffee in the railroad station, I had observed that the fat conductor in his old black uniform with a gold watch chain attached to his belt had their belongings put carefully on the old station's wooden platform. The conductor looked at me and smiled. Then he shouted, "All aboard," even though he knew that there was nobody to get on the train. We both knew it could be a one-way journey.

The old train pulled slowly out with its cars clanking. Its steam and smoke covered everything in sight. When all the black coal smoke and steam disappeared, the train was gone. A short time later, the passengers walked out of the station house. It was interesting to see how they would react to the train being gone. At first, they just stared at the train tracks. Everything was deathly quiet. The whole place was deserted. The only thing left was the station and the rusty train tracks that seemed to go nowhere. I could see them talking to the old man who would only show up with his dog when the train delivered passengers. By now, the group must be wondering what was going to happen next. I could feel their misgivings about this trip. They had a wide range of emotions about them. Some of them were excited, and some were apprehensive, but everyone was confused. It was too late for them to back out now. There was no other option but to continue.

As they started walking toward me, I recognized everyone in this group. In front of me was the most unusual or unique collection of characters who I had ever had the pleasure to observe. They certainly were not the run of the mill folks. I looked at the list on my roster on the clipboard. I started checking each one off my list of names. There was one thing that they didn't have any idea about. I had selected each individual with a purpose in mind. Each one was chosen for several reasons: chakra, astrological sign, and heritage.

This wilderness expedition would not be anything like they would have expected. There would be many trials ahead of them. If they had the ability to work together, they would be instrumental in saving a mysterious and mystical land from ruthless beings. In doing so, this group would become legends. If the great spirits are pleased, they would forever be known as: **The Keepers of the Yawi**. Only one thing stood in their way. They would have to survive the journey first.

The group arrived in front of me. I introduced myself to them. "My name is John. I want to congratulate you for being selected for this expedition to The Land of the Eagle Feathers. Only a very few have ever been invited to go there. I am very glad to have you with me on this journey. I am going to explain why you were selected for this expedition."

Everyone looked at each other. I knew that they couldn't wait for an explanation about why they were chosen to be here. I would tell them only what they needed to know for now. The spirits of The Land of the Eagle Feathers would test them before allowing them to continue to the next part of their journey. If they didn't pass their tests, they would not be allowed to live or return. It would be a one-way trip for them. The same would be for me. If I failed this time to have selected the right individuals, I would not return. I had failed too many times. The Great Spirits of this land had given me one last chance to remain alive. It didn't matter anyway. If this group failed, there would be no Land of the Eagle Feathers left to save. I would choose my words carefully to explain as best I could what laid ahead of them.

"I know you have studied what you can about the legends surrounding The Land of the Eagle Feathers. I will tell you that this land does exist. It is a mysterious and mystical land. I will take you to this land. You were chosen for this journey for one reason. Each of you have special skills and powers. The Great Spirits of this land need your gifts. They need them because The Land of the Eagle Feathers is under siege. There are many groups that want this land for their own purposes. Some want the riches and wealth of the land; those groups are easier to handle. It is the groups that want the most important thing that The Land of the Eagle Feathers possesses that are the most dangerous. I know you know what that is." Before I could say it, several of the group answered at once, "The powers of this land."

"I know you know about what would happen if anyone would ever get their hands on such knowledge. Nobody or anything could stop them from controlling everything. They would destroy The Land of the Eagle Feathers and anything else that got in their way."

"So why do the Elders of this land need us?" asked Nick. I answered his question, "Because pretty soon the Elders and Spirits of The Land of the Eagle Feathers will be too weak to protect the land from those wanting it for themselves. The centuries of protecting the land has weakened them while the groups have become stronger. The Elders and Spirits need the knowledge of the universe to stop them once and for all."

"The legends say that they hid the knowledge, and even they don't know the whereabouts of the books that contain it," said Lo Ming.

"It doesn't take a genius to figure out that we have been chosen to find them," stated June.

"There's only one problem," said Moses. "The legends say that most people that have tried to find them died trying,"

"Each one of you will have to make that decision. It goes something like this. Unless all of you go, we might not have the powers and skills needed to survive the quest to find the books."

"We will need to go through a passage in the Great Green Mountains. This passage is well hidden. We will need to reach a sacred mountain top before the first night of spring. We have a council meeting to attend with a Great Elder of this land. It will take us several days to get there. It will not be an easy journey to the mountain ridge top of the sacred mountain where a council meeting will be held.

I know that you know the legends about this land. The legends are right: to meet with the Great Elder is a great honor. I only hope that you will prove worthy to meet with him. If you do not prove you are worthy of such a meeting, you may die on the way there. The Great Elder will explain the ways and culture of this sacred land. First, you must prove yourselves worthy to the Elders and spirits of this land.

An invitation to this expedition is for only those who are deemed worthy of such a privilege. This is your last chance to leave. Remember this. There are people that will stop at nothing to find out more about this mysterious land. They want to exploit it for their own gains. They are dangerous. They may even try to hurt or kill you to obtain your knowledge. Eliminating you would be no more to them than swatting a fly.

Each of you has special talents or powers. These skills could make a difference in our survival. It will take all of your knowledge and skills to survive. If you still want to go, get dressed in suitable clothes and take your gear to the horses over there. Don't take anything that you can't carry on your own backs. The horses are only for the first part of the trip. The rest will be on foot in the rough mountain ranges. Remember that I am in charge. You will need to follow my orders to stay safe."

I looked at everyone and asked them individually if they were going. June, Rose, Nick, and Antonio said 'yes' quickly. Mary, Lo Ming and Moses hesitated for a few seconds before answering. I would have to wait to see if their hesitation meant anything. Everyone did answer "Yes." I didn't want anyone saying that I had forced them to go. There was one thing that I didn't tell them. Once they had stepped foot on that train, they didn't have any other choice but to come. It was their destiny.

As the group headed back to the railroad station to change, June spoke first. "I have heard from my grandfather about this land John is talking about. There are great legends about it. In my tribe, many braves have tried to find it. Many never returned from the quest to find it." Several others in the group said the same thing. Their grandfathers or other close relatives had told them stories about this land, but they all agreed that they had thought that it was just a myth or legend. June told them that one thing is clear. "I know why several of us received invitations. We have something in common. We were chosen for this expedition because of our ancestors." If the others agreed with her, nobody acknowledged it. June was the Libra, the peacekeeper. She would inspire to seek peace, harmony and co-operation in the group.

Everyone wondered who this John was. Could he be trusted with their lives? Did they have any other choice? There was only one thing to do to find out: follow him.

The group decided to have a little meeting on the railroad station porch before going back to the corral to join John. Soon, everyone had changed their clothes and had gotten their belongings. There were several chairs and benches on the porch. Lo Ming was the first to speak. "I have studied ancient legends and cultures. I feel that I should tell you something about the legends associated with The Land of the Eagle Feathers. As the legend goes, The Land of the Eagle Feathers holds many secrets. It is said that this land contains the secrets to unleashing unimaginable forces. These forces are so powerful that only the Great Spirits of this land were entrusted with them. These secrets are contained in four books. Each book relates to a season of the year, Spring, Summer, Fall, and Winter.

For generations, groups of people wanted these secrets. Some wanted to control the world. Some wanted the resources of this land, such as jewels; gold; silver and other precious materials. It is the secrets hidden in this land that they want the most. To keep anyone from taking the greatest secrets, the Great Elders of this land hid the knowledge in four books. They titled each book by the season they were written for such as: ***The Book of Spring; The Book of Summer; The Book of Fall*** and finally ***The Book of Winter***. The only way one could access any of these books is to have the Great Elders give the first one to you. To do that, you must be worthy of their respect. To obtain the other books, you must return to meet with the Council and the Great Elder the first night of each season. Each book contains clues to the next book.

There is something else that I know. In order to protect the knowledge in the books, the Great Elders had a Great Medicine Man hide the last book in a special place. The Great Medicine Man took all the most important knowledge and put it in the last book, *The Book of Winter*. To protect the location of The Book of Winter, even the Great Elders of this land do not know where the last book is located. You must decipher the first book and use clues contained in that book to locate the next book, finally obtaining clues to the most important book: *The Book of Winter*. That's probably why Antonio is here. Only a person gifted in ancient languages and codes could decipher the pages of each book. Lo Ming is the Aries in the group. Considering that Aries is a fire sign, her battle cry is "Let's get started." Her passion and bravery will be great assets in the quests ahead.

"Now let me get this straight, to obtain the riches and secrets of this land, it takes collecting four books. The first book contains clues to find the next book with each book containing clues to the next one until the last book, which contains the greatest knowledge of all," stated Nick. "But why should the Elders want anyone to obtain these books?" It is not surprising that Nick would ask questions. Nick is the Aquarius in the group and has a curious nature. He is not what he seems.

"Remember what John said, the Elders do not have the strength to keep the evil groups out of the land by themselves anymore. The many years of fighting them has taken a toll on their powers. They need the knowledge contained in *The Book of Winter* to strengthen themselves. With that book, no force could conquer them," said June.

Rose had listened to the others talk. Very softly, she said, "There are things that some of you left out. The Great Medicine Man made it almost impossible for the Elders of the tribe to get the books. The knowledge of the last book is so powerful that it would be difficult for anyone to resist having it, even one of the Elders. That is why he made one thing to keep even them from getting it very easily. It would take an incredibly special group of people to obtain the last book. Legends say that several groups have tried but were not successful." Rose is the Scorpio of the group. She understands the rules of the universe. She will be the most loyal member. She will keep the other members on their mission. She will be able to see through the others.

Mary had been listening to the others talk. She knew all about the legends. She was torn. She knew that with each legend there is some truth and some fiction. She was trying to sort this out. "How do we know this?" said Mary. Mary is the Pisces of the group. She knows the truth already. Her emphatic and intuitive skills will always be correct.

Antonio is a player. He was analyzing each member of the group. He is a survivor. He would have to depend on the other members of the group to survive. Antonio stated to the others, "We must get one thing straight right now. We will need to depend on each other. I only hope that each of you have the skills that we need. Nobody can let us down." Antonio is the Capricorn of the group. Capricorns are known to be ruthless in going after what they want. However, they are also quite sensitive with those they care about. These traits will be helpful. Eventually, the group will see both sides of Antonio.

Moses is a man that speaks his mind. He looked at each member of the group. "I agree with Antonio. We will see if each of us measures up to this task ahead. We must think as one. In nature, only the strong survive. We will see if you all are strong enough. I will make this my mission to see that you measure up," Moses laughed. Moses is a natural born adventurer. He is the Sagittarius of the group. Nobody knew whether Moses was serious or not. He did have a sense of humor. One thing he did have was that when he sets his sights on something, he does not quit until he gets it.

I interrupted the group on the porch. I asked them what they were meeting about, but all I got in return was something about them getting to know each other better. I intuitively knew that that was not the full truth. I would let that go for now. I knew that this group would figure everything out sooner or later. They had all heard of the legends of this land. They knew that nobody had ever been able to find the last book. They knew legends say that everyone who has tried to get the books has not been heard of since.

I laughed to myself. It seems that each one will not tell everything they knew. Each one still wants to come. That is why I thought that they just might survive this journey. It would not take a genius to figure out why we were starting in the last days of winter, the most dangerous time of the year in mountain terrain.

I led them back to the corral. I had a surprise for them under the shade of the great oak tree, I had fixed a Southern Style Barbeque for them with all the fixings. I told them to eat up. This was the last big meal they would be having for a while. It didn't take long for them to dive into the food. I took another look at this group. I knew what they were not saying out loud; "What did I get myself into?"

Chapter II
The Journey Begins:
Are We Worthy?

Within an hour, we were mounted and on our way. I could see that most of them were good on horses. One or two could use a little more practice. I was impressed with June and Moses. Mary seemed to be a natural. There was something about the way that she rode that was eating at my memory.

The logging trail that we were following hadn't been used for years. It was mostly overgrown and covered with grass and weeds. A small mountain stream was to the left of us. The fast running water that ran over and through the boulders and rocks made a loud rushing sound that drowned out any possible conversation. Being the first day, everyone was alert. I noticed that Moses looked uneasy. Maybe, this was because this was not his usual habitat, but that wasn't it. He was on the lead horse with us following him. I had told him to just follow the trail. I was on the last horse, following the others. I wanted to watch how everyone dealt with the trail.

Suddenly, Moses jumped off his horse and ran ahead of us. He was fast. Before I could stop him, he leaped up and grabbed something from a low-lying branch. The large rope like thing in his hands curled up, but his hands moved quickly and caught it by the back of its head. We all stopped. Moses had probably one of biggest Timber Rattlers that ever existed in his hands. It was over two yards long and about a foot in diameter.

Bending over, Moses said something to the large rattlesnake and carefully placed it in the brush by the trail. It was as if they could communicate to each other. I had wanted to know if Moses truly had this special skill. Only the most gifted of Bushman had this power. If Moses did not have this power, I wouldn't have needed to worry about him. The snake would have killed him. I was glad old Levi, the snake, didn't. If he did, Moses' mother would probably kill me.

The others behind me observed this scene. They were worried that the snake would be by the trail and strike us when we passed. The only thing Moses said was that the snake was now our friend and would always be and not to worry about him anymore. This pleased me because I now knew that Moses had proved himself worthy. By worthy, I mean that he did not have to kill to take care of the snake. He used his abilities to prevent harm to the snake and others. His father and mother would be proud of him. They had taught him well.

Nobody said anything about what Moses had done. Rose seemed to be studying Moses carefully. She had questions about what had happened, but she would wait until the time was right. There was one thing she did know, and that was that Moses had special powers. Her crystal ball had told her some things about him. He had skills that would prove to be useful in the future. She smiled to herself. Lo Ming would be a good match for him. Lo Ming was more than an equal to him in many ways.

Nick could sense that something was amiss. Not only could he sense the presence of the timber rattler, he thought that something or someone was watching our every move. Its presence worried him. The last time that he felt a presence this strong resulted in a disaster. He knew that everyone thought that he was just a dumb surfer bum with his dark tan and almost white blond hair. They all looked at him as a spoiled, rich brat that didn't have any business being here. Why should he care about what they thought? What they didn't know was that he was more than that. He had to find out why the voices and dreams didn't stop each night, and why was he drawn to come here?

June rode her horse like she was born to the saddle. Her horse and June were like one. I recognized that she was probably what one would call a "horse whisperer." As we crossed the difficult mountain stream and around the steep terrain, the horse instinctively moved to her slightest touch or voice command. No matter how hard the trail became, one would think that she was just taking a stroll in the park. Her grandfather had taught her well. That was not the reason she was here. Her tribe and ancestors once lived here. It would be her skills as a great medicine woman that would be needed in the future.

June noticed that the trail was slowly starting to disappear. The trail was growing fainter. The weeds, plants, and tall grasses were reclaiming it. It reminded her of the many miles of trails she had walked or ridden in her life. It was like a principle of nature: the longer the trail, the more it would slowly start disappearing. This meant that hikers would start turning back as the trail got further from civilization. If we kept going, one thing was for sure, we would be on a faint trail that nobody had been on for many years. Now that's when things could get interesting for all of us, she thought, and that brought a smile to her face.

The day was quickly turning to night. I had decided to take them to a secret place that was one of my favorite spots in these mountains. I rode my horse to the front, motioning for them to follow me off the main trail. We pushed our way through some thick brush and around several stands of tall trees. Carefully and slowly, we made our way down to a mountain meadow that had good grass and water. What made this place different was a hot spring with a small pool of hot water which was large enough for several people.

The steam from the hot springs gave this place an air of mystery and resembled something almost mystical. Many years ago, I had taken another group here. Things with that group did not go well. It seems that the hot spring makes it easy to tell people what you think even if it hurts others. These opinions can cause problems and can even turn people against one another. The result of that was nobody returned from that expedition.

I had assigned each member of our group certain jobs to do when it was time to pitch camp. I would observe how well this group would work together to get things done quickly. Being located half-way up the narrow mountain valley, the sun would be setting quickly.

I studied the interactions between the members of our group with each other. I was pleasantly surprised in the way they worked together. They respected each other. Even though they had only met early today, they were bonding in ways much differently than I had ever observed in any other of my guided groups through the years. This group just might prove to be up to the tasks ahead.

Nick proved to be more talented in the field than most of our group expected. He had been assigned to cook our first meal. His resume stated that he had taken a couple of years of culinary arts training. I decided to see if he could cook. Anyone can cook in a modern kitchen, but it takes a lot of skill to cook over an open fire. I had given him the last of our fresh food and vegetables. In a Dutch oven, he made a stew with dumplings. The seasonings were perfect. He had even found some herbs in the meadow to spice it up a bit. The wild onions gave it an aroma that spread through the camp. For dessert, Nick made cornbread filled with blackberries and dried fruit.

The group's opinions about him were changing. I knew that Nick was more than what met the eye. He was more experienced about the out of doors than one would think. I didn't select him for this trip due to his cooking talent. We would need his other talents in the future. I had seen him in action. He had a dark deadly side. The army had trained him well. There's an old fable about a wolf in sheep's clothing that fits Nick. He had dressed in old faded desert army khakis with worn boots, the way many hippies dressed years ago. He looked harmless enough, but I knew different. I would have to keep a close eye on this boy.

After the meal, we still had enough time to go to the hot spring to relax. It didn't take any persuading for everyone to start down to the hot pool. It seems that modesty was not a trademark of this group. Nobody had brought a swimsuit. Everyone put on shorts and t-shirts.

Everyone was in great shape. That is when I noticed something that would shock me. Mary had a small colorful butterfly tattoo in the small of her back and one on her right shoulder. At first, I could not stop looking at them, but Mary spoke first. "Haven't you seen a butterfly tattoo before?" she softly whispered in my ear. I looked at her and whispered, "Only once on a woman that I knew long ago, and I thought was long dead." She whispered back, "Maybe, she just got lost and has come back to haunt your soul." With that, I jumped out of the pool and went back to our camp.

I didn't stay at camp long. I needed to see the chemistry of this group. I slipped back through the forest at the edge of the meadow to observe. That's when I noticed him and the white wolf by his side. On the opposite side of the meadow, I could faintly see that a Native American brave in buckskins was watching from the woods. I had felt his presence before. They had sent him to watch and observe us.

Everyone in the hot spring seemed to be having a good time. The whiskey and rum that I had left was being drunk and passed around. Rose seemed to have taken a shine to Nick. She was teasing him with her charm and beauty.

Nick had what you would call a six pack and muscular arms and legs. Rose's eyes seemed to linger on his body. Her smile was wickedly sensual, and her eyes flashed at him. He was spellbound by her. He started splashing water at her. She returned the favor.

He grabbed her and pushed her under the water. To his surprise, she easily tossed him off her. She smiled, placed her forefinger on his chest, and said, "Not so fast, young man, I'm not so sure about you yet." With that, she slowly and very sensually climbed out of the pool. Looking like a picture of Venus, she walked back to her tent. She smiled. She knew she was driving young Nick crazy.

All the others started to have fun splashing and talking. I noticed that Moses and Lo Ming just stared at each other's eyes. They seemed to be communicating somehow and were very serious. Whatever they were sharing with each other nobody could know, but there was something there. Antonio was busy talking to Mary and June. You could see that he had the gift of gab for sweet talking women. His accent was very appealing to them especially because he was a man of mystery to us.

As I left them all to their fun, I made sure that the Indian Brave and his wolf were gone. Tomorrow the trail would be getting more difficult. Let them have their fun tonight. It would be no picnic from now on.

Everyone was up and ready for breakfast. Nick had fixed some pancakes. He had found some wild honey for them in a nearby hollow tree. Carefully, he had smoked the bees out and didn't even get one sting. After breakfast, we packed our horses. We started out through a faint trail in the hemlock trees to the main trail. Moses noticed that the terrain was getting much rougher and difficult for the horses. He thought that he saw something in the dark brush on the other side of the mountain stream. He knew it was not a man or an animal. Spirits have a way about them. They are not always friendly. I watched the others to see if they sensed it. I could see they did seem uneasy. Some were nervous and unsure about something.

As we started to cross the narrow gap between two high peaks, June stopped her horse. She was in the lead. This stopped us all. She turned her horse to us and said, "This land before us is dangerous." It is full of spirits and other creatures that you have not encountered before. My elders taught me about such things. To some, they are only myths and legends, but I know better. The spirits are restless. They will be testing us to see if we are worthy to continue.

She raised her arms to the sky and closed her eyes. High above, a golden hawk was flying, gliding on the updrafts of the mountains. It circled us and dove straight at June. In an instant, the golden hawk landed on her right outstretched arm and vanished in a few seconds into a cloud of smoke. A cold wind blew the trees around us. Suddenly, everything was silent. She turned her horse back to the trail. Starting up the trail again, all she said was that we had permission to go on.

We crossed the mountain gap. There was a small valley about a half a mile long with rich flowing grass. A stream was on the right side of it. Moses noted that there was a horse and mule at the far end of the valley grazing. Soon, everyone realized that we were not alone. Stopping the group, I told them that I had sent for Morning Star to take care of our horses. They asked, "Why?" I told them that we would have to leave the horses here. It was too dangerous for them to travel further. We would pitch camp here for the night. I told them that nobody was to go alone to any place from now on. There were too many things that could harm you here. Antonio began to wonder what he had gotten himself into. It was a feeling that was spreading amongst the others.

Reaching the far end of the valley, Morning Star came out to greet us. She had on a dark brown buckskin dress that was short. It had many symbols on it of the moon and stars embroidered on it. The ladies were happy to see another female. They had so many questions to ask her. Having already built a campfire, Morning Star had fixed supper for all of us. Quickly making camp, everyone made their way to the campfire to eat. Moses, Nick, and Antonio had taken care of the horse's gear. It didn't take long for the horses to start grazing on the tender green grass.

As Morning Star started to fill everyone's plate, there was a tremendous roar that filled the twilight that rumbled down the valley. The roar sounded like it was a cross between a lion and a bear. Morning Star only said Great Bear has come. We need to be careful. He is angry and promises to try to stop you from entering the Land of the Eagle Feathers. Only with the sacred words will he allow you to pass. However, you will have no trouble while in the valley. Our meal of fried trout from the stream and beans with bacon was a treat. Sweet cornbread with wild berries and honey was the dessert. After eating our fill, the ladies noticed that Morning Star was missing. I told them that she would be back in the late morning long after we were gone. She had family in these mountains that she needed to visit.

It was getting dark. I told Moses to picket the horses near camp for their safety and make sure the ropes are tied tightly to the two trees that were near. There were mountain lions and bears here. We don't want anything happening to them. Moses felt for the black leather whip that was tied around his waist. Like most men that worked

32

the cattle and horse ranches in Australia, he never went anywhere without it. I told everyone to get a good night's sleep and fill their water bottles or canteens from the stream. If you wanted to bathe, you can in the stream. We would leave at first light but remember to take only what you need and can carry.

Everyone said good night as I headed to my tent. Looking back, I observed that everyone had decided to stay up awhile to talk. It would a fine night to stay up. The air was cool and without a moon. The stars in the black winter's sky were brilliant, shiny like diamonds. Just before I fell asleep in my tent, I could hear June talking about the different constellations.

June was pointing to the different constellations. She named several of them, not by the white man's names, but by the Indian names. Being that there were bears around them, especially Great Bear, it reminded her of a story she heard when she was very young.

Taking her time, June found the constellation she wanted. She asked if anyone had ever heard the story about the seven sisters and the bears. Several of the group said that was one story that was new to them. June with her right arm outstretched toward the sky pointed to a constellation of seven stars. "Those stars together are called The Seven Sisters. Let me tell you why," June said. I know that everyone likes to tell stories by a campfire at night. Our group was no different. She had gotten everyone's attention.

When I was a little girl, my Grandfather, who is a great medicine man, told me this story. He said that there is a special group of stars called "The Seven Sisters." I asked him how did the stars get that name? He replied it was because of a bunch of bears and seven young Indian girls. The young Indian girls were playing in a large mountain stream. They realized that several large bears were coming toward them. They knew that if the bears caught them, they would probably die. One of the young girls saw a large rock in the middle of the stream. She told everyone to follow her to the large rock. They might be safe there. They all ran, splashing through the stream toward the large rock.

Quickly reaching the rock with the bears just behind them, the seven young girls climbed to the top of the rock. The bears begin looking for a way to climb up on to the rock to get the girls. Knowing that eventually the bears would find a way to get up to them, the young girls called to the Rock Spirit to help them. Each rock has a spirit that molds it and shapes it.

This Rock Spirit had never had anyone ask it for help. The Rock Spirit asked the seven young Indian girls why they had called. The seven young girls told the Rock Spirit that unless they could find a way to get away from the bears that they would surely die. After thinking for a few minutes, the Rock Spirit said it would be honored to help them because nobody had ever asked this Rock Spirit for help before.

By now, the big bears were starting to get on the rock. The rock started to rise. The rock shuddered. It started to grow under their feet. Up and up into the sky it went. The bears below found that they could not get to the girls. As the rock grew, the sides of the rock became steeper and steeper. The bears soon realized that they could not climb up the steep sides to get to the girls. The bears could only watch as the girls went further and higher away from them. Before long, the rock had become very tall and large. The bears knew they would never be able to reach the girls. It wasn't long before the bears gave up and decided to leave.

The seven young Indian girls rejoiced because now they were safe. They asked the Rock Spirit to make the rock small again. The Rock Spirit sadly said that it would not make the rock small because of the bears below. The Rock Spirit told the young Indian girls that it could do nothing. The Rock Spirit would not be responsible if the bears came back and caught the girls.

As the girls watched below them, they hoped that their tribe would come looking for them. Soon, they saw them below, but they were too far away. They couldn't hear their screams from that distance. To their dismay, they watched as the tribe left and gave them up for dead. The members of the tribe had found the many big bear tracks on the stream banks. They thought that the bears had eaten the young girls. They got their belongings and moved their camp to a safer place.

The girls realized that their tribe was going away. They became very upset. They felt that they would die on this rock. The sides were too steep for them to climb down the rock. It was getting twilight when one of the girls said that she had an idea. Maybe, the Great Star Spirit could help them. They all called out to the Great Star Spirit as loudly as they could together. The Great Star Spirit heard their voices.

The Great Star Spirit commanded the stars to come down and pick up each young Indian girl until all of them were in the great sky above. The Great Star Spirit commanded that each of the seven girls become a star. The girls were happy. They would forever be together in the sky. Also, they knew that each night they would pass by the Rock Spirit below them that saved them. In gratitude, they would shine brightly together to thank the Rock Spirit for saving them. That is why that constellation of seven stars is called the Seven Sisters. You can see it now shining brightly as it passes over us tonight.

Moses asked, "June, why do you call it a story instead of a legend."

June smiled and answered back, "Because it's true. Don't you see the Seven Sisters shining down on us?"

With that said, everyone laughed, but you could see on their faces that they weren't so sure if June was kidding or serious. It wasn't long before everyone went to bed. June was delighted that it seemed that everyone looked toward the constellation before they entered their tents to get some needed sleep.

Beans, bacon and cornbread were what I fixed for breakfast. Everyone was soon packed and ready to go. I gathered everyone together. Under my blankets, I told them I had parting gifts for them. As I drew back the blankets, I watched their faces. "Where we are going there are things that can harm you and others. I have chosen a few things to give you that can help us in the land called The Land of the Eagle Feathers. This place doesn't allow any modern weapons. The only somewhat modern weapon is black powder. Modern weapons do not work in the Land of the Eagle Feathers.

Here are the gifts that I have for you. June, I have several golden hawk feathers to give you. I know you know how to use them along with a tomahawk and knife. Rose, here are some crystals that you will need. I know you will use them wisely. Moses, you don't need anything, you have your whip and special skills. Mary, I understand that you are an expert Archer. There is a long bow and several special arrows. Nick, I know that you are an expert in martial arts. I will give you a frying pan anyway. Your grandfather will someday show you how it works. Antonio, you were the hardest for me to choose something for. I chose for you something that may surprise you: a wand. That is all you will need. Now for Lo Ming, I don't need to give you anything. You have your martial arts and walking cane to protect you along with your special gifts. I know you will wonder what I will be carrying. It is this black powder 50 caliber Hawkins rifle with special loads and a bowie knife. You need to hope I don't ever need to use it, because it would mean one of you failed to protect us.

Everyone was a little startled about the weapons. I knew that they were also wondering why I knew so much about them. I explained to them that where we were going had dangers. These dangers will come from those that would want to exploit this land. The people who want The Land of the Eagle Feathers are much like the people that took the Indian Lands from Great Native Tribes in North and South America. These people didn't care if they killed to get it. There are evil beings that would not care if we vanished if we got in their way.

Nick, I know you know that we are being followed. You can sense their presence. Nick replied that he could feel several hostiles. "How far?" I asked him. Nick tilted his head and took a deep breath through his nose. He listened to the wind and replied, "About two miles away to the west, coming fast."

We wasted no time in breaking camp. We packed the horses with the rest of our gear. Morning Star had returned. I told her to go quickly and take the eastern trail back. She would be safe on that trail. We watched as she took the horses in a long pack train on the eastern side trail of the clearing. As soon as she was out of sight, I pointed to June to move up the trail. Moses pointed to the sky. Dark clouds were forming ahead of us. I didn't like it, but it was the way of the spirits.

We had begun our climb up the rocky mountain trail. In the distance, the sound of thunder echoed down from the mountain range. Each of us had a pack, weighing approximately fifty pounds or more on our backs. The traveling was slow due the rocky trail full of large rocks and boulders. I judged that the rain would probably start in about one hour. If we got caught in the open or by the flooding of one of the large mountain streams, it could cause us a lot of trouble. In fact, it could be downright dangerous.

We had started to cross a large mountain stream that was at least 60 feet across. I had crossed here many years ago. A clap of thunder so loud it made the hair on the back of your neck stand up startled us. But it wasn't the thunder that worried me; it was the roar coming down the mountain. Moses shouted at us to get across the stream bed as fast as we could. He knew that sound. Anyone who has been in the Outback during the spring flash floods recognizes the sound of a flash flood coming downstream.

June was the first to cross to the other side. Standing on a large crystal boulder, she could see the wall of water coming in a white mass of foam. The water carried debris with it down the mountain. Every one of us left in its path started running to the other side. Moses; Mary; Rose; Antonio and Lo Ming barely made it to the other side of the stream bed when it hit. I felt the water hit me with all its force. The force knocked me off my feet and was carrying me. I had no time to think or look. I could only swim or guide myself down the swollen stream.

I tried to look for Nick. He had been behind me. All I could see was whitewater; tree trunks; branches and debris around me. In the corner of my eye, I spotted a large low branch of an oak tree. As I was being carried by the rushing water, I made a desperate lunge for the branch. My arms instinctively grasped it and wrapped around it. I tried to climb onto the branch. My heavy backpack full of water was too heavy for me to climb up. I could only hold on hoping not to lose my grip and be carried away by the force of water downstream to a certain death.

Nick was not doing any better than I was. He saw the water just before it hit him in mid-stream. His quick thinking saved him because he had just enough time to take off his backpack and use it as a life raft. I saw him float by me on it with the swift current taking him downstream. Where it was taking him, I didn't know.

After about twenty long minutes, I felt someone taking ahold of my pack. A female voice told me to let go of the branch. Antonio, Lo Ming, and Moses caught me as I fell into the stream below. They were all wet and covered in mud but safe. Mary and Rose had gone on downstream to try to find Nick.

As they helped me out of the stream, I told them that we had to go help Nick. June said that I would need to stay here with her. I was in no shape to help anyone. I had several deep cuts on my arms and back that were bleeding badly. She would have to stop the bleeding and clean up my wounds before they became infected. Before I knew it, Moses had placed me on my front, and June had started working on my wounds. I was going to say something, but the words wouldn't come out because everything went black.

Lo Ming, Moses, and Antonio left their packs behind taking only rope and first aid kits with them and headed downstream. It was difficult to navigate the stream bank due to the slippery debris covering the stream and banks. They were yelling for Nick, but they never received an answer back. After about a mile, they found Mary and Rose. Rose had found Nick's backpack but no sign of him. They were getting more worried by the minute. The distinct sound of roaring water was coming from downstream. That could only mean a large waterfall was near. If Nick had gone over it, he could be dead from the fall or drowned in the pool below.

Frantically, the group moved toward the sound as swiftly and cautiously as they could. Lo Ming was the first to yell and point to the falls ahead of them. As Antonio reached the edge of the falls, he carefully leaned over to look down. Everyone asked him what he saw. Antonio shook his head. He told them that Nick was lying face down on a ledge about forty feet below the edge of the falls. He could make out some blood beside his head, but there was no sign of life. Nick was not moving at all.

Mary grabbed her first aid kit. She pulled its straps over her shoulder. She told them that she must go over the side and reach him first. Since she was a medical doctor, she was the one who had to go. Moses tied his climbing ropes together to make sure that there was enough rope to reach Nick. Taking one end of the rope, he tied it around Mary's waist. The other end would have to be held by everyone else since there were no available trees or boulders close enough to tie to. That meant it would take everyone working together to lower Mary to Nick's location.

Mary slowly moved over the side of the cliff by the waterfalls. It took everyone's strength to hold Mary as she was lowered down to the ledge below. After a few minutes, Mary shouted for them to stop lowering her. She had reached the ledge. They waited for Mary to give them a report on Nick's condition. Mary shouted to them that Nick was alive but hurt. He was unconscious, but it appeared that no bones were broken. He did not have any bad cuts, only bruises.

Mary carefully tied her rope to Nick's body. She jerked the rope twice to tell them to start pulling him up. She would have to remain on the small ledge until they could throw the rope back to her once they got Nick to safety.

It took all the combined strength of the group to get the unconscious Nick up to them. Finally, Antonio pulled the unconscious Nick onto the top of the cliff. They moved Nick over to the side of the stream bank. Dropping the rope down to Mary, they helped her up the side of the cliff to safety. They asked Mary what her prognosis for Nick was. She told them that she didn't know. Nick had received a concussion from the fall. Until he wakes up, she would not know how much damage had been done.

Moses had fashioned a stretcher out of two six-foot branches he had found. He used his ropes to make a small bed between them to carry Nick out. They must get Nick back to a safe place to camp for the night before it gets dark. Nick would need the warmth of a fire. It gets cold in the mountains at night this high up. Our clothes were soaking wet. We needed some food as well. Putting Nick on the stretcher, they started the long trek back upstream to June and me.

June cut off my shirt to survey the damage. Several of the wounds in my back would require her to stitch them up. She took some fishing line out of her backpack. Using a hook out of her fishing kit, she attached the fishing string to it. Before she started, she cleaned out the wounds. Reaching into a small pouch in her medicine bag, she rubbed some special herbs into each wound. The native medicine should hasten the healing process. She remarked to herself that John has many scars from wounds in battle. He must be a great warrior. June smiled a wicked smile. If she stitched up the wounds in an artistic way, they would look like a planets and stars in our solar system when the scars healed. This is what she did. One thing that she was glad about was that I was still unconscious when she finished. She took a blanket out of her waterproof backpack and covered me up.

Realizing it would be getting dark soon, June found a small clearing away from the stream to pitch camp. It took a while, but June dragged or carried the group's backpacks to the clearing. Then June half dragged me to a tent she had set up. The stream had returned to clear water, so she took off my clothes and washed the rest of the dirt and mud off my body and pulled me into the tent. Covering me up with the blanket to keep me warm, she took out an herb and grounded it up, added water to it, and forced it down my throat. He will sleep well tonight, but he will be very sore in the morning, she thought to herself.

Soon she heard the others coming up the stream toward the camp. They saw the fire she had started in the clearing. Moses and Antonio placed Nick's stretcher by the fire to keep him warm. Without saying a word, the rest of the group fixed their tents. Rose decided that she was going to take care of Nick. Combining their tents, she fashioned a much larger one that would allow her room for the two of them to be together.

Moses looked at Lo Ming. She knew what Moses was thinking. Rose was like a mother bear taking care of its cub. She told him that that wasn't it. Rose was more like an older cougar taking care of its younger mate. Moses nodded in agreement. Rose stripped off Nick's dirty clothes and scrubbed him clean before having him put into her tent. She wrapped two blankets around him to keep him warm. The weather was getting colder with a north wind blowing in from the mountains.

Mary had looked at John. She was satisfied with what doctoring June had done with John. June told her that she had used medicine that her grandfather had taught her. John would sleep all night from the powdered drink she had made him drink. Mary told her that she would watch him tonight.

Mary informed Rose that Nick had a bad concussion from his fall at the waterfalls. Rose stated that she knew how to cure him of that problem. She would use some of her unique knowledge to cure him. She had special stones and crystals that she could place by his head which would repair anything that was damaged. She pulled two gemstones out of her pouch. One gemstone was amethyst.

The other was agate. Both gemstones had healing powers. Her mother had taught her about such things.

"Don't worry, he will be as good as ever tomorrow," she assured Mary. If you hear him scream or yell, it will mean that the stones are working their magic. Then she told Mary how she knew of such things. "You see, my mother is a Voodoo Priestess from the Bayou near New Orleans." This didn't surprise Mary. She had already guessed that Rose had that type of knowledge. Mary had learned long ago that native medicine or even voodoo treatment could heal. She had studied about such things and had seen firsthand that they worked. The major factor in such things working was the power of those administering the cure.

Lo Ming had made a soup out of some of the food packets that were in their backpacks. The group sat around the campfire in the middle of the circle of tents. Enough firewood had been brought in to keep the fire burning all night. It would help to keep them warm. Moses had placed a series of flat rocks to reflect the warmth of the fire toward each tent. Everyone, except Nick and John, was sitting on small logs near the fire eating. It was dark with only a few stars in the winter's sky. It was still winter. The first day of spring would be several days from now. Winter had not yet decided to give up. It was getting just plain cold.

June was the first to speak. She loved to tell stories which had been passed down. Many of these stories had wise teachings that should be followed. She was gifted in this way. It had been only a few days ago that they had met each other. They had been strangers on a train. They were still strangers to each other. John had told them that he would let them know why they were given the privilege to be part of this expedition after the meeting with the

Great Elder in The Land of the Eagle Feathers on the first night of spring.

June wanted to express some of her misgivings about this group before her. She knew that they were bonding into one, but she also knew that not everyone here was here for the same reasons. She had learned long ago that sometimes it was better to express your doubts in stories. You can get your point across and not say it exactly. June looked at the group before her and said, "We are here on this mountain tonight. We were strangers a few days ago. I have studied the ways of my people for many years. My grandfather is a great medicine man of my tribe on the plains. He has given me insights into the hearts of men. Let me tell you a story that relates to this group. You be the judge of what this legend means."

Long ago, there were two scorpions and two large frogs by a riverbank. As everyone knows, scorpions are very difficult creatures to deal with because you can't trust them. The two scorpions asked the two frogs if they could ride on their backs to the riverbank to the other side of the river to visit their scorpion friends and relatives. The two frogs were not very receptive to that idea. The frogs asked, "Why should we do such a thing? You are scorpions, and you kill frogs." One of the scorpions replied, "Because if we sting you crossing the river, we will both drown." Both frogs looked at each other and thought it over. Then one frog said, "We think what you say makes sense. We will take you up on your offer."

So, each frog let one scorpion on their backs. When one frog had finished crossing the river and let his scorpion off his back, he looked for his friend and the other scorpion. They were not anywhere to be found. He asked the scorpion, "What could have happened to our friends?" The scorpion replied, "He must have stung your friend, and they drowned in the river." The frog upset asked,

"Why?" The scorpion answered, "A scorpion is a scorpion. It is in their nature to sting frogs. He stayed true to his nature." "But why didn't you sting me?" asked the frog. The scorpion replied back, "I am still a scorpion, but I have learned. If I did not go against my basic instincts and stung you, I would have drowned. I have other scorpions depending on me. Sometimes, you must go against your nature for the greater good."

Observing the people around her, June said, "We are like the two scorpions and the two frogs. We have scorpions in this group. I hope that those scorpions among us learn from this journey. If they don't, we will fail or even worse." Everyone in the group looked at each other. Then Rose said, "I know what June says has truth. I have felt this too. But I am an optimist and a romantic. I am going to look after Nick tonight." Rose excused herself and went to her tent to take care of Nick. Soon, the others did the same going to their tents to get some needed sleep. Antonio decided to stay up to attend to the fire.

Rose's tent was getting colder as the cold north wind blew. She had placed the stones and crystals close to Nick's head. After about an hour, Nick started yelling in his unconscious state. Rose knew that the cure was working. She tried to make sense out of what Nick was saying.

Nick had shouted out, "I didn't mean to kill them. I didn't know that they were there. Please forgive me!" There were other things he said like "I am tired of killing; this war doesn't make sense for me anymore. I have seen too much of this." Then he was quiet and said nothing. Rose could see that Nick was shaking because he was cold. Rose felt the temperature of his head. He had a fever. It's an effect from the cure. The cure had worked. She still had two things to do to save him. She knew that she had to comfort him and keep him warm. She did what she knew she had to. She would use her body to warm him up and give him comfort. Stripping her clothes off, she got into the blankets with him using her body warmth to keep them warm. She wrapped her arms around him and told him everything is going to get better because Rose is here.

Mary went over to John's tent and went in to check on his progress. She noticed that John had a slight fever. That was to be expected. She took out some medicine from her doctor's bag and applied to his wounds. Being careful to ensure that he was warm enough, she covered him with his blanket. She knew that she had met him before. She didn't know where or how, but she had this feeling about him. Maybe, it was in the time of her life before her accident. She was a quite different person now. She felt a warm feeling whenever they were together that she couldn't explain. She brushed these thoughts aside. She would check on him every two hours to make sure that he was doing better.

Moses; Lo Ming; June and Antonio were still sitting by the warm campfire. What June had said to them was starting to sink into their minds. If that wasn't bad enough, what Moses had to say added to it. Moses told them that he knew that more than two people were following them. One was a young adult Native American Indian, a young brave, with a large white wolf at his side. Moses had caught glimpses of them in the thick cedar forest. The one thing that bothered him was that the young brave was not behind them. He was in front of them. He was traveling parallel to them slightly ahead of them. Moses was sure that the brave knew where they were going.

The other person was following them about 500 yards behind. Whoever they were, they were very skillful. They left very few signs behind them. Of the two, he was more worried about the one behind them. Lo Ming thought the same thing. She had felt the same way. Antonio said that was news to him, but they should be careful. If someone was following behind them, then it meant they wanted to gain access into The Land of the Eagle Feathers. If they did, that could be very bad for all of them.

They decided that each of them should keep watch. Moses would take first watch, followed by Lo Ming, June, and then Antonio. The others would be needed to look over the wounded members of their group. June left to get some sleep before her watch. Even though Antonio knew who was following them, he wouldn't tell the others. After all, a scorpion is a scorpion. He went to his tent. He would sleep well. He knew he didn't need to worry.

Moses looked into Lo Ming's eyes. He thought that she would look away, but she didn't. They were the only two people up. Moses wanted to get to know Lo Ming better. Before he could say anything to her, she spoke to him first. She didn't exactly speak to him out loud. Her lips did not move. She used her powers of communicating directly to his mind. "I know you want to get to know me," she said to his mind.

"Yes, I do. You are the only person who I can communicate with like this. You know that I have powers to communicate with animals. There is a legend in my land. It goes something like this: if you meet another person of the opposite sex who can talk to your mind and you to their mind, you are destined to be together," Moses replied.

Lo Ming replied back, "I have heard of that legend. We will see if it is true. I have never been able to talk to anyone this way before. I can feel that you have not been able to do that to anyone else. We have a long trip ahead of us to learn about each other. I am going to get some sleep. Wake me when it's my turn to take a watch." Moses watched her as she left to go to her tent. Then he heard in his mind, "I know you like my figure, I like yours, too." Moses couldn't help but laugh. He knew he would have to watch what he was thinking around her.

Large snowflakes started falling around midnight. The North wind was blowing harder causing some snow to drift. The campfire was no match for the storm. No matter what Moses did, the snow was choking out the fire. Finally, Moses gave up and just watched the fire go out. About 2 o'clock, Antonio relieved him of his watch.

Moses never did like cold climates. His body was shaking from the cold. Antonio told him to get to his tent and change into some dry clothes. He would take the rest of the watches tonight.

Since Antonio didn't have to tend to the fire, he decided to go over by some cover in a small grove of scotch pine and stay out of the wind and snow. He could still see the trail behind their camp. He didn't worry about the trail in front of them. If there was anyone in front of them, they would ambush them when they moved up the mountain trail tomorrow.

Moses was making his way to his tent in the snow. As he passed Lo Ming's tent, he heard her call to his mind. "It's too cold in this tent without a fire. Moses, go and get on some dry clothes. Then bring back your sleeping bag and blanket back here. We can use each other's warmth and the extra blankets to stay warm. Now, hurry, before I change my mind." Moses didn't need to be told twice. He went straight to his tent and changed.

Lo Ming heard Moses at her tent's entrance. Unzipping the entrance to her tent, Moses climbed into her tent after he carefully cleaned off the snow from his boots and clothes. Lo Ming told him to get in her sleeping bag with her and put the other items on top of it to keep warm. She told his mind not to get any ideas. He told her not to worry. He was too cold to do anything. As he settled into her sleeping bag beside her, he welcomed her warmth. Soon, they both were fast asleep in each other's arms.

Mary decided to stay in John's tent after she stopped by to check on him around midnight. It was much too cold to go out and come back. John was still fast asleep from the medicine that June had given him. Mary was getting cold. Taking a blanket, she curled up behind him and used her body heat to keep them warm. It didn't take much time before she was fast asleep.

June was getting cold. The wind seemed to find a way to cause a draft in her tent. Knowing she needed something to help keep her warm, she had a plan. Taking a small charm out of her pocket, she waved her fingers over it. Even though it was dark, she knew that her spell was successful when she felt the warm wolf's tongue on her face. Her wolf had come to her. She asked the black wolf to lie next to her to keep her warm. The black female wolf seemed happy to join her. June put her arm around the wolf with her blanket. Now, she could go to sleep.

As June was starting to drift off to sleep, she remembered how Midnight had come to her. One night several years ago, she had been working late reviewing some old manuscripts about spells and folklore of the Cherokee Tribe. It was research for a college term paper. A great medicine woman had written down a special spell. June had translated it. It said that if you are lonely and sad this spell will brighten your day. It did say one other thing. If you use this spell, you must promise to forever care for what comes to you. June had been feeling sad that night because it was the anniversary of her parents' death. She didn't know why. She just said the spell. The clock in the old college library stuck midnight as she finished the last word of the spell. There was a flash of light. Before her appeared a black female wolf with bright red eyes staring at her. She didn't know what to do. A warm feeling came

49

over her as she stared back into the wolf's eyes. The wolf smiled at her. June opened her arms for the wolf to come to her. Before she could react, the wolf jumped into her arms, knocking her down. The wolf started licking her face. She soon realized that the wolf needed her as much as she needed the wolf's love. She named the wolf Midnight. They have been with each other ever since.

Even in the shelter of the pines, it was hard to stay warm. Antonio was about to call it quits and go to his tent when he saw a figure in the distance in the snow. This had to be who was following them. Watching very carefully from his hiding place, he studied the figure.

He could tell it was a female form by its shape. The figure did not have any weapons that he could see. The person he was watching was very graceful and skillful in being silent. She used the terrain to her advantage to be concealed. As the dark figure got closer, he realized that her movements were familiar to him. The figure stopped about 50 yards from him.

He looked at the terrain. If he moved silently through the pine thicket, he could sneak up behind this person and take them out. Using combat skills that he learned a long time ago in the Scottish Highlands, he silently moved to the right of the figure in front of him. The boulders and pines gave him great cover.

This person must be studying the camp. She was probably sent here to find out how many were here and what they were doing. This was to Antonio's advantage. The stalker would be too busy observing to be looking for someone coming up from behind. Antonio was only about six feet from his prey. The intruder was just on the other side of the boulder in front of him. He knew from the steam of their breath that she was on the left side of the boulder. With the utmost skill, he quietly moved around the boulder. The person was only three feet in front of him looking directly at the camp in front of them. Antonio lunged at the figure, knocking her down and landing on top of her.

He instantly knew who it was. The person couldn't talk because she had the wind knocked out of her. Before she could speak, he put his hand over her mouth. He couldn't believe it. The one following them was Angela!

Seeing Angela here was not a good sign. He had met her many years ago in Italy. They were on different sides at that time. It is funny to think that now she was his boss or let's say partner. The two things that Antonio did know about her was that she was not to be trusted and that she was deadly. Her reputation was legendary in that regard. He knew that from personal experience. She had tried to kill him once. He had forgiven her for that because he would had deserved that fate.

They had double-crossed each other in Italy. They had been lovers back then and so were they now. Their relationship was complicated, and they were playing a dangerous game. If her boss ever found out about their plan, he wouldn't hesitate to kill both of them. Knowing her boss, it would be like him to send her to check on him. It was no secret in the underground that he wanted The Land of the Eagle Feathers for himself. The rumors were that he wanted to be the most powerful man in the world. Antonio had used that to his advantage to get this job.

He was both elated and furious to see her. At least, he didn't have to worry about anyone trying to attack the camp tonight. She was supposed to let him go on this mission alone and not call attention to anything.

When he had found out that he had been selected for this expedition, he had called her. Antonio wanted to make some extra money. In his line of business, he knew that her company wanted The Land of the Eagle Feathers for themselves for many years. It wasn't difficult for him to get her to hire him. Her company wanted to buy, lease or plainly take the land for development. They needed more information about it. That was his angle.

"Why are you here?" Antonio whispered. Angela replied that she wanted to slip into the land and see for herself if there was anything to be interested in buying. Antonio didn't believe a word that Angela said. There had to be something else to get her to come out here. Besides, she never traveled alone. She always had her bodyguards with her.

"Where are your men?" he asked her. "They are down the trail camped about two miles from here. They are too clumsy to follow you without being seen. That is why I am alone," she replied. That was probably the only truthful thing she had said. It would be like Angela to do the job herself. She wouldn't trust others to do what she could do herself. He knew the camp was safe from her especially if he could keep her busy tonight.

Angela was worried that Antonio would not believe her. She decided that she would need to reassure him. Angela knew how to get to Antonio. She told him that her camp was near. They needed to get out of the cold and could talk there. Antonio didn't have to be persuaded because he could feel the warmth of her body through his cold jacket. After walking about 200 yards, Angela led him to a small cave.

Antonio and Angela met each other in Italy. Antonio was working for the Vatican. He had been a priest, but he had lost his priesthood. It seems that his behavior was not at all priest like. He liked women too much and worldly goods. He did have some needed skills that the other priests did not have. The Pope recognized these talents. They offered Antonio an assignment to investigate cults and priests. It was on one of these missions that he met

Angela. She was a member of a cult working for a priest whom he was investigating.

Antonio befriended her one day at an outside café. Before they knew it, they had become lovers. Antonio had observed Angela in action. She was ruthless. She could kill without emotion. Even though he was able to break up the cult, Angela never knew about his role in the cult's demise. She vanished when the Italian Secret Police arrived to capture members of the cult and the priest leading it.

It took years for Antonio to find Angela. Apparently, she had gone into business with a ruthless organization. The Vatican wanted to know more about this group. It wasn't hard for Antonio to get with Angela again. He had special skills that she needed.

Antonio was growing tired of working for the different Popes over the years. He had worked for himself between jobs with the Popes. Just maybe, it was time for him to double-cross them. With Angela's help, he could just do that and end up extraordinarily rich and powerful. He never told Angela about working for the Popes or any of his other business adventures. Angela just knew what he wanted her to know. He did know one thing. Angela was not who anyone thought she was. She had special powers. Where she got them from, he did not know. Did he trust her? No, but she did have one weakness. She wanted the same things he did: power and riches.

Taking him inside, she soon had a small fire burning. Antonio thought this was a cozy place. Angela had already made a bed by covering branches of a pine tree with her blankets. All Angela had to say was come to bed. To Antonio, Angela was one of most beautiful women in the world. Her long dark straight hair hung down her back. Her dark eyes sparkled in the firelight. Her dark red skin contrasted against her white t-shirt.

Lo Ming woke up early. Even though she enjoyed the warmth of Moses' body, she decided to go out and check on Antonio. She was glad that the storm was over. The sky was clear but cold. The sunrise was bright, the color of gold, as it rose over the eastern mountain range. Lo Ming looked everywhere for Antonio. He was nowhere to be found. Finding where he had been in the pine grove, she started following his tracks. She could tell that he must have been carefully moving toward something by the way he was using the terrain to conceal himself. She was by the boulder where Antonio had jumped on Angela. As she started to move around the boulder, she heard a voice behind her. "You are out here early," Antonio said to her.

Lo Ming turned around and saw Antonio behind her. "Why are you down here, Antonio?" she asked. "Because I saw a figure here last night and followed them back to their camp about 2 miles from here," he replied. "How many were there?" she asked. "At least 10 men, maybe more," he answered. "Are you sure?" said Lo Ming. "Yes, we better break camp and get on up this mountain," answered Antonio.

Lo Ming agreed by nodding her head. Lo Ming turned and followed him back to camp. What Antonio didn't know was Lo Ming was aware that he was lying about one thing. Lo Ming could smell the scent of a woman on him. She would have to watch him carefully from now on because she knew Antonio couldn't be totally trusted.

Nick awoke with a start. Where was he? As his eyes adjusted, he could make out Rose getting dressed. Rose was putting on her blouse. "I see you are better. It was nice having you keep me warm last night," she teased him. Nick could only remember something in his dreams about feeling a soft warm woman against his body. His head was hurting, and he was a little dizzy. "What happened," he wondered? Rose filled him in about what had happened.

She told him about his concussion and how they rescued him. Nick was a little worried about what he may have said in his sleep last night. If he did say anything, Rose didn't appear to let on what he said.

I felt the warmth of the body next to me. Opening my eyes, I could make out it was Mary curled up to my back. My movement woke her. She told me what had happened. She let me know that I was a little battered and bruised, but no bones were broken.

I could feel the stitches in my back. Mary told me how June had doctored me. She did laugh about the stitches, however, "June had an artistic way of stitching your cuts. Your back resembles a map of the universe," she said.

Mary gave me some clean clothes she found in my pack. I tossed my blanket aside to put them on and realized that I didn't have any clothes on causing Mary to smile at my embarrassment. Mary smarted off by saying, "For an old man, you keep yourself in great shape, but by the many scars on your body, you must have trouble staying out of trouble." Mary left the tent while I was dressing.

The weather had changed drastically. The snow was melting fast. Moses and the others were breaking camp quickly. Antonio told me about the group of men behind us. June had cooked some breakfast for us. We swallowed it almost whole. We needed to get up the trail before our uninvited guests arrived. Nick seemed a little dizzy but said he could make it. The others asked me how I was. I told them that I was fine.

I reminded everyone what was ahead of us. In order to get into the passage to reach The Land of the Eagle Feathers, you must get by the Great Bear. The bear is known as E-qua Yonv. He is the guardian of the passage. The Elders of The Land of the Eagle Feathers use him as a test to see if you are worthy to enter. If the sacred words that are inscribed into the rock cliff are not said exactly, the Great Bear will kill everyone there. We cannot kill the Great Bear. We can only slow him down. Our job is to give Antonio time to decipher the writings on the rock wall to open the passage.

Antonio was the first to speak, "I remember that Morning Star stated that if we don't say the sacred words, Great Bear would stop us." I replied to him, "You mean if you don't say those words, the Great Bear will prevent our passage. You will have only a few minutes to translate the symbols on those rocks ahead to stop him or we may all die here." Nobody needed to hear anything more.

We broke camp and headed up the mountain. I put Lo Ming and Moses in front with Antonio right behind them. After about a fifteen-hundred-yard climb up the trail, we could see the wall. By now, all the snow had melted making the footing slippery. As soon as Antonio saw the wall, he ran toward it. Immediately, he started to study the signs and symbols inscribed on it. The symbols were from an ancient language of what is known as the Ancient Elders. He had seen them in Mexico once. There were also symbols that were Asian, African, and Middle Eastern. If he had hours, he could be sure of the translation, but he only had minutes. He wasn't so sure he could do it. He had no choice, but to push those negative thoughts from his mind.

The roars came from far below the valley at first, with each one coming nearer and closer. I spread out the group in a semicircle. "Everyone needs to protect Antonio. He's our only chance," I yelled to them at the top of my lungs. "He must translate the symbols and say them out loud. We can only slow the bear down. This creature is quite different from anything you have ever encountered. It's all up to you to work as a team to survive."

Then we all saw the Great Bear Creature coming. He was a giant brown and black spotted bear. If there was anything meaner than a junk yard dog, it was this creature. His mouth was full of the largest white teeth looking like they were dripping out of his mouth. He was like a mad dog roaring and snapping at anything in sight. Antonio yelled that he was only half through with the translation. He needed more time to finish.

Rose was the first to react. She took some green jade crystals out of her pouch and threw them on the ground. She held on to her crystal necklace with both hands and said something. A bright light blinded all of us including the large creature. Rose yelled that this would only last for a minute and her powers would be used.

As Rose slowly fainted to the ground, June held up her golden feathers. She raised them skyward. As the blinding light faded, several golden hawks appeared. They dove at the bear creature and seemed to distract him. June knew that this would only slow him down. They were no match for this creature. The giant creature raised his paws and swatted at the hawks, hitting a few. They were like bees attacking a bear stealing their honey. Soon the hawks would have to retreat because of their wounds.

Antonio yelled, "I'm almost there, I need only two more minutes." Mary took her bow and landed two arrows into the front paws of the bear's raised legs. This stopped the bear. He was startled to see the arrows in his paws. He started to shake his paws and tried to pull them out. Moses tried to communicate with the Great Bear creature. His realized quickly that this was not a normal creature but a great bear spirit in animal form. His powers were useless. That's when Moses took his whip and cracked the bear's nose. Then he whipped the long whip around his back legs. Not to be outdone, Nick took his frying pan and hit the creature directly on the head in one leap, but the giant bear swatted him back. He fell unconscious to the ground.

Lo Ming saw her chance. She took her walking cane and lunged at its neck. This caught the bear off guard. It made a coughing sound and fell to the ground rolling over. I knew that this only stunned the bear. He would be on us shortly. I lowered my rifle as the creature quickly removed the arrows and other objects. It started to walk toward us, and its power was too great to stop. It was useless to try to stop him.

The creature was about to reach us, and I was slowly tightening my finger on the trigger of my gun, when Antonio finally yelled at the creature. **"We come in peace. We are you. You are we. We are all kindred spirits like the animals of the forest and the leaves of the trees. We are one with Mother Earth. The eagles of the sky fly high to the Great Spirits. You have protected this land for many moons. The earth has circled the sun many times. The Great Elders have called to us to come. Your spirit is great as were your ancestors. Our spirits want only to help the sacred land that you protect. Let us pass to see the Great Elders to see if we are worthy as you have been worthy."** With that said, the Great Bear creature looked at us and turned down the trail.

The stone wall behind us opened, and a tunnel appeared that would lead us to the Land of the Eagle Feathers and the judgment of the Elders. I knew there was a chance that the Great Elders would find this group was worthy of the quest to find the sacred books. They had made it past the first great test. They had worked together. They would have given their lives for each other. There would be more tests ahead of us. We collected our belongings, lit our torches, and started through the tunnel.

Chapter III
Entering the Unknown Land:
Who and What Awaits Us?

The tunnel looked like an old railroad tunnel. It had train tracks. The funny thing about the tracks was they looked as if they had been used recently. The rails had fresh shine on them like a train had just been through here. We had to somewhat steady Nick because he was still a little shaky from the incident with the Great Bear. It didn't appear that he had any head injury. Mary had checked him out. Rose was assisting him. I was wondering if Nick was hurt or just enjoying Rose's attention.

The smell of burnt coal and ash was in the air. The light from our torches was being reflected on the walls of the tunnel. After examining the walls closely, we discovered they were covered by some sort of crystals. Antonio decided to collect a few of the crystals to examine them later. Walking through the tunnel was like walking among the stars in space with each crystal shining like a star in the night sky. Finally, after about a mile, we neared the other end of the tunnel. Ahead of us, we could see daylight shining into the tunnel.

As we walked out into the sunlight, our eyes were blinded by the daylight. We could hear the songbirds in the trees. They were gathering bits of grass and twigs for their spring nests. The train tracks went on to another tunnel, but we discarded the notion of following it. There was a large white boulder with markings on it.

Antonio looked at the symbols. His translation indicated that we needed to follow this trail to get to our destination. He seemed somewhat worried. I asked him why. He only said we need to hurry because the ridge top on White Eagle Mountain was three days from here. The stone said to be there, no matter what happened, by the first night of spring which was three days from now.

The sun was directly overhead so I decided this was as good of the place as any to take a break and have some lunch. The fight with Great Bear had taken a toll on us. We were all a little dirty and covered with dust and dirt. The tunnel must have had some silt from coal on it because our faces were almost black from it. Near the tunnel entrance, there was a small spring dripping water from the side of the mountain. This gave each of us a chance to clean up.

After eating our rations, we were back on the trail. Moses and June took the lead. I decided to stay in the back. I was still uneasy about someone watching us. Nick was feeling better. We were making good time. Rose was busy talking to Mary. I noticed that Lo Ming was deep in thought. Antonio was just ahead of me in line.

I asked Antonio what was troubling him so much. He told me it was that the stone writings said that not all could be trusted. Also, they said there was a place to stop for the night in a meadow with a spring that would make us feel young again. We are not to get off the trail at any time. The meeting with the Elders could mean life or death for all or only one.

I started to wonder if the only one part meant Antonio. That would be the only reason for Antonio to worry. There was something about him that made me feel he was not what he seemed. I had no choice. I had to take him on this journey. I needed him for the trials to come. In fact, I needed all of them to survive what would lie ahead of us.

This land seemed enchanted. It was beautiful. Even though I had been here many times over the years, I could never get over its natural beauty. The forests were dark and full of life. We saw deer, elk, and even a few buffalo.

In the corner of my eye, there was the Brave and his white wolf following us again.

Moses had stopped several times to listen to his friends. The animals and spirits of this land were talking to him. You could hear their voices coming from everywhere. If the others heard them, they didn't say anything. Mary was oblivious to everything. She was not used to the world around her. Where did I know her before? Was it in a past lifetime or just someone I had met long ago? I knew she was thinking the same thing by the way she would study my face when she thought I wouldn't notice her.

There appeared to be an opening in the thick forest ahead. Rays of light were coming through the trees as they were not as thick as before. We had been traveling uphill for several miles. The trail was opening into a valley with a small meadow below. This meadow was full of bright colors of spring flowers. There was a spring just as the boulder had said there would be, with a bubbling pool that was bubbling. We made camp.

Our camp was close to the spring. Moses and Lo Ming gathered some wood for the campfire in the woods nearby. It didn't take them long because there was plenty of wood available. They stated that it looked like someone had left the wood for us.

Nick had started a fire and put his frying pan on it. He asked us all to chip in some of our rations, and he would make a good hot meal for us. I swear, Nick could take anything and make a gourmet meal out of it. After eating, I was surprised nobody had taken advantage of the small warm spring's pool. Everyone appeared reluctant to get in. We all were dirty, sweaty, and could have used a good bath. They said that Antonio had told them about the legend of the spring. They were a little hesitant to use it. I did what I thought was right. I took off my shoes and jumped in with all my clothes on in one big splash. My clothes needed cleaning away. I had never felt anything so good in my life. The best spa in the world had nothing on this.

Everyone jumped in after me. The waters of the spring cleaned our clothes leaving no dirt and magically mended the torn holes in them. The water was intoxicating. It made you feel young and free like a teenager with no cares in the world. Moses and Lo Ming took off their clothes and carefully placed them in the water. We were all like kids going skinny dipping. It just felt so good. The rest is just a blur in my mind, a good blur.

The next thing I knew, it was morning. I got up to look for my clothes. I located them by the spring. They had dried during the night. I dressed myself.

Mary was stirring by her tent. She jumped up and looked beautiful in the morning light. She looked at me. I thought I saw a little smile on her lips but didn't know why. I didn't say anything to her because I didn't know what had happened last night. Probably nothing, she didn't seem too disturbed.

One thing for sure was Moses and Lo Ming must have had a good time because they got out of her tent together to gather their clothes. In a few minutes, everyone was dressed. We ate our rations without anyone talking or at least anyone wanting to talk. It seems that the spring had a magic of its own and it would keep its secrets from us.

We started up the trail which led us to a deep forest. Nick said he had a bad feeling about this place. We stopped for lunch by a small beaver pond. Rose had a puzzled look on her face. She was in a trance for a moment but said nothing later about it. The trail was easy to follow. I took time to think about each member of the group in front of me.

They reminded me of another group that I had taken before to this land many years ago. Most of that group survived that journey but refused to return to this land. They said it was too dangerous to return. Many of that group had special skills and mystical powers. If it hadn't been for their powers, I would not be here. Like this group before me, they had been invited to come to The Land of the Eagle Feathers. We had become very close that year long ago. The trials that we faced made us stronger. We had become blood brothers in a matter of speaking. But that's another story, I needed to concentrate on the members of this group.

I knew that the members of our group couldn't resist an invitation to come on this expedition. The legends about this land were thought to be myths carried down through history. Most anthropologists had dismissed the notion that such a place existed. There were many people who had been invited to join an expedition that never took up the invitation because they believed it was a scam or hoax.

Those who studied what little had been written about this land sometimes thought otherwise. The one thing that intrigued them was that in The Land of the Eagle Feathers were several ancient books guarded by a Council of Elders. These books contained wise knowledge. Some would state the true philosophy of life that should be followed. The legends said that those who followed such a lifestyle would inherit the true meaning of life. The most important part was that only a special few could gain the meanings and enormous forces.

There was a dark side to these legends. Because of the knowledge that these books contain, it is believed that those who possess these books would have the knowledge and forces unknown to the world at their disposal. This would make them invincible and all powerful. Not only could they rule the world, but they could rule the universe.

There is a name for one such group. They are called the "Dark Ones." I have fought them for many years. I had never been able to completely stop them. The council knows that it is only a matter of time before they would be able to take over this land. They know that if the "Dark Ones" do obtain control of this land, evil would triumph. The Dark Ones would not only control this land, but the world and beyond. I had heard of rumors there were other groups interested in this land. Some of these wanted the knowledge for themselves. The opposite was true for some of the other groups. They felt nobody should ever have such knowledge because such knowledge would corrupt anyone.

If the Council of Elders believes that our group is worthy, they will start our group on a journey of knowledge about this land. First, they will try to explain the culture and history of this land. Then they will give them access to the first three books to find the clues for locating The Book of Winter. Each book will require them to return to this land to gain more knowledge.

There is only one problem for this group. The "Dark Ones" will stop at nothing to obtain this land and **The Book of Winter**. Our group must accept a vision quest to obtain the knowledge they need. This quest comes at a steep price. You must accept that your life will forever be changed. They must make that decision for themselves. I can only lead them to the Council Meeting on the first night of spring. I hope that I am not leading them to their death like I have for so many others. My only regret was I had lost many good people trying to save this land. I wondered what the Elders would do next to test our group. It didn't take long to find out.

The weather was warm on this side of the mountain range. The vegetation was turning green. The hardwood trees were beginning to sprout buds for the leaves that would follow. After about two hours of hard hiking, we came to a valley. This valley was full of green grass with patches of small brush and trees scattered across it. A large mountain stream was at one end with several large pools full of trout. The valley was at least two miles long and almost as wide. This was a perfect location to set up camp for the night. I noticed there were several large boulders close to one of the pools of the mountain stream. I chose that for our campsite.

Antonio had taken the lead in line. He started across the valley heading straight for the boulders at the other end. We were about halfway across the valley floor when the weather suddenly turned. In a matter of just two minutes, the sky turned pitch black with large thunderhead clouds. Lightning bolts flashed across the sky forming webs of light. Thunder was shaking the ground with every lightning bolt that flashed. Lo Ming saw it first. A tornado was forming at the far edge of the valley. Judging by the direction of the wind, the tornado would be heading right toward us. Seeming to know what he should do, Antonio stopped dead in his tracks.

I was beginning to think that this could be one of my shortest excursions ever to this land. To make matters worse, the rain fell in torrents blurring our vision of the valley. The wind had picked up speed as well. Dead brush and leaves were swirling around. Nobody could see much of anything. Each of us grabbed the hand of the person in front of them. Antonio turned and led everyone to form a circle. Antonio yelled for everyone to get on the ground face down and to join hands. He yelled that, no matter what, everyone must not let go of anyone. Moving to the center of the circle, Antonio pulled out a metal tent pole out of his pack and stuck it deep into the ground. He tied several what looked like metal strings to the top of the metal pole. He quickly gave one string to each of our group, telling them to tie it to their right arm and turn around so their heads were facing outward with their arms stretched out in front of them. This placed everyone's bodies inside the circle.

The tornado must have been getting very close to us. The sound of a freight engine could be heard near us. Antonio took out the wand that I had given him and pointed it to the center of the pole. A flash of electricity shot out of it and lit up the metal pole in the middle of our circle. The electricity traveled up the pole and pulsated up and down the strings attached to our right arms. The wind and rain stopped moving inside our circle. Antonio had somehow formed a force field using the electricity.

The tornado was right above us now. We could see inside its vortex. I wondered if the field would hold. The metal pole was starting to waver. June turned over and yelled something at the tornado. Rose managed to take a black onyx crystal out of her blouse pocket and place it outside the circle. The crystal turned bright red. It seemed to be absorbing energy from the tornado and storm. The winds started to slow in strength, but the danger was not over.

Lo Ming motioned for everyone to stand up together and shout the ancient words. "We are strong. We are one. We are invincible. We cannot be conquered by forces of nature because we care for each other. Nobody can defeat our souls." We repeated these three times holding our arms outstretched to the dark sky above us.

June slowly reached down and took out a hawk feather from under her leather blouse. Letting the feather go, the tornado pulled the hawk feather into the center of its vortex. June yelled, "By the great medicine of my ancient ancestors before me, I command you to leave us and this valley forever." There was a great flash that knocked us all down.

The storm disappeared in the flash. We were on the ground looking up at the bright sky. The only thing that told us that something had happened was the metal pole in the center of our circle and the strings tied to our right arms. There was another thing. Outside the circle next to Rose was a large red crystal boulder that pulsated with energy. Somehow, we were alive. We were wet and bruised, but we were alive.

Moses pointed to the sky, "The spirits of this land are pleased. The large bird high in the sky is an eagle. It is flying toward the large mountain to the south of us. That is where we must go." I didn't have to tell the others that he was right. We just got our packs and made camp by the large boulders.

I had everyone put their tents up in a semi-circle with the open side facing the boulders. The nights were still cold this time of year. The campfire would be placed on the open side of the circle. This would allow for the heat of the fire to reflect off the large boulders back to the tents giving maximum warmth to everyone.

Nick asked Moses, Lo Ming, and June to fish for trout for supper while he got the campfire started. Antonio and I volunteered to gather firewood. Rose said she would assist Nick with the cooking. Mary decided she would look for some wild plants to season the food. I was a little worried about Mary. She seemed to be the only one who was not participating with the others. Something about her demeanor bothered me.

Our fishing party came back with several large trout. Nick remarked that they looked as big as largemouth bass. There would be plenty of trout to go around. Mary had returned from her foraging. She had found some wild sage, onions, and some other exotic plants that we weren't familiar with for seasoning the food. Nick had taken out some dried potato flakes and added water to them to make whipped potatoes. Mary added some of her exotic plant seasoning to them. It wasn't long before supper was done.

We dove into the meal. The excitement of the day had made everyone hungry.

After we had finished eating, Antonio told everyone that he had found a warm water spring in the woods to the north of us. The water wasn't too hot, more like lukewarm. It sure beat the cold water of the mountain stream. He was going to go there to relax and get clean. He asked if anyone would like to join him. Naturally, everyone said yes. Rose had fashioned a clothesline to dry out our clothes by the fire. Within minutes, the clothesline was full of clothes. Our group headed out to the spring following Antonio. I decided to stay back to guard our camp. Not so much from any person, but from animals like bears, coyotes, or any other small animals that might like our supplies. Before he left with the others, Nick said, "I see that you have the same feeling I do. Someone is still following us." I just nodded my head.

After about forty-five minutes, June came back from the pool. She gave me some herbal medicine and told me to bathe in the warm pool and make sure my wounds were clean. She said to put the medicine on my back mixed into a paste with the warm water. It would help relieve the pain and keep the wounds on my back from becoming infected. I asked her if she minded being alone. She said she didn't, she had her black wolf, Midnight, to keep her company. I could see that she was looking intently at the forest behind us. She was looking for more than animals. One thing I did know for sure was that the brave and his white wolf were more the hunted than the hunters.

When I got to the pool to join the others, I noticed Antonio paying close attention to Mary. Mary seemed to be enjoying Antonio's conversation. There seemed to be some chemistry between them.

I took off my shirt and pants. Wading into the pool with the others, I asked Mary if she would mind if she would put some of June's medicine on my back. I could see that Antonio wasn't happy. I had interrupted their conversation. Antonio muttered that he needed to get back to camp anyway. Antonio excused himself and left.

I had a green washcloth with some soap in it in my hands. Mary took the soapy green washcloth. She asked me to turn around. Taking the washcloth, she carefully cleaned each wound. Her hands were warm and soft on the back. It had been a long time since I had felt warm soft fingers touching my back. Mary asked if she was being too rough with my back. I told her not to worry. She was doing just fine. When Mary finished her cleaning of my wounds, she slowly and sensually started putting June's medicine on the wounds. Mary was being so gentle.

She was so close to me I could feel the warmth of her body on my back. It didn't take me long to ask her if she was about done. "I am almost done, just a little more on the lower wounds on your backside."

It didn't take me long to put on my pants and shirt and head back to camp. I can still see the wicked smile on Mary's face as she watched me go. She had a little disappointment in her eyes as I looked back at her. She was starting to get under my skin. Only one person knew how to do that, but I lost her long ago.

Lo Ming and Moses left the warm pool together. Lo Ming couldn't help but wonder where this was leading. She had found that they could communicate without saying a word. It was as if their minds could talk to each other. Sometimes, it was words and sometimes feelings.

The first time that this happened was when their eyes met after the incident with the Rattlesnake. She had looked deeply into Moses' eyes as if she could see what was in his soul. It had worked with other men before, but what she got in return upset her. Words flowed into her mind: "Hello, I can hear your thoughts, don't worry, this journey should be one to remember," She stared back at him, and her mind said to him, I'm not so sure. This is nothing like any trip that I have been on before." "Don't worry!" he replied. "Your mystical powers will keep you safe. Remember, we are like one in thought and deed. We can achieve great things together. In the legends of this land, remember if you can read another one's thoughts, you are destined to become lovers forever."

Lo Ming was full of contradictions. Mixed feelings and emotions were flooding her mind, invading her thoughts. She had never known anyone who had these powers before. She must be crazy to have any feelings about this man. Moses was so different from her. Their cultures saw things in different shades of the spiritual world. How would her relatives and mentors think if anything became of this? What did he want from her anyway? She was also rich from her business in Asian Antiques which her family ran in San Francisco. As if on cue, Moses broke into her thoughts, "Your worries are unfounded. I am rich in both spirit and money. The reason I am here is to explore the Spiritual World. I want to find those who are like me. We are more alike than you think. I know that you will find out that this journey is only the beginning of our journeys together. Look at the stars and tell me that what I say is not true."

Lo Ming didn't need to answer his question. She knew the answer. She carefully slipped into her tent taking Moses by his hand with her. The tent was twice its normal size because Moses had attached his to hers.

June caught a glimpse of something in the shadows of the dark forest. John had only left to join the others a few minutes before. A white male wolf appeared. The white wolf had a ghostly look especially with the dark background of the forest behind it.

June had been playing with Midnight. Immediately, Midnight could sense the male wolf. Midnight took off to meet the white wolf. June tried to command her Midnight to stay with her. Her wolf stopped and turned around to acknowledge her command. When the white wolf howled, her wolf turned and ran straight for him. June jumped up from the log she had been sitting on to run after her wolf. She was fearful that the two wolves would fight each other. She knew that her wolf would not let any other wolf close to her. Midnight would always protect her.

In about three long leaps, her wolf was beside the white male. June grabbed a tree branch to scare off the white wolf. Before she could do anything, she heard a male voice saying to her, "Don't bother them." "Why not?" she asked as she turned around to see the handsome young dark-skinned brave standing next to her. "It is for the wolves to decide, not us," answered the brave. "They have just met each other," June replied. "That does not matter to the wolves. They have their ways. They just know. It's what you call instinct," stated the brave.

June's wolf had just reached the white wolf. June held her breath. After the two wolves stared at each other for several minutes, the two wolves touched noses and ran into the forest together. June had to admit to herself that the two made a romantic sight. June turned around to talk to the brave. He stared at her. He seemed to be studying every inch of her. She didn't like that the way he was looking at her. "Why are you looking at me like that?" said June. "Only because you are so beautiful, I couldn't help myself," replied the brave.

"Have not you seen a Native American woman before?"

"Yes, but never one my age. You make me feel a little crazy inside."

June could feel her face blush with his words.

"Why do you stare at me?" asked the brave.

71

"I am like my wolf. My medicine man grandfather said that I always go after what I want," June blurted out before she realized it.

"I was sent here to watch your party of travelers to our land by the great Elder of my tribe," the brave said. "Before I leave, I will give you this white hawk feather. Wave it any time, and I will come. I am glad we had this chance to meet. I can feel that your heart is glad too.

June gazed into his eyes. They were not brown, but sky blue. She had seen those eyes before. She said, "I will be seeing you again." The brave turned and disappeared into the dark green forest. Soon, she heard a howl of a wolf and her black wolf appeared next to her. "I see you had a good time with your new friend." Her black wolf answered by wagging her tail and howling back at the forest to be answered by the white wolf.

June's thoughts were of only one thing. Her thoughts were focused on the young brave with the white male wolf. She knew that they had met before. It may have been in a different lifetime. Each time she had got a glimpse of him watching from the woods made her feel emotions and feelings that she never thought possible. He was her soulmate. They had to be together.

She thought she was losing her sanity. It was if one of her romance books had become real. She had realized that studying Native American Culture didn't pay well. Her Elders recognized that her storytelling talents were one of her strengths. It didn't take long for her to weave this into her writings about the research she had done. One of her English professors had challenged her to use her unique knowledge to write a short story for a class assignment. She wrote that short story.

Her friends suggested for her to turn the short story into a romance novel. To her surprise, it became a best-selling novel. The rest is history. A worried expression started to grow across her face. In this mystical land, were her stories starting to become real?

When I got back to the camp, I saw June setting on a tree log by the campfire. She looked deep in thought. I asked her if anything was wrong. All she said was that this land changes you. My Elders told me that it would. I suggested to her that she should get some sleep. We have a long day ahead of us tomorrow. June yawned in agreement. She got up and went directly to her tent.

Nick and Rose came back from the warm spring. They were both dripping wet. Nick told Rose that he needed to get some sleep. Rose looked into Nick's eyes and asked him if he would like to put their tents together. He told her that would be fine with him. Rose told him to change his clothes and join her after he fixed their tents. She reminded him that this was just a friendly gesture on her part and not to make too much out of this. Nick replied to her that he would be a perfect gentleman. Rose said that she knew that he would. "You have trouble being alone," she told him. Nick only nodded. "I have been alone too long. The darkness of my dreams haunts me," he replied, "You seem to make them go away. Being close to you does that for me."

Antonio stopped by to tell me he would take the next watch. I told him not to worry. He should get some sleep. He would need it tomorrow. With that said, he headed to his tent. I decided to head to mine. I had noticed the young brave and his wolf at the edge of the forest. I knew he would watch over us tonight.

I had just arrived at my tent when Mary appeared out of the darkness. She was carrying most of her clothes. Her t-shirt and white underwear were wet from the pool. She certainly was a beauty. She asked me if my back was better. I told her it was. I told her that I had made a rack out of branches near the campfire and that she could dry

73

her clothes on it. She smiled back at me and stated that was a good suggestion. She threw her dry clothes into her tent. Then she started back to the campfire. I couldn't help but watch her from inside my tent. She took off her wet clothes and headed toward her tent. Mary pulled on a large sweater inside her tent.

She couldn't believe that she was enjoying this trip. When her father, David, had encouraged her to go on this trip, she wasn't too surprised. He was a famous businessman worth many millions. His company was always on the lookout for more places to buy or exploit to make bigger profits. He was a tough man to do business with because he prided himself on getting the best deal. Nobody was allowed to get in his way. If they didn't want to sell, he would have done about anything from blackmail or extortion to obtain want he wanted. She had learned a lot about business from him.

Her stepmother, Benita, was not the best mother in the world. She was heartless and cruel. Benita was a good match for her father. Benita was from Colombia, South America. It was rumored that her family was in the drug trade. Her white hair, flashing dark eyes, and pale skin gave her an exotic appearance. For a woman in her early forties, she was in excellent shape. Benita took pride in her physical strength and beauty. She would spend hours each day in exercise classes. The harder the class, the better she would say. Mary hated her. Benita was very cruel and did not have a warm bone in her body. For some reason, sometimes Benita would be nice to her.

Whenever she asked her father about her real mother, her father would not answer. He would only say that her mother was a good woman who died in childbirth. Mary only saw her in pictures. Her father did tell her that her mother was too soft to deal with the harsh world outside their house. He did tell her that he wished her mother had been more like Benita. The one thing that her father didn't know was that Mary planned to get rid of Benita. That was one thing she had learned from her stepmother. You must get rid of those who oppose you before they get rid of you.

Mary knew that Benita would do that to her. Benita had tried to get rid of her several years ago. Mary had survived Benita's attempt to kill her and it cost Mary her memory. Mary could remember some things. She couldn't remember other things. It was as if Benita had taken selective parts of her memory and destroyed them. Mary did remember that Benita had tried to drown her in the jungles of the Amazon River. The rapids and rocks in that part of the river had damaged her face so much that she had to have plastic surgery to reconstruct her face. Only a small scar on her temple was a reminder of that incident. She never told anyone that she knew that Benita had intentionally pushed her out of the canoe.

Mary wondered why she was thinking so much about this. Ever since her so-called accident, Mary had become a cold, calculating to those around her. There was something about this land that she felt was changing that side of her. The more she was around John, the more she thought she knew him from somewhere before. He looked like a man who lived two hundred years ago. It was that faint scar on his left cheek that kept bothering her. She had seen it before. She did admit to herself she liked teasing him, and she recognized that they had some chemistry. She would use that to get what she wanted out of this trip.

Nick finished putting his and Rose's tents together. He had put on his newly washed clothes. Rose noted that Nick smelled like lilac. She liked the smell and asked him about it. Nick told her that he had found some of it growing near the mountain stream. He told her that he had been thinking about lilac, and it seemed that the lilac just grew out of nowhere.

He had crushed the flowers to make a lotion. He thought it would make a good scent. He asked her if she liked it. Rose replied that it was better than how he smelled before taking that bath in the warm pool. What she didn't tell him was that it reminded her of her first lover long ago. She had first met him in a city garden one spring that was filled with lilac brushes. She told Nick to lie down close to her and get some sleep. Nick moved close to her. turning his back to her. Rose put her arm around him. Nick enjoyed the warmth of her body. Rose had the ability to make him feel safe and warm. It wasn't long before he was fast asleep.

Rose couldn't help herself. She had been drawn to Nick the moment she saw him sitting in the seat beside her on the train. Even though she appeared years older than he, she knew that that wasn't so true. She had seen how he cried out in his sleep. She had pieced together some of his dreams. Nick had apparently done or seen many very disturbing things. He must have some sort of PTSD (Post Traumatic Stress Disorder). Before letting him into her life, Rose felt that she had to know Nick better.

As for Nick, he had been thinking before he fell asleep about how he liked her being around. He liked that she was mysterious. Her beauty was more than skin deep. He had no mixed feelings about her. He knew it would only be a matter of time before Rose would come around to having him around in a more permanent basis. Nobody had been able to make him feel so much better.

He was starting to feel alive for the first time. He had been in a very dark place for so long. One day, he would explain to Rose about his past. The war had changed him. He had seen too much and done too much. He had to live with that. He only hoped she would understand when he finally told her. For now, he had all the time in the world.

His grandfather and The Elders in the desert of the great Southwest had taught him that it would take time for him to heal. They had taught him many wise things. They had told him to go on this journey. It was his destiny. It was the way back for him.

The warm morning sun had just cleared the tops of the valley as Nick had begun fixing breakfast. The birds were quite festive today, I thought. The songbirds were celebrating something.

Moses smiled as he opened his eyes. The tent was aglow with the soft light of the morning sun. Lo Ming was already awake. She was beautiful in this light. She couldn't keep from smiling at Moses. It was the first time that she had seen him smile. This told her that Moses would be back for the summer trip.

Moses' thoughts were filling her mind. They were good thoughts, maybe a little bit racy. They were of her, like a replay of a movie, from his perspective. He reached over and touched her cheek. A small tear appeared and slowly made its way down his face. Her mind asked him if something was wrong. He replied by kissing her. The symbols that she gathered from his thoughts were of love and caring. She returned his thoughts with hers. This was going to be a good day.

Lo Ming got up to join the other women to go to the hot springs to bathe. All the women couldn't wait to ask Lo Ming what happened the night before. I have always noticed that women had to talk about everything. Men will talk about some things. They usually steered clear of conversation about their relationships, especially the special ones. From where we men were, it sounded like the women were having fun chattering about something. Moses seemed at least 10 years younger today. He had that old spring in his step. I swear I even saw a twinkle in his eye.

Everyone gathered around the campfire to eat. Nick had made some pancakes. He had taken some trout from the mountain stream and fried up some homemade trout patties. They were something like salmon patties. Naturally, I had brewed a pot of hot coffee. One thing I had to have in the morning was hot coffee. I did have some hot water for those who liked tea.

Before long, we broke camp and headed up the faint mountain trail. We needed to be there by dusk before dark. June took the lead. I told her to follow the young brave and his white wolf. They would appear to her from time to time on the trail ahead of us to make sure that we would not get lost. They would lead us to the ridgeline campsite on top of this sacred mountain named White Eagle Mountain.

It took us most of the day to get up the steep rocky trail. There were many large boulders and trees to go around in the first two thirds of the way up the mountain. I was glad that it was a little cold. It was just right for hiking a steep mountain trail. The cold air was fresh with the scent of the green pine trees. Being cold, the sky was crystal clear. The sunrays were shiny in beams of light that looked like spotlights flowing down from the tall green tree branches from above. You could sense that spring was near.

June didn't have any trouble staying on the trail. I could tell when June noticed the faint shadow of the brave and his white wolf by the smile that would form on her lips. Her eyes would light up like new money. I swore that he returned the smile back at her. June had made her black wolf appear. She let her wolf go ahead of her. She told us that her wolf would let us know if there was any danger ahead. I think her wolf had other things in mind.

We made good time hiking up the mountain. After a few breaks to catch our breath and for lunch, we arrived at the ridgeline on the top of the mountain as dusk was starting to descend. The sunset was beginning to form. Soon, the last rays of golden sunlight would be gone. We had arrived at what is known as a bald on this mountaintop. I explained to our group that this is a sacred place. A bald is where no trees grow, only grass on a mountain top. Because nobody knows how a bald is formed, many legends have tried to explain them. The native Indians believe that a bald is a spiritual place. They believe that the great spirits formed a bald. It would allow mankind to see the power of the great spirits. If you were worthy, you could communicate with them. This right is reserved only for a select few.

Carefully we pitched camp. I asked Moses and some of the others to go back to the forest and gather some firewood. I would make a fire pit for the campfire to cook on and keep us warm.

I didn't tell them that I had to make it a special way. I moved rocks around to make seating in a semi-circle, so everyone was looking toward the east. The direction east represents salvation and spirit. This will be our group's beginning together. It will officially begin when the Great Elder arrives later tonight at midnight on the day that begins spring. Our group has much to learn about this land and its sacred teaching. Tonight will be the start of such a journey of learning much like spring is the start of the great cycle of life.

After a simple meal, I had everyone remain seated looking toward the east. Night comes early this time of the year in the mountains. The cold night air had cleared the sky of clouds. The stars covered the night sky. Your thoughts could get lost in this canopy of planets and bright stars. The greatness and vastness of the universe is always a wonder to behold.

June pointed toward the North Star. "My people used the North Star as a guide to travel where they are today. It is a sacred star to us." A beam of starlight came down from the heavens. It landed near the edge of the forest about fifty feet away. In its light was the young brave with his white wolf by his side. The starlight gave their figures a shiny silver glow. His white buckskins were covered with bright crystals that shone like small stars. He raised his flute and pointed it directly at June. He started to play an ancient Indian song. June could not help herself. The melody was one that she recognized that her Great-grandmother sang long ago. The name of the song was *Forever with You.* June stood up, raised her arms toward the North Star and started to chant and sing.

Where are you, my brother?
Where are you, my father?
Where are you, my sister?
Where are you, my mother?

We are in the touch of the wind.
We are in the trees that bend.
We are in the drops of the rain.
We are in the memories that remain.

We are in the halls of the mind.
We are in the times left behind.
We are in the stars above.
We are in the moments of love.

We are in the leaves of a tree.
We are in the shadows you see.
We are in everything you do.
We will be forever with you.

Hey yi, hey yi, hey yi, yo.
Time will come. Time will go.
Hey yi, hey yi, hey yi, yo.
Remember us from long ago.

As the song finished, a strong breeze blew in from the North. The campfire's flame puffed up and become brighter. We all could feel a powerful force. In the night sky above, several shooting stars formed and disappeared like fireworks on the Fourth of July. The stars seemed to move around from an unknown force. They swirled around much like leaves do in the wind on a fall day. Silence covered the mountaintop like a blanket. There was a flash of light followed by a loud explosion that echoed down the mountainside. We dared not move. We all knew a force that was more powerful than anything we had ever experienced was coming.

Chapter IV
The Council of Elders:
What Will They Say?

In the distance, a faint sound of drumbeats could be heard. The drumbeats became louder, moving like a slow breeze in the summertime. A flute joined the drums. Its melody was mystical and spiritual. Only an Indian flute can produce such a sound. The eastern sky in front of us turned a reddish tint. The sound of the drumbeats came faster, and the flute's music became more urgent. The sky's color turned red before us. A form of some kind was approaching us.

He came out of the edge of the red light, more spirit than substance. The form soon became an old man in full Native American dress, like a Great Chief. He was more like a Medicine Man who possessed great medicine of the Great Spirit. His white, almost bleached buckskins were trimmed with gold, red and silver thread. In the background, a lonely wolf howled, followed by an owl's call. The owl hooted three times. He was not alone. A young brave stood straight and tall in the shadows with a large white wolf at his side. They chose to stay in the shadows.

The man or spirit approached us. He seemed old as the mountains of this land but full of life and spirit. His eyes sparkled like the stars above. The drumbeats slowed their tempo. The flute's music became a whisper. The old man spoke saying, "I come in peace to give you a message, Lak'ech (I am you; you are me)." The music and drumbeats stopped. The mountain became silent in the still of the night. He began his prayer by raising his arms and pointing an eagle feather toward the heavens:

Oh, Great Spirit, creator of all things
We send our prayers on the eagle's wings
Oh, Mother Earth and Father Sky
Hear our voice, hear our cry

We were told many moons ago
About the man who is known by Antonio
He would be the chosen one to understand
The secrets to the passage to our land

We need help from this dark stranger
The Elders have said our land is in danger
Please hear our cry as yesterday becomes today
Show this stranger your secret ways

We pray for answers in the sacred wind
We pray for answers that you can send
We pray for answers from the sacred birds
We pray for answers without words

Oh, Great Spirit, Creator of all things
Giver of all space and what time brings
Oh, Grandmother Moon, Oh, Grandfather Sun
Hear our prayers, let your will be done

The Great Elder looked down at us as he finished his prayer saying, "As the Great Elder of The Land of the Eagle Feathers, it is time to welcome you to our land. We will conduct a Friendship Dance, di'sti, to show you that you are welcome." The Great Elder took an eagle feather from his medicine bag. He waved it in a circular motion. Several male Indians appeared in a circle in front of him. The young brave with a flute and an Indian Woman appeared next to him. The woman had several tortoise-shell rattles bounded to her legs. The Great Elder with a groundhog skin drum in his hands started to chant and sing. "I am "The Gotogwashi or Caller of this dance. I will sing our Friendship song."

As he started his song, a woman in a red dress with the tortoise rattles on her leggings starts to dance around the men in the circle. The male members started dancing as well in their circle. The Great Elder gradually sped up the beat of the drum, and the young brave with the flute joined in. They joined the men in their dancing circle. A group of Indian women appeared. They started to form a line behind the lead woman who was dancing around the circle of men. The Elder sped up the song faster and faster. The women circled the men moving faster, keeping up with the tempo of the song. Both circles moved faster and faster. trying to keep up with the speed of the music. It seemed impossible to dance to the speed and volume of the music.

We could feel the heat of the dancers and the energy that they were generating. The air was heated by this energy. When it appeared that they could not go any longer. all the dancers turned and rushed out of their circles and disappeared into the night. The only one left was the Great Elder, standing in what would have be the center of both circles.

The Great Elder looked at our group. He spoke in a way that demanded respect, "It is time for you to learn about this sacred land." He told us to listen. What I am saying is sacred to us and this land. You must understand why this land is called The Land of the Eagle Feathers. You have been summoned here for a great quest. I do not have to tell you about what the great quest is, because you already know. You know about the four books. If you do not obtain all of them, this land is doomed. I will give you the first book. You will have to find the others. Before I give the first book to you, you must know what you will be fighting for. You must be willing to die. or you will fail.

You are warriors. A warrior must know that to risk their life, the cause must be important to them. If your heart is not with this land, you will fail. You will need its spirit to protect you.

The Old Great Elder took a pause. He started to speak. "The eagle is our symbol of this land. We all dwell in this Land of the Eagle Feathers. No matter when or where, our dreams and visions are shaped by the Eagle as it crosses the vast regions of sky and time.

In the beginning, the creator gives each bird a song to sing. He chose the Eagle to be the Master of all the birds. That is why the Eagle can only give commands and does not have a song to sing like the Nightingale. The Eagle is the messenger of the Creator. It was chosen because it soars so high. It can go between Earth and the land of the spirits. When the Eagle soars so high, it can bring messages from the Great Spirits to man and return to the heavens to communicate the needs of mankind.

The Eagle embodies everything that we know about our existence. In the spring, it lays two eggs. These eggs remind us of how everything is made up of two parts. Man has two legs; two arms; two eyes, and many other parts of man's bodies contain. He has both a physical and a spiritual side. The greatest part of all is that man can create himself by joining his two sides to create himself by the joining of a man and a woman.

The world we exist in has the range of things that are in twos, whether they be the same or opposites. There is the spiritual world and the earthly world. There is the range of land that is as high as the mountains and the low of its valleys. There are birds that can fly and birds that can only run or walk. There is what is true, and what is false. We have the heat of the sun and the cold dark of the night. Lastly, we have the believers and the non-believers.

Everything has a beginning and an end like our lives, which start and stop, on our worldly journey. The Eagle is one with the land and the heavens above. We should all look and learn from The Eagle in this Land of the Eagle Feathers. We all have songs to sing, stories to tell in the songs of words that are the poetry of man's thoughts. *The Book of Spring* lies at the end of that log. Antonio has been chosen to decipher it for you to study and understand what I have said. You have been chosen to fulfill this quest and journey. In the days ahead, only you can save this land from the darkness that wants its light."

The old man took his staff and stirred the dying fire. The sparks flew up like lightning bugs, lighting a dark, moonless night. He pointed the staff to the spring sky and said, "We have much more to say, and I will come again on the first night of summer." Suddenly, sparks from the fire rose up like a swarm of bees, and he vanished into the night. We watched as the brave faded into the dark forest much as smoke fades and disappears into the night. The only sounds we heard were a lonely howl of a wolf with three hoots of an owl.

Several moments went by before anyone dared to speak. They were puzzled by the event that had unfolded. Thoughts and feelings moved throughout their minds like the winds of a hurricane, scattering bits and pieces everywhere, but not making any pattern of reason to its design. Was this real or just a vision? Why did they appear to us? How did we get picked for whatever was to come? This group was somewhat a unique one, but why were we chosen? At first, they looked at each other, and then they stared at the bright spring sky as if to find the answers to their questions.

Everyone seemed to be in a daze. Nobody spoke for several minutes. It was hard to tell what they were thinking. This group had so many hidden talents and each one's perception would be slightly different in what they had experienced. I couldn't wait to see or hear what they thought.

Antonio was uncomfortable as I handed him ***The Book of Spring.*** Everyone's eyes were on him. He was mystified by what the Great Elder had said about him. How did the Great Elder know so much about him? There were many other people who had great talents at deciphering symbols and words besides him. If the Great Elder knew about his talents, what other things did he know about him? Hopefully, he didn't know those other secrets that he had. These other secrets that he kept to himself could be dangerous for him if the others of this group found out. He had come along on this expedition because he was invited. To be invited by John was one thing, to be invited by the Great Elder was another. Antonio decided very quickly that he had to explain a little about himself to the group to have them believe that he was just picked because of his knowledge.

Antonio looked at the group of faces staring at him. He said to them, "I know what you are thinking. How did the Great Elder know about me? Why would the spirits of this land pick me to decipher anything? Frankly, I don't know. I have done a lot of work with archeologists throughout my life. Perhaps they found out about this. How, I don't know. I feel that John knows more about this than I do." This was a favorite tactic of Antonio's. When in a tight spot, try to point to others to get out of the limelight. When everyone's eyes turned to John, Antonio knew this tactic was working.

Before I could try to answer Antonio's statement, June spoke up. "I know several other things about this land and their spirits. My grandfather told me about this land when I was young. He told me that legends say that this land is where my tribe once lived. He said that this land possesses the knowledge of the universe. It is protected by a Council of Elders. Many years ago, evil men or spirits tried to take this land. They wanted its resources, but the most important thing they wanted was the knowledge that this land possesses. There was a group that was evil. This evil group was called the **Dark Ones.** Many battles were fought with them. Many of my tribe died fighting them to protect this land. After one great battle, where so many of my tribe died, my tribe decided that it was not worth losing every member of our tribe. They left this land once and for all."

Nick interrupted her, "My grandfather told me that the names of the other books reflect the seasons when they can be opened to be studied. Only one man has the ability to decipher the books. Deciphering is just one part. He will need to have the help of others to obtain them especially the last book: *The Book of Winter.* The other three books *The Book of Spring, The Book of Summer, and The Book of Fall* can only be opened on the first day of their corresponding season. *The Book of Winter* must be opened by a special person on this mountain during a specified day in winter. June was right when she said that we are here because of our ancestors. That is the thread that runs through some of us. That's why we are here, but some of us are..."

Before he could say anything else, there was a bright flash of light from the campfire. Standing in the center of the lit campfire was a woman dressed in a beautiful Red Buckskin dress. The dress was trimmed in diamonds, rubies, and other precious jewels. Her long blackish gray hair was adorned with a headdress of eagle feathers and sacred stones. Her eyes were black as coal. She appeared to be about early middle age, but that didn't distract from her beauty. There was a dignified way in which she stepped down from the fire on to the ground. Her moccasins were red with white trim but were not burnt from the fire. She spoke to us. "I am the Red Woman of this land. I know that each of you have many questions about why you are here. Follow me to the Great Council Meeting, and we will explain to you. You must be careful in what you say. If it does not please us, you could be banished from this land and have your spirit taken from you. Choose your words carefully. Follow me." This is what we did. We followed her to a great cave lit with many torches. Inside the cave was the Council of Elders seated cross legged in a semi-circle around a great fire.

Our group sat down in front of the Council. Mary was staring at the Red Woman, who was seated next to the Great Elder of the Council. Mary was searching her mind as to where she had seen this woman before. When her eyes contacted the eyes of the Red Woman, Mary jerked back as if a lightning bolt had hit her. Mary knew instantly that she knew the Red Woman from somewhere. "That's impossible," she thought.

She concentrated on where she had seen the Red Woman. All she could see in dark recesses of her mind was a picture of an old wooden door with a padlock on it. The door had a light shining behind it. The door was shaking as if something was trying to get out. The door flew out for just a split second and then closed. The only thing she saw was the Red Woman holding a baby. The baby was crying. Mary could feel several conflicting emotions: sadness; pain; need and disbelief. She hadn't felt any of these emotions for a long time. Perhaps, she was getting too soft as her stepmother would say. She knew better than to let herself feel. Feeling only causes pain.

Moses was deep in thought. He remembered some of the stories his mother used to tell him. These stories were about a mystical land called The Land of the Eagle

Feathers. Her stories were always exciting. His father was always in the stories with his mother. They would be fighting evil forces who were trying to take the land for themselves.

He thought the stories were just tall tales like the ones people made up for bedtime to get the children to go to bed. There was one thing that she told him that stuck in his mind for all these years. It was the name of the leader of the warriors they fought with in many great battles. The leader's name was John. John was a great warrior who rode a white horse. He wondered on this journey if their guide could be the same man, because John's horse was white. The only thing that didn't fit was that John had died in a battle along with his father. His mother did say that John came back later. Somehow, he returned from the dead, but at a price. He had come back as half man and half ghost.

Moses felt that it was his destiny to journey here. On his manhood trip called a walkabout in Australia, he had a dream under the stars one night. He had been bitten by a poisonous snake. In his delirious state of sleep between life and death, he saw his father and a man walking together toward the setting sun. His father told his friend that he must go back and finish the fight. It was not his time yet.

He had done his father a great service by saving his mother. The man argued with his father. His father pushed him back and left jumping into the light of the setting sun's sky. The last words his father said, "I will be back. My son will come and get me. You must take him to the place that I am going. He will bring me back to my wife and his mother. My son will grow up to be a brave warrior." That was the last thing in his dream that he remembered before he woke up.

When he woke up, his arm was bandaged with medicine that was made from local plants. Without that medicine, he would surely have died. The great medicine man of his tribe in the Outback would only say that it was the will of the spirits that saved him. Only a spirit would have the ability to have knowledge of such medicine. It must have not been his time to die. Moses had a great destiny to fulfill. He also had a lot of questions that needed answered.

The group snapped out of their thoughts. The Great Elder stood up to start the meeting. He turned his head and looked at me. "John, we have tested this group of people that you have brought us. The hardships that your group faced to get here have demonstrated to us that this group may be worthy to complete the quest for *The Book of Winter*. We used the storms and other events on your journey here to test your group to see if they had the ability to work together and skills needed for this quest. You know that the **Dark Ones** are getting more powerful each day. It is only a matter of time before they will be able to penetrate our defenses that have kept them out of our land. One Dark One leader is already able to cross into our land. The only thing that is keeping us safe is that they can only bring a few warriors with them.

Your group is strong and made up of many different races of mankind. It is in this mixture of their many colors and special talents that they possess that gives this group the advantages that your other groups did not possess. This group will be the last chance we have in keeping this land from those who will take it for evil instead of good. We must get *The Book of Winter* to obtain its secrets to give us the power to stop the Dark Ones once and for all.

We know that everyone in your group is not who you think they are. You have no choice but to work together. It is written in the stars that your journey will be in four parts. First, you must decipher and study ***The Book of Spring.*** Then return each season with the last season being the start of a very dangerous quest to locate and return ***The Book of Winter*** to us. This will not be easy. Many people have died trying to get this book. If this book ever got into evil hands, everything here would be no more. The world outside of this would become under control of very evil forces. This would destroy mankind.

The people you have brought here are now part of the destiny of this land and their world. You have no choice but to complete your destiny or die trying. On the table, there are several marbles and an earthen jar. Each one of you must take one marble and place it into the jar. If any one of you puts in a yellow marble, your quest will end today. But if everyone puts in a blue marble, then your quest for ***The Book of Winter*** will start today. If everyone chooses the quest, then you have no choice but to complete it. If you do not complete the quest, everyone in your group will die. It is written so. You are all in this together. You must trust each other to complete this and keep coming back. If any member of your group does not return from your world, everyone will die. That is your choice.

The Red Woman pointed to the table. "There are marbles in that red bag on the table. Do not show your choice to anyone. Go, one at a time, and put your marble inside the jar. Your fate will be decided by each of you. Mary, you will be the first, followed by Antonio. Then, whoever wants to go next."

Mary got up and walked over to the white marble table. She took her time in choosing a marble and placed it into the jar. Nobody could see what color she put into the jar. Antonio followed her. He seemed to have trouble deciding. Antonio looked at the Great Elder and the Red Woman. He slowly looked at the other members of the

Great Council before deciding. He picked out a marble and placed it into the jar. The rest of the group followed. They didn't take much time to decide. After everyone had put a marble in the jar, they looked at me. I told them that I did not have a vote in this. Antonio asked me why I didn't choose a marble and put it into the jar. I replied to him that every one of you will decide my fate. If you have chosen not to take on the quest, I will die like I did many years ago.

The Red Woman went over to the white marble table. She carefully reached into the jar and took out the marbles, one by one. The first marble she picked up was a blue marble. Each marble was a blue marble. There was only one marble left. She picked it out of the jar and held it in her hand. She did not show it to anyone. She said, "This marble is Antonio's. He is the one who we trust the least of all of you. Let us see what he chose. Without him, the quest could not be completed. Antonio had to choose. He knows that he has a lot to lose if he makes the wrong decision." Before the Red Woman opened her hand, Antonio jumped up. He said to the Red Woman, "Throw the marble into the fire. The smoke of the fire will give us the answer. As you know, the spirits determine our destiny. I will let the spirits decide. They know our destiny."

The Red Woman nodded to Antonio. She threw the marble into the fire. At first, nothing happened. The smoke of the fire started turning colors. The first color was yellow. Finally, the smoke turned a bright blue. The Red Woman looked at everyone, especially Antonio. She stated, "So be it, the Great Spirit has decided. I only hope that everyone here follows their word. Go back to your camp. John must remain here."

Everyone left to return to camp. I stayed as the Red Woman commanded. The Red Woman looked at me. The whole Council was wondering what she would say. The Red Woman started her speech, "We had been waiting for you for a long time. Many moons have passed into many seasons. We were starting to doubt. You have come to us like you had promised. You have done well to get this far."

The Red Woman kept speaking, "You do know that Antonio's marble was yellow. He is a man of magic. For some reason, he changed his mind at the last moment. The Great Spirit made the smoke turn blue instead of yellow. Why did Antonio decide to let the Great Spirit decide?" I looked back at the Council and replied, "Perhaps, he has been affected by being here in this land. I remember that he read the first pages of *The Book of Spring.* He already knew his fate. He just wanted some proof." The Red Woman laughed saying, "As June said, "Once a scorpion, always a scorpion! For all our sakes, I hope he has changed. You are the one who bet your life on him. You now know your destiny. Now go! You have your one last chance to live as you are: half man, half spirit. We will not save you this time. The Great Spirits of this land have spoken."

They were waiting for me by the campfire. Rose spoke, "We have been talking. We all know that it was you who sent us the letters to come on this journey. I saw it in your eyes. We need to know why." I looked at them and said, "What you say is true. I did write those letters inviting you. I spent years looking for people that had powers such as you have. That is not why I chose you. None of you is perfect. Each of you has something missing in your life. This journey gives you a chance to fill that void. That's what makes us so strong. All of us must to fulfill that need, including myself. I will not make you follow me. That is up to each of you. We are all destined to travel on this journey together. Antonio isn't what you used to say many years ago in France with the Musketeers: "All for one and one for all."

June spoke up, "I had heard of such Councils from my tribal elders. I know only a few are ever allowed the chance for such a quest. The wise medicine chiefs of my tribe say that you don't get to choose your fate. Your fate is written in the stars." Moses just sat in silence and said nothing. He looked at Lo Ming as if she knew something more than all of us. He had developed respect for her knowledge of the spiritual world.

Rose touched her crystal necklace stating, "The vision I saw yesterday in the still waters of the beaver pond relates to this. We had become different kinds of animals. Two of us were animals that cannot be trusted. The vision showed that every animal was needed for a special ceremony to fulfill a special quest. You see! We never had a choice. It is everyone's destiny to go on this great quest."

After Rose finished her speech, she pulled out a small pouch filled with gems and precious stones. She gave June several yellow amethysts. Lo Ming was given several bright red rubies and white pearls. Mary received a bright red turquoise. Nick was given blue topaz gems. Moses was handed green emeralds. Antonio knew that he would receive yellow agate. Rose held up black Onyx with tiger eyes and red jasper stones. Antonio knew there was one gem missing: Red Diamond. This was one of the rarest stones in the world.

"There's one stone missing, Rose," Antonio stated. "Yes, you mean the Red Diamond," replied Rose. Rose took out a large Red Diamond and gave it to me. I will never forget what she said next. "This is for your son. He is the most important one of all." Before I could protest and say that I do not have a son, the Red Woman appeared out of the shadows. "Yes, John, you have a son. He is the last piece of the group of chakras that will give your group the power to obtain *The Book of Winter.* You will meet him when you come back for *The Book of Summer.* Antonio or Rose can explain what a chakra is," she stated as she disappeared into the shadows of the night.

Rose stated that she felt the power the group generated. She had never encountered a group of people who could produce that much individual power. She knew that they were chosen for that reason. It must have taken John much research to find them. One thing that puzzled her was where was the person who represented the Red Diamond. She could feel it wasn't John. She could feel the power within John. It had to be his son. Much like she had more power than her parents in this regard, John's son would have more power than he does.

Antonio interrupted Rose. He stated that he has realized what this is all about. This is about what is called The Sacred Bridge Ceremony that requires strong chakras. This is a very ancient ceremony that bridges two worlds; the one you can see and the one that is mystical. The precious stone and gems represent various symbols, such as green for plants and animals that are special to that person.

They say you are born with the knowledge of this ceremony. It is passed down through generations to a select few. Chakras are vital energy centers that reside in everyone's bodies not detectable by modern medicine. Antonio had read from the ancient scripts that great powers can be released by people with especially powerful chakras. He realized that our group was made up of members with strong chakras. Each one of us has one specific strong chakra part. Chakras are based on parts of the body. Everyone has seven chakras. These are: Crown or top of the head; Brow or third eye; throat; heart; solar plexus; sacred or ovaries and prostate and base or coccyx.

Now Antonio knew why John had selected each member of our group. Each one of our group has an especially strong chakra. Another thing Antonio remembered was that most cultures have some sort of chakra base throughout the world.

In his readings of ancient text, he remembered that if a group of strong chakras were used in this ceremony, representing one chakra part each, they could unleash mystical powers of unbelievable force. With four powerful women as a base, this would be even more powerful. The one thing that they had to have was an Akasha. An Akasha could combine and direct their powers into one force. That is why John's son is so important. He must be the only one who is pure. The rest of us are not. He must be the Akasha.

Antonio stated that finding **The Book of Winter** was their quest. It was going take more power than anyone has ever produced to complete it. This could mean that we could be destroyed in the process of obtaining the book. Lo Ming stood up and smiled saying, "There's an old Chinese saying, without risk, there is no fortune." Everyone nodded their head in agreement.

The group looked at me. They could see that I was still in shock about having a son. I didn't say anything. I didn't have to. The group had come to realize that I was always more than what I seemed. To be able to select this chosen group, I had to have the knowledge of the ancients. My mind must had started to play tricks on me. Suddenly, I saw a vision of a young pregnant woman who I knew several years ago. It couldn't be she because she and my child had died in childbirth. I quickly erased the thought from my mind. It was too painful. I was angry with the Red Woman. How could she tell such a story? My son is dead.

Lo Ming looked at each of us. "I know much about spirits, myths, and legends. I have studied with the great mystics of the ancient eastern world about mysterious and mystical events. We must follow this to the end because it is our destiny. We will succeed because the Great Council of Elders know that we are **The Keepers of the Yawi**. Remember what I say, there is danger ahead of us. When dealing with spirits or whatever, there is always danger." Then she grabbed Moses' hand. She led him away back to their tents that they had pitched together. They made an interesting pair.

I could sense that Nick knew more than he let on. He could feel it better than the rest of us. I felt that his grandfather had been teaching him his tribe's sacred ways. It didn't surprise me when Nick said it is late, and we needed to get some sleep. Rose's eyes lit up as she looked at Nick and agreed. I could see that there was something more as their eyes met.

I told the others to go back to their tents and try to get some rest. It would be a long day tomorrow. I picked up *The Book of Spring* that was lying next to Antonio. "This book and the others that will follow will be your responsibility, Antonio. You are the only one who can translate the symbols. It's your job to guard it for us. Like it or not, that's your job from now on," I declared. Antonio smiled and mockingly replied, "I guess that I don't have any other choice." "Not if you want to stay alive," I whispered in his ear. "You know that I have more at stake than anyone here."

Antonio had many problems facing him. He was not here because he wanted to be. This journey was more than he had bargained for. He would have left long ago, but he had to stay. He had many reasons to be here. The most important one was to show a special woman in Houston, Texas that he was more than a playboy. Even though he was one of the best experts in languages in the world, he was not someone you would take home to momma. He had been the life of the party and was famous for his conquests of women and adventures. For him, this was more than adventure, this journey would be the answer to all his troubles. He would impress her associates and her when this adventure was over. He would have their respect.

For the first time, he felt something that he had not felt for a long time. He felt that he had friends. It had been many years since he had ever had true friends. He had lost that feeling many years ago. All of his friends had died doing various missions with him. He had promised himself not to let anyone get close to him again. He had found something different here in The Land of the Eagle Feathers. He had found friends. How could he betray them? Why are so many people trusting me? He looked at the stars. A bright shooting star shot across the night's sky. It was a sign. He smiled. He knew his fate had already been written in the last book: ***The Book of Winter.***

Antonio was worried. He wasn't in Houston. He was in The Land of the Eagle Feathers. He had to deal with the members of this group. He had to hide who he really was, but who was he? He remembered June's story about the two scorpions. He was one of the scorpions, but who was the other?

Chapter V
The Journey Back:
When Will We Get Home?

The bright red sunrise was full of color with some light gray clouds in front of it. From this mountaintop, we could see for many miles. The views in all directions were beautiful. It would take us most of the day to get back down the mountain. If we hiked at a fast pace, we could get part of the way back before nightfall.

I never could figure out why food cooking outdoors always smelled so much better than indoors. Nick was up fixing breakfast. He had taken some dried bacon and fried it with some powdered green eggs. Nick had put some cornstarch in the water with the powdered eggs to give them a bright yellow color. Green was not too inviting a color for eggs. The instant pancakes he made with hickory nuts covered with honey were excellent. I told everyone that we needed to be on the trail in 45 minutes. Moses told me that the red sky was a warning that the weather was about to change for the worst. Moses smelled the air. He said that we would be having a hard rain in about eight hours. I replied to him that there was nothing better than a spring thunderstorm in the mountains to start the growing cycle of life.

I put Nick in the lead with Moses right behind him. Lo Ming would be next followed by Rose and Mary. Antonio was directly in front of me. I had already sent June ahead with her black wolf to check the trail. She would attract the young brave and his white wolf. She was to report anything out of the ordinary.

Since we were about two days from the passage back out of this land, I didn't worry. It would be after we get through the passageway that we could have trouble. Rose and June had talked to me about their feelings about the journey back. They both could sense that people were waiting for us at the far entrance of the passageway. I told them not to worry about anything until then. We should be alert at all times. The Council did say that the barrier to keep people out was weakening. Nobody should be able to get into this land unless they had special powers to do so

I was worried about the trip back to the Eagle Train Station. I could feel that something was not quite right. After about six hours of hard hiking, we arrived at the bottom of the mountain. I told everyone to take a short break and eat some snacks. We still had about four good hours of daylight left. We were going to push on toward the entrance to this land. Moses pointed toward the sky where he had spotted some large dark rain clouds. He told us that we would have about four hours until it would start raining. I told everyone that I knew a different way back. We should be able to get to a good place to stop for the night in about three hours of very hard hiking to camp for the night. It also had boulders that offered a safe place to camp from a storm.

I took the lead to guide them to the new campsite. I set a very fast pace. This would be a good test of everyone's stamina. I had been a little surprised that there was not that much talk about the events of the last few days. I didn't worry about June finding us. The young brave would show her the way to our campsite.

This land had a way of changing its shape. It takes a little practice to adjust to the changing features. It had been a pleasant day to hike. The temperature was a little cool. Except for the storm clouds moving in from the north, the sky was clear and sunny. The mountains in spring was my favorite time of year. There's a certain smell to the earth as dirt starts to warm to the new season of renewal. We crossed several small mountain brooks and streams. There were many meadows filled with wildflowers divided by small patches of woods. Each meadow was bigger than the last. Animals were grazing in the tall grass. The large elk used their horns to push the old dead grass away to get to the budding tender grass below. The songbirds were singing and gathering the old dry grass for nests. The larger birds were drifting in the updrafts between the mountains. If this wasn't paradise, nothing was.

About halfway across the meadow, I could see two people in the distance by several boulders. The boulders were in a circular pattern with room inside the circle for us to set up our tents. The two wolves were playing with each other in the meadow. One of the figures left with his wolf. As we approached, June greeted us. Her wolf jumped up to be petted by Rose. I guess you could say June and her wolf were our welcoming committee.

Moses reminded us that the storm would be here quickly. I had everyone pitch their tents in a circle with room for a campfire in the middle. Antonio decided to put his tent on one end of the circle. I put mine at the other end. Moses told us that we had only about 13 minutes before rain would start falling. The boulders would protect us from flying debris from any of the winds from the storm. Moses weighted down the tent ropes with large heavy logs that he had found in the forest in front of us. Nick had taken his tent shovel and dug some small drainage lines to take the rain away from the tents. I looked at my watch. The rain started falling at the exact time Moses said: 13 minutes.

Nobody had to say a thing. They just got in their tents. June and Mary had pitched their tents on opposites sides of the circle with Moses and Lo Ming combining their tents. Rose and Nick also combined their tents. Several strikes of lightning were followed by thunderclaps that seemed to roll down the valley. The flashes of lightning could be seen through the fabric of your tent. The wind had picked up speed, but the boulders broke it up and protected us. You could hear a few trees come crashing down in the forest around us. The large boulders protected us from any chance of being hit by limbs or tree trunks. Moses had told me it would be about three hours before the rain would stop. I knew it would be dark by then. One thing I did know was that if Moses said the rain would stop in three hours, it would.

The rain stopped at 8 o'clock. With the amount of rain that came down, it would be very difficult to start a fire. As I crawled out of my tent, I observed that Nick was trying to start a campfire. He had put some wood down inside a circle of some rocks. I decided to watch him. It would be a miracle if he could get the wet wood to start.

Nick looked carefully around to see if anyone was watching him. He couldn't see me. He raised his hands toward the star filled sky. He said something. As he lowered his hands, a small ball of fire was between each of his hands suspended in the air. He directed the ball of fire toward the wet wood. When the ball of flames hit the wood, the wood burst into flame. I smiled at this sight. I knew that his grandfather had taught him well on his trips to the Southwest deserts of North America.

It didn't take long before the smell of Nick's cooking got everyone out of their tents. Trout was on the menu again. June had caught some just before we arrived and had put a stringer of them in a small pool between two rocks to keep them fresh. Luckily, she had tied the stringer to a small tree to keep them from washing away. There were several small boulders to sit on. We sat together, eating the meal Nick had fixed.

Lo Ming asked Nick how he could start such a large fire after so much rain. Nick look at her saying, "I just raised

my hands and picked at the wood, and it started by itself."
Lo Ming laughed, "If I didn't know that what you were
saying was the truth, I would say you were pulling my
leg." About that time, Lo Ming pointed toward the night
sky at a large falling star. June said, "I guess it is time
for us to contemplate the meaning of the universe."

Everyone laughed because isn't that what many people
say when looking at the stars at night. Antonio pointed out
the names of each star. Mary wanted something deeper, so
she decided to talk about the different philosophies of
tribes she had studied in her travels around the world. I
told the group to have fun. I was going to bed. As I got to
my tent, I signaled the brave to keep watch. He was at the
edge of the forest with his white wolf.

It was just before dawn as I woke everyone from their
sleep. I could tell that they must have had a lively
discussion about the universe last night. They were slow
to get up. I reminded everyone that we must get to the
passageway by 3 o'clock. I tossed each one a small bag of
some fried cornmeal filled with dried berries and nuts that
I had Morning Star make up for me. I told them to be
ready to go in 15 minutes. As I suspected, June's tent was
already gone. I didn't have to say anything about her
because everyone knew where she was.

The shortcut we were taking back was a steep trail that
crossed one mountain. I wasn't too surprised that
everyone made it easily. I must say that I would rather
have taken the valley trail instead, but that would have
taken too much time. We needed to get to the other end of
the passage before dusk.

June and the brave were waiting for us as we arrived at
the passageway. I signaled by sign language for the young
brave to go back. It was time for us to return to our reality.
I told everyone to be ready that we were going to have a

different type of welcoming committee after we got to the other side of the passage.

Before we entered the passage back, I asked each one of our group if they were planning to return. Everyone agreed they would. I told them to be back at the Eagle station five days before the first day of summer. We needed that much time to travel to the next Council meeting.

As we entered the tunnel, I told them to have their weapons ready. They would soon find out what we will be facing for the rest of our journeys together. All of us must stay alive for us to complete our mission. The wall of the passageway was now in front of us. I turned to Antonio saying, "Now say the words that will open the passageway to the outside world." Antonio said, **"We have met with the Great Council. They have given us their blessing. We must return to our homeland. Open the passage for us to complete the first part of our journey."** The wall started to open. I could see they were waiting.

I had told everyone they could not fire or do anything until they were completely out of the passage. You were not allowed to kill anyone while in The Land of the Eagle Feathers unless given special permission by The Council of Elders. We rushed out of the passage.

Antonio had his wand out. Two arrows flew directly at June. Antonio directed his wand at them. They exploded in mid-air. In front of us were at least twenty men dressed in Ancient Chinese armor. Some of these men had swords or spears, and several had crossbows and knives. The warriors had a distinct look of anger and rage. They appeared to be more animal then human.

Moses jumped down onto a warrior. He took his large Australian hunting knife out in one smooth motion and knocked a sword out of a warrior's hand close to him. A warrior next to that warrior swung his sword at him.

Before Moses could block the sword, a sound of metal on metal could be heard. Nick had taken out his iron frying pan and used it like a shield to deflect the warrior's sword. Nick swung the iron pan at the warrior's head. Nick's frying pan caught the warrior on top of his head and knocked him unconscious.

By now, everyone was out of the passageway. A pile of backpacks was next to the outside wall where we threw them to get them out of our way. I yelled to Antonio to close the entrance to the passageway. Antonio turned and looked at the passageway. He said a special chant. The wall returned from the air and closed.

June had taken one of her hawk feathers and shot a bolt of lightning from it. It hit a warrior who was about to shoot Antonio in the back. Antonio started to use his wand again, but a sword hit it. Antonio immediately ran to his backpack and pulled out a rapier that he had been hiding in the pack. Turning to face a warrior behind him, he felt a sharp pain in his right shoulder. This caused Antonio to drop his blade. Antonio thought that this must be his last fight. As the warrior pulled his sword blade out of Antonio's back, Antonio fell to the rocky ground. The warrior lifted his blade to finish off Antonio. Just as the warrior started his swing, a spear point appeared in his shoulder. An arrow hit the warrior's sword hand. The warrior turned to see who had done this to him.

Lo Ming was standing behind the warrior with her walking stick. Her walking stick had a large blade attached to one end. The warrior fell to the ground. Lo Ming looked to see who had shot the arrow into the warrior's hand. She couldn't see anyone. Antonio had a smile on his face. There was only one person who had put such symbols on an arrow. It had to be Angela.

I was too busy with three men trying to surround me. I had out my knife. I blocked one sword lunging at my heart. Grabbing the warrior's sword, I lunged at his middle and hit him in the arm and shoulder. Another warrior simply took his place. This warrior had a spear. This gave him the advantage. Using the long spear to keep me away from him, he started to strike at me again. Leaping and then rolling over several times before the warrior could react, I smashed my fist into the warrior. I heard Antonio yell "Duck." As I did, a rapier flew by me directly into a warrior's leg right behind me. He fell to the ground holding his injured leg. I turned to look at Antonio. He was falling to the ground unconscious. He was bleeding badly from his wounds.

Moses had two warriors fighting him. He used his long knife to block the thrusts of their swords. As if he was bored with this type of fighting, he took his free hand and gripped his whip in his belt. Swinging his whip in one fluid motion, he caught both warriors by their necks and pulled them close to him. With the blunt end of his knife handle he hit both in their heads and knocked them out.

Mary had shot arrows at the other archers. She didn't hit them. Instead she hit their crossbows. This destroyed the functioning of the bows. The archers knew instantly that she could have easily killed them. They simply nodded at her in respect for her skill. Dropping their bows, they ran back into the forest for cover.

Rose flung several of her exploding beads at several warriors. The warriors were not expecting the explosions. This dazed them. The sound of a loud horn could be heard. The warriors started to retreat. They quickly picked up their fallen warriors and ran for the forest.

Nick seemed to be disappointed that the two warriors in front of him retreated to the forest at the sound of the horn. Realizing that the short fight was over, we ran to where Antonio was. Antonio was starting to regain consciousness. I noticed that his pack by the passageway

107

was gone. Before I could do anything, Antonio smiled and said, "Don't worry, the book is safe. It's in Nick's pack where I put it this morning when you weren't looking. I thought someone might try and take it from me." Then Antonio passed out.

Mary quickly put a pressure bandage on his wound. It didn't stop the flow of blood from his deep wound. I told Moses and Lo Ming to quickly put up Antonio's tent in the clearing below. We would need to work on Antonio. His tent would work well for this. Moses and Lo Ming did this within a few minutes. They put blankets in it for Antonio. Nick and Moses carried Antonio to the tent. Carefully, they placed Antonio on the blankets.

Mary and Rose started working on Antonio. They tried to stop the flow of blood. I went over to Nick's backpack. Putting my hand in it, I touched something made of leather and jewels. I pulled out *The Book of Spring.* Antonio was full of tricks and surprises. I couldn't help wondering if he hid this here for safekeeping for us, or did he have other plans in mind? This was a question I couldn't answer. I had to laugh. June and the Red Woman were right: once a scorpion, always a scorpion.

Inside the tent, Mary and Rose removed Antonio's shirt. They could see that Antonio's wound was serious. I had already assigned Moses and Nick to be on guard duty. They left with June and Lo Ming following them.

Mary summoned me to come into the tent. Mary looked at Rose and me saying, "Without some type of blood, Antonio will die tonight." I asked Mary how we can give him blood out here. Rose replied, "Mary knows how. I can feel she knows something about this."

Mary replied, "Yes, I do. I don't know if it will work. It is extremely dangerous." "What is? I asked. "Go get June. She is the only one who can help him now," Mary commanded.

Rose returned with June. Antonio's breathing was becoming labored. Mary looked at June saying, "There is a legend that your people know a way of giving blood to each other to cure people of great sickness." June turned to look at Antonio and Mary. She stated that it was a dangerous ceremony. Both people involved could die if it was the will of the Great Spirit. Besides, it had to be two members of the same family to give blood to each other. The wrong blood would kill the wounded one, and the loss of blood might kill the other.

I told them that we have not got any alternative but to try. They asked who would take such a chance to save Antonio. I told them that I was the only one that I would allow to do it. I have nothing to lose. If Antonio does not survive, I won't. The Council told me that unless our mission is successful, they would not let me remain alive. Antonio must live. We have to have him. Without him, we cannot complete this mission. You see failure is not an option for me.

June left to get her medicine bag with its special herbs, sacred stones and symbols. I asked Mary how she had knowledge of such things. She reminded me that she had studied medicine of different cultures throughout the world. Being a professor of ancient medicines, she had to have knowledge of many things. She had gone even further to study sacred ceremonies of various cultures. June returned before Mary could explain more. She told me to lie down beside Antonio. She told me to take off my leather shirt. June told everyone that they must remain completely still and quiet for this to work.

June said one last time to me, "You do know that this sacred ritual of healing can save Antonio or kill both of you." I replied to her with a "Yes." Taking out her sacred stones, she placed them on my chest and placed some on Antonio's chest. She started chanting some sacred songs as she waved a hawk feather around each of our bodies. Beside us, she drew a circle with two bodies inside. In a small pipe, she lit some sacred leaves of a special herb. She took the feather and moved the smoke around us toward both our faces. I felt myself drifting off into a deep sleep and a dream. In my dream, there was a white buffalo with a great medicine man asking me to answer a simple question, "Are you willing to die for this man named Antonio?" I could only nod my head. "So be it!" he explained.

Several hours must have passed before I awoke. A candle was lit inside the tent. Antonio was on his stomach. A fresh scar that looked as if it had just healed was on his back. That scar seemed to match a few old scars on his back as well. I couldn't hold up my head for very long. Mary told me to lie still and rest. June said to me that I must have the same type of blood as Antonio for both of us to be alive.

June said, "Like it or not, you are now officially "Blood Brothers." The sarcasm in her voice could not be missed. It was not missed on me. She already knew that I was Antonio's Blood Brother because he had saved my life. That was the way of her tribe, and I agreed that that was the way of my people as well.

Moses was talking to the others outside while Antonio and I were sleeping. They had pitched their tents around Antonio's in a circle. Nick had tried to follow the warriors' trail. It was no use. Their trail just vanished into thin air. It was as if they were never here. Nick did find a track of a woman's footprint just before the trail ran cold. It also vanished with the other tracks.

Moses stated to the others that he believed we were attacked to gauge how good of fighters we were. Someone wanted to know about our fighting abilities. Someone was feeling us out. They would be back someday but not for some time. They would be waiting for us again, probably, when we return this summer. Moses said, "When we return this summer, they won't stop. They will be prepared for us. Everyone must weigh this fact before you return. We may not be so lucky next time."

June and Mary told the rest of the group that it would be at least another day before Antonio and John might have enough strength to walk back to the Old Eagle Train Station. Nick asked, "Why doesn't one of us try to find Morning Star? She would have the horses in the meadow about one day's walk from here." June replied saying, "I will do something even better. I will send one of my hawks to find her location and come back and tell me where she is. That will save us time. Then I will go and bring back two pack mules to carry Antonio and John back." Everyone agreed to this. June took out one of his sacred hawk feathers. She moved the hawk feather above her head in a circular motion. A large golden hawk appeared high in the sky above them. Saying something in an ancient language, June motioned her feather toward the valley below. In a few moments, the hawk was flying out of sight.

In about 15 minutes, June's hawk landed on her outreached arm. The golden hawk leaned forward to June's ear. June nodded her head. She turned to us, "I have good news. Morning Star is only about five miles down the valley from us. If I leave now, I can get there some time tonight. There is good light of the moon tonight. I should have no trouble in finding my way to Morning Star's camp. Mary can look after Antonio and John while I am gone."

Moses looked at Nick and told him to go with June. There may be other warriors in the forest who could ambush June. June started to protest that she didn't need anybody's assistance to protect her. Moses laughed and

111

made that toothy smile of his, "It's not for your protection, June. It's for the warriors' protection. I want you to leave some of them for us to fight later." Nick and June grabbed their things and left on a fast run. Moses and the others figured that they would be back with the mules about noon tomorrow.

Rose had a campfire going in a few minutes. Nick was not the only one who knew something about fire. Lo Ming had gathered some plants and found some wild mushrooms for a soup. She had only seen these plants and mushrooms together in the same place once before. She knew that this was a sign.

Lo Ming thought it was time for some of them to find out more about themselves and the other members of the group. This soup would let them release their innermost thoughts and feelings. Perhaps, it would give them insight into the importance of this journey to their lives. If this group was to ever become what it could be, they must deal with who they are.

Taking out Nick's frying pan, she put the plants and wild mushrooms into the pan to simmer. She added some spices and more water. She made a very spicy soup. She filled Moses' and Rose's food bowls with the wonderful mixture. She warned each of them, "This is a special soup known only to a very few. I discovered it on a trip to Tibet many years ago. This soup will make you dream of events and happenings, both in the past and future. You must never tell anyone of the dreams that you will have tonight, or they will not come true; or worse, the dreams will become nightmares.

I will watch Antonio and John tonight. Since I have already drunk some of this soup before I joined you on this trip, I don't need to drink it. I encourage each of you to drink it. It will give you needed insights about each of us and what is in store for us in the future. Our enemy is gone from this land for now. Sleep well. Don't worry about Nick and June. They already know much about their future." Lo Ming turned and went to the Antonio's tent to relieve Mary.

Lo Ming told Mary the same thing about the soup. As Mary left her, Lo Ming reminded Mary to be careful when she drinks the soup. It might tell her more about herself than she already knows. Lo Ming told Mary, "Don't say that you won't drink the soup. I know you will. You can't resist knowing." Mary smiled back at Lo Ming saying, "We all have secrets, don't we, Lo Ming?" With that said, Mary walked down to the campfire. Lo Ming stared back at Mary as she left. "Yes, we all have secrets don't we, especially these two men in front of me. One day, they will find out a secret about each other. Then there will be a price to pay."

Mary found that Moses and Rose were already fast asleep on some blankets they had placed by the campfire. There was still some hot soup in the flying pan. She took a blanket and placed it on the ground beside the campfire. Pouring herself some soup, she drank it. The soup wasn't like any soup she had tasted. Each swallow was better than the one before. Putting the empty bowl down beside her, she pulled the blanket around her. She looked at the bright spring's night sky. She closed her eyes to discover another time and place.

In Moses' dream, he was looking at the great desert. The red rays of the sun in the east were only beginning to rise above the morning clouds. The gray clouds were small and bunched together with the red sunrise as a background. The few small trees dotted the barren landscape. His grandfather, a great elder and medicine man of the desert, told him that every lesson and knowledge that you need could be found here in the great desert. What did a little boy of eight care about that? He was too busy playing and exploring to care. The deserts and high country of Australia was his playground.

The faint voice of his mother was calling him to come back to the house and get some breakfast. It would take about 5 minutes of hard running for him to get back home. He loved to run. He liked the freedom of running in just his loin cloth with no shoes. He could feel the earth under his feet and the sky above. His grandfather told him that he had a great sense of the world around him.

He was approaching the large ranch house with the circular porch. He could see the outline of his mother cooking in the kitchen. She was young and very pretty. At least, he thought so. Her smile could melt your soul. Even as a boy, he wondered how could someone be so loving one moment and be so strict the next?

He opened the screen door to the kitchen. The smell of fresh biscuits and bacon filled the air. She was cooking on the old wooden fired stove. Her long shiny straight black hair almost reached her hips. "I know you are there behind me. It's time for breakfast. I have some rice, eggs, bacon and honey for us to eat. Go and wash up. You are sweating from running. You need to learn to run without making so much noise."

He didn't think much about it at the time, but when she turned to look at him, he noticed her race. She was Asian. He had never really thought about it before. She had told him about how his ancient ancestors had conquered the world many years ago.

His father was sitting at the table. He was a big man with muscular arms and legs. He was a gentle giant. He never raised his voice, even if he was angry at someone. It had to do with his father's native Australian heritage. His father didn't have to say anything, just give him that look for him to know that he had better do what his mother said.

They were about halfway through eating breakfast when a man on horseback stopped in front of his house. Moses didn't pay much attention to him. His mother and father welcomed the man inside for some breakfast.
They talked like old family friends, mostly about small stuff like the weather and lack of rain. Moses finished his breakfast before the man had his second cup of tea. He remembered that the man said he sure missed his coffee in Australia. His mother smiled at him and said that this cup was coffee as she handed it the cup to him. She told him that she knew he was coming this morning. She saw it in the tea leaves early this morning. Moses excused himself and went outside. He would leave the old folks to talk to each other.

Moses decided to listen to the conversation his parents were having with the stranger. He moved to the porch and quietly made his way close to the kitchen window. This took time because the wooden flooring made creaking noises. He positioned himself below the kitchen window to listen. He was exited to listen to their conversation. He had never done this before.

"I don't know about this. We have fought with you before, and nothing ever gets resolved, only more fighting," his mother said. "I agree with my wife. We have fought this enemy many times. They keep coming back. Why do we need to do it again?" his father added.

The visitor answered, "They are getting closer to obtaining entry into the land. If they do, they may get access to the books. You know that the fate of our world is wrapped up with this land." My father replied, "Yes, we do. We will meet you at the secret passage one last time. You must promise me to always keep my family safe if things do not go well." My mother said back to them, "I do not like this, but we will do as you ask. We will meet you in two weeks. Go before I kick your butt out of my house!" I knew my mother was upset. She never used language like that before.

Moses moved toward the front door. The man was at the front door. He turned and looked at Moses. He wore an old faded white hat much like the ones in the movies from the United States about the fighting between the white man and the native Indians. It had a number on the front of it. Moses could see it clearly now. It was the number seven. He didn't wear boots like most white men. His shoes were made of wild animals, like deer.

He could clearly see the man's face. It had a faint scar on the left side of his cheek that faded into his week old grayish black beard. It was his eyes that startled Moses. One was blue and the other was brown. He smiled at Moses.

Moses recognized him. He still has that white horse. He mounted his horse and sat on the old cavalry saddle, looking back at Moses. John nodded at Moses and rode off into the desert. Two weeks later was the last time Moses ever saw his father after his father left with his mother.

Moses started to awaken from his dreams, but another took over. He was a man now. In his dream, he saw a great army marching into battle. They wore black ancient Chinese armor. A woman rode beside him dressed in black leather, carrying a fighting staff. She smiled at him and pointed to the army in the valley below them. "You know we will need to fight them before long, Moses. We are a good team. No matter what happens, I will always love you," Lo Ming said to him as they rode down to meet this army with their weapons drawn. Moses jumped up from his dream. He awoke and saw Lo Ming standing beside him. He then knew why he loved her so much. It was written in the stars.

Rose had just fallen asleep when her dreams came. She was in a bayou in the Louisiana swamps. Being a teenager, she wanted to go outside the swamps to visit New Orleans or any place with people who might be her age. She loved her parents, but she needed more than this life in the backwaters of Louisiana.

Her parents were loving and taught her many things about the world. You could say she was homeschooled. There were some subjects that most kids weren't taught. Her mother taught her the ways of the arts of voodoo, and her father taught her the ways of the gypsy and witchcraft. Both of her parents told her that she had powers that only a few could ever possess. They had never seen anyone like her who could absorb their teachings and expand on them. She knew that they were both proud of her.

The dream shifted to a time that Rose had a shop of her own in New Orleans. She looked older. She had been through several trials in life. A small box was being delivered by a man dressed in old blue jeans and an old long-sleeved shirt. To her surprise, he had on a cowboy hat; she didn't pay too much attention to him because she wanted to open the box.

She signed for the small post office cardboard box. The man left and hurried down the street. It was raining hard outside. She looked back to see if the man was getting wet. He had put on a long off-white canvas raincoat. The rain was running off his old cowboy hat. He nodded when he saw her. Their eyes met for just a moment. Like most people do, they both looked away.

Turning back to the cardboard box, she started opening it. There was a long neck chain with two metal tags attached to it. The metal tags were not in good shape. She couldn't read the name on them because they were charred from a fire or something. She recognized them as being what the military called dog tags.

As she touched one of them, she had felt a man in pain. A picture of a young blond man, wearing a combat uniform in a battlefield that was exploding around him touched her mind. He was injured and being carried in the arms of another man. The other man was not a soldier. Then the scene faded from her mind. She fell to her knees from his pain. This young man had seen too much pain. He needed help.

She dropped the dog tags, and the vision stopped. She got off the floor in shock. Looking into the box, there was a handwritten note. All it said was that you must always keep these tags with you . You will meet this man soon. Only you can help him live again.

The mailman had stopped by at that moment. He asked her if something was wrong. She did her best to say everything was fine. He asked her to sign for a special delivery letter which she did. He left after she signed for it. Opening the letter, her heart stopped. It was the invitation to go on the expedition to The Land of the Eagle Feathers. There was a short message at the bottom of the invitation: Bring along the dog tags. Her mind raced back to the man who gave her the cardboard box. She could clearly see his face. The faint scar on his face and those eyes could only have been John's.

The next scene was Rose lost in a dark green forest. Men, carrying swords and spears, were chasing her. She was trying to get away. A young man was running beside her. He told her to run to her left. He would lead them away from her. She told him no, but he told her not to worry about him. She did as she was told and ran to her left and hid behind some brush. Nick smiled as he realized that they did not see her. He turned and ran. She awoke from her dream with a start still worried. As she opened her eyes, she realized it was still dark with the night stars shining brightly.

Mary's dreams were very confusing. Bits and pieces of images flashed in front of her. She found herself in a hot desert. She was a young woman dressed in an off-white man's work shirt and short cut off blue jean shorts. The hot sun was beating down on her. There was a man standing in front of her. She couldn't see his face with the sun behind him.

The man briefly held out his arms and pulled her close to his body. His body felt so good against her. His strong arms wrapped around her. She felt safe in his arms. If this could last forever, she would have been happy to just stay in his arms. They kissed, and his unshaven face slightly rubbed against her soft checks.

A loud noise interrupted her peaceful scene. It was a gunshot. A soft pain started growing in her chest area. She could see blood starting to pour out on her chest area close to her left shoulder. The man laid her down in the soft sand. Just before she blacked out, she saw her father with a gun in his right hand pointed at her. The last thing she remembers hearing was her father, yelling at the man, "I meant to kill you, not shoot my daughter. You should have left her alone." .

In the next scene, Mary was waking up in a hospital. She was upset. She didn't know who she was. A woman said to her that she was her stepmother. Mary didn't recognize this woman. The woman who claimed to be her stepmother was next to her beside the hospital bed. Her stepmother wanted to know what happened to her. All Mary could reply was that she knew nothing. Mary didn't even know what had happened to her. She couldn't remember anything about herself.

Mary's side and head hurt. The pain was almost blinding. Her stepmother said that Mary had hit her head during the accident. A doctor came in before Mary's stepmother could say more. The doctor looked at her wounds and her head. The doctor seemed a little displeased. "I know that you are more than a little confused. It seems there was an accident. You were accidently shot. You fell and hit your head on a sharp rock. You suffered a traumatic brain injury. You have been in a coma for almost a whole year. You are lucky to be alive. I'm not too surprised that you have some memory loss associated with that. Your memory may return some day. Your condition is improving each day. As much as she tried, Mary could not remember anything or especially anyone who had been her boyfriend in her past.

One thing that did startle her was she looked different from pictures of her from the past. The doctor said that her face had been seriously cut and bruised. He had only one thing that he could do to save her face from severe permanent facial damage. He performed plastic surgery. The only other thing he told her was that during her coma she had been pregnant and lost her baby. She had asked what happened to the father of her child? All they told her was that he left her and never returned. Benita, her stepmother, told her that her boyfriend had been no good. It was better that he had left.

Several other scenes appeared before Mary in her dreams. One in particular was very difficult for her to understand. It was a little boy, playing in a big valley surrounded by mountains. An older woman was watching him carefully. She was teaching him the names of the different animals and plants around him. The boy called her "Grandmother." She was dressed like a Native American. Her red buckskin dress had many decorations on it. The little boy was asking what the designs meant. The woman told him about the names of the stars and phases of the moon. The last question the boy asked his grandmother was: "Will I ever know who my mother is?"

His grandmother smiled and replied, "Yes, you will. She will come here one day and meet you. That will be not for many years. For now, you must learn much about this land before she comes." At that moment, Mary recognized the woman's voice. Mary knew who the woman was. The last thing Mary saw was The Red Woman of "The Land of the Eagle Feathers" nodding her head at her.

These dreams were very difficult for Mary to understand. She could not understand their meaning. Who was the mysterious boyfriend of hers in one of the dreams? Why did he leave her? What did this small boy and the Red Woman have to do with her and the dreams she had? As Mary awoke, she wanted to talk to Lo Ming about them. She couldn't because as Lo Ming said you couldn't tell anyone about them. You must figure them out yourself or lose them forever. Mary's nature was cynical. She would take these dreams for just dreams induced by the soup. But in the back of Mary's mind, thoughts were forming about them.

After Moses was fully awake, Moses asked Lo Ming how Antonio and John were doing. Lo Ming replied that Antonio was doing much better thanks to John's blood transfusion. Moses asked how was John doing? He understood that John had taken a big risk if the spirits did not agree to the exchange of blood. John was very weak, but he is sleeping. Lo Ming told Moses that she had given John a powerful powder in some water that would speed up his healing. He will probably sleep until midmorning. Moses told her to get some sleep. He would watch them while she got some sleep. Moses took Lo Ming to his tent. "Now get some sleep. I will wake you when they become conscious."

Moses noticed that Rose and Mary were still sleeping as he walked by them. He entered the large tent where Antonio and John were. He and Nick had put both

Antonio's and John's tents together to give them more space.

Moses lit a candle and placed it in a small lantern. He attached it to a string between the two tent posts to give him some light. Antonio was having a dream of some sort. He must have been fighting someone in his dream. Antonio said the name Angela several times. There was one phrase he was repeating that caught his ear. "I will do this mission, but I don't want to because I will have to betray people. You say, I have no choice. The Religious council says that the world is at stake." Then Antonio fell silently into a deep sleep.

Moses looked at me. He spoke out loud as if he wanted me to hear him. I pretended to be asleep. "I have searched for many years to find you. My mother would never tell me about you. She said you were too dangerous to find. You and I have a destiny. I don't know whether to kill you or thank you for saving my mother's life. All I know is that because of you, my father is dead. She told me that you were dead, but I knew better. People like you never die. Whoever you are, you won't have to worry about me not finishing this mission. When we do complete this, if we live through it, we will have a day of reckoning. I will promise you that we will have a day of reckoning. I owe my father that much."

Moses sat down between Antonio and me. He knew from the start that this journey was different from any other he had been on over the years. He sensed that everyone here was linked to each other in some way. He would find out what that link was. His Grandfather told him that he had special gifts. He could talk to animals, but he could also sense when things were not the way they should be. He could feel that the people here were not what they seemed to be. Everyone here had secrets. They also had great powers. John had put this group together.

But why this group of people? Did John know who he was?

Moses looked at Antonio. Antonio was one who everyone didn't trust completely. Even the Elders of The Land of the Eagle Feathers did not trust him. Antonio seemed to have many reasons to be here. He wondered what the truth was behind Antonio's presence. It wasn't just that he could decipher ancient texts. Whatever his true reason, Moses would be watching.

Moses did not worry too much about June, Nick, and Rose. Mary was one who he did worry about. He had watched her. Her actions were not normal. She didn't seem surprised by any of the events of the trip. She certainly was not one to trust. If there was ever a wolf in sheep's clothing, she was one. She didn't fool him. She had another agenda for being here. Moses just wondered if John knew all of this. There was only one way to find out and that was to follow this journey to the end.

Moses had one thing that he was not going to give up. Lo Ming and he were destined to be together. She, also, was not what she seemed to be. He didn't care. Someday, he knew she would tell him. They had all the time in the world. He was a patient man. His Grandfather had taught him that.

One gift that Moses did have was that people usually underestimated him. It was an advantage he had with several of the others except for Lo Ming and maybe, John. A cold sensation of ice on his back made Moses suddenly start to laugh out loud. This sensation always came when he under-estimated others. He realized that he had. The spirits of the Outback were telling him that everyone here felt much the same way he did. The members of our group didn't completely trust everyone, either.

How John was going to hold this group together was his problem or was it? John was highly intelligent. Moses smiled to himself. He had just figured out detail of John's plan. John had picked everyone because of each one's personal problems and weaknesses, not just each one's powers. It will be our weaknesses that will somehow give us an edge over what will come. Why, he did not know. One thing was for sure: things will get more dangerous in the coming seasons. Moses could only hope that John knew what he was doing.

Mary came into the tent. She told Moses to get some fresh air. Moses left to fix them some breakfast. He wanted to see Lo Ming. Mary sat down between Antonio and me. We were still sleeping. The sunrise would begin in about half an hour. This is a time, they say, when magical things happen. She looked at me. She couldn't explain it. She just knew that we had met before. There was something about me that was driving her toward me. She just knew there was a connection. As she watched me, she noticed that I was growing paler. I opened my eyes and told her to get Rose. Mary ran to get Rose. Returning quickly to the tent, Rose told Mary to stay outside. Rose was not too surprised at what she saw in the tent. I was almost transparent. "How long have you been like this?" Rose asked. I replied, "For many years."

Rose said she had heard of this condition. "When did you die?"

"Many years ago, the last time I tried to stop the Dark Ones," I said.

"I knew about your condition the first time I saw you. My mother is a Voodoo Priestess. She told me about people like you. You are half alive and half ghost. That is why you must do the Council's bidding. You must prove that you are worthy to live once again. You failed once. I do know one thing. Redemption has a cost of its own. The Elders are giving you a chance to succeed. We are your last chance, are we not?" asked Rose.

124

"Perhaps, I cannot say if you are. I only know that we have this year to save this land and our world. You must not tell the others about my condition. Your parents taught you well. When you see me getting in this condition, you know what to do," I stated to her

"Yes, I do," replied Rose.

After a while, Rose came out of the tent. She told Mary that John was better. She had given John some medicine. John would be weak for a while longer but probably could travel later today. Mary said she would watch Antonio and John until Nick and June arrived. Mary wondered why John needed Rose to help him. Mary could only reason that on this journey nothing was what it was supposed to be.

It was getting close to midday when June and Nick arrived with three mules that Morning Star had given them. They also had some fresh food. Antonio had been awake for a couple of hours. Mary had made him some soup to eat. He asked what had happened. Mary told him about the loss of blood from his wounds in his shoulder and back. Antonio didn't seem that surprised that John had risked his life to save him. Antonio muttered something about John was always doing something like that. Mary wondered what Antonio meant by that. Before she could ask, Antonio changed the subject very quickly. It didn't escape Mary that Antonio had information about John that he hadn't shared with anyone.

Mary dressed Antonio's wounds. The wounds were healing very quickly. There were no signs of infection. Mary marveled at the speed of the healing. What should have been fresh wounds were now closed with only small scars left where she had stitched the wounds. Antonio told her that he felt like he could walk or ride out of here soon. Antonio looked over to where John was sleeping. He noted that John didn't look that good to him. The transfusion must had taken a lot out of him. He didn't have to say anything about that. He knew Mary had already noticed.

June immediately went to see about Antonio and John. She asked Mary to come out of the tent and filled her in about their condition. Mary stated to June that Antonio seemed to be healing quickly, but John did not seem to be recovering as well. Mary told June that she didn't think John could travel today. June replied, "In this land, don't give up so quickly." Morning Star had given her some sacred water and medicine. "He should be able to travel in about two hours. Go and get something to eat and gather up your things. We will be leaving in about three hours. That will give us enough time to get back to Morning Star's camp before dark. Take Antonio with you so I can work on John and get him well enough to travel."

Someone was shaking me. I opened my eyes and realized it was June. Before I could say anything, June filled my mouth with water that tasted terrible. She made me drink it all down. My mouth was on fire, and I started shaking. June sat on me until my shaking stopped. She got off me and told me to get up. It was time for us to travel down the trail to Morning Star's camp. She seemed to be angry with me. I asked her why. She said that she would tell me someday but not now.

Everyone looked at me as I left the tent to sit down by the campfire. They had already eaten. I started to get the last of the food, but June stopped me. She said that I must not eat anything for several hours. She took the last of the food and ate it herself. Moses had packed one of the mules with most of the tents and other belongings. Nick and Moses helped both Antonio and me on to the back of the remaining mules. Moses told us just to hang on until we got to the Morning Star's campsite.

June took the lead with the others following on foot. Moses had the lead mule with Antonio. Nick had mine with the last pack mule roped to my mule. The rough, rocky trail made slow going at first but soon we were making good time as the trail became smoother. In four hours, we had arrived at Morning Star's campsite. She had been cooking supper for us.

Antonio must have been doing a lot better. He slid off his mule without any help from anyone. He walked over to my mule and said let me help you, old man. I could see that he was enjoying that I was not recovering as fast as he was. As he helped me down, he whispered in my ear, "I owe you one, Blood Brother." I was still a little weak as he helped me sit down against a log by Morning Star's cooking fire.

Everyone was eating. Morning Star knew what was on the group's collective mind. She looked at everyone and said, "The spirits had come to me in a dream and told me to take the sacred trail to get here several days ago. It takes permission from the spirits to be allowed to use it. We will take the trail back where it ends close to the train station. It will take us three days to get there. Nobody is to get off this trail. You must stay close to the trail all the way back. If you stray from the trail, you will become lost and will never find your way back. That is what the spirits told me. Tomorrow night, we will camp by the Pool of Youth. Everyone must bathe in that pool to cleanse yourself. The sacred trail only appears at the will of the spirits. It will fade away after three days. You do not need to worry about anyone harming us. Sleep well. Take John to the shelter that I have built. I will take care of John tonight. We leave at first light."

The next thing I remember was being put on my white horse. Morning Star tied my hands to the saddle horn. "That is so you won't fall off if you fall asleep," she told me. She took the lead horse with the others following. I don't remember much of that day.

It seems that we traveled very hard that day. We reached the campsite of the Pool of Youth just before dark. Moses had everyone set up camp. I was still very weak. Moses combined Mary's tent and mine to make a larger tent for me. Morning Star said that she would be back at first light to guide us back the rest of the way. She pointed to the large pool that was bubbling with water. Steam was coming off the hot water. Everyone knew that they must bathe in the pool tonight.

Moses and Lo Ming, wearing very little clothing, were the first to go to the pool to bathe. After a while, they returned to their combined tent. The night was very pleasant. The temperature was warm for this time of year. Rose and Nick took their turn in the pool. When they returned to their combined tent, June helped Antonio to the pool with her. They returned shortly. June helped Antonio into his tent and said that she would take her turn later after Mary and me.

I was still a little weak, but I could walk. Mary steadied me as I walked to the pool. When we got to the edge of the pool, she sat me down on the grass bank. She made me stand as she took me under my shoulder and led me into the pool. The warm water was wonderful. I felt at peace for the first time in years. She sat down in the pool, holding me close to her. My body started to shake again. I tried to stop it but couldn't. Mary held me tight to her. She put my head on her soft chest. She started humming a song. I knew that song. I had heard it long ago. The only woman I ever loved would hum that song. Tears started flowing down my cheeks.

Mary must have felt my tears. I had stopped shaking. She turned my head toward her and looked into my eyes. I thought I saw a tear in her eyes as well. She helped me up. She led me back to our tent, and I fell fast asleep.

When I woke up the next morning, Mary was still asleep. She had laid beside me. I could see the butterfly tattoo on her right shoulder. This flooded my mind with unsettled memories. I got up and pulled the blanket over her. I felt like a new man as I dressed and went outside in the dark of the early morning. This was the first time in days that I had my strength back.

Mary awoke from her troubled sleep. The dreams she had under the influence of the tea were bothering her. Were they true or not? There was something about the dreams and John. She couldn't connect John to the dreams. She knew they had to be connected. She could only push those thoughts from her mind.

She cursed herself. She must be getting soft. John was starting to get under her skin. She knew better. There was something familiar about him. She felt different around him like a young schoolgirl. She didn't have time for this. She had other things she needed to attend to. She had work to do when she got back. Last night was nice in a way, but she quickly dismissed it from her mind.

Morning Star returned at first light. We had all the animals packed and saddled. Morning Star led the way for the next two days. She left us midday a few miles from Eagle Train Station. The trail seemed to fade into the forest behind her as she rode back.

When we reached a little clearing in the trail, I told everyone we would stop for lunch. We would need to have a meeting before we got back to Eagle Train Station. I needed to know where everyone stood.

Everyone had just finished lunch. We were sitting in a circle. I congratulated everyone for getting back alive. I told them that things would be different once we returned to the Eagle Train station. Time in The Land of the Eagle

Feathers doesn't match time in the modern world. They should not be surprised about what day and month the calendar says.

I needed to know if everyone planned to return to get the next book on the first night of summer. We must have all of you return. Please raise your hands if you are returning. As I gazed at the group before me, I watched as each one raised their hands. I wasn't so sure about some of them, but I took it that they would all return. I stressed to them that they should not speak about this trip to anyone unless it would help us later. Don't be surprised if you observe people following you. You need to be careful. There are forces that would like to have some of the knowledge about the land you saw. You could be in danger.

Antonio will be sending each of you copies of what he has deciphered. He will only send you certain pages that pertain to your expertise. None of you will have a complete copy of the manuscript of *The Book of Spring*. The reason for that is obvious. That means if anyone obtains your copy, it won't give them the whole book. I have given Antonio your addresses. Study what he sends to you. You need to be on the Eagle Train from the valley below seven days before summer. Be careful, your lives depend on it.

I didn't give them time to discuss anything that I said. We saddled up and headed to Eagle Train Station. I took a shortcut so that we would be at the Eagle Train Station by early afternoon. The train was due at dusk. This would give us time to make sure everyone had their belongings packed and ready to go. I noticed that Antonio looked a little anxious. I wondered why. He told me it was about his job and boss, but mostly about his boss. We arrived at the Eagle Train Station about 3 o'clock. Mary had gone to look for the train schedule and came back surprised and confused. Even though, I had warned everyone.

It appears that someone had marked off all the days in April and most of May. She said that it should only be about April 12nd, and no train was due today. I asked her what day the train schedule indicated it was. She said it showed May 22nd. I then told everyone that that must be today. They all looked at each other with disbelief. It couldn't be May 22nd. That would mean we had been gone for over one month. Mary said in disbelief, "How could that be?" I told them again, "When you go into The Land of the Eagle Feathers, time is a dimension that changes. Remember, you must be back here in only a few short weeks to continue this journey."

Some things don't ever change. The old man and his dog were sitting on the porch like they had done for so many years before. The group stopped to talk to him while waiting for the train to arrive. The old man asked them if they had had a good trip. Antonio laughed, and said that it had been a boring one.

The old man smiled, replying to him, "Yes, sonny, I thought so." Antonio asked him why he said that. The old man said with a twinkle in his eye, "It must have been boring because you all made it back. My dog and I had a bet that one or more of you might not make it back." Antonio asked why he said that. The old man looked at the group as he replied, "Because you are the only group that everyone returned. Sometimes, nobody returns; sometimes, only a few. My dog and I have never seen everyone make it back." The old man's dog barked at the group. The old man said to his dog, "Yes, I know." Lo Ming asked, "What did the dog say?" The old dog barked again. The old man said as he and the dog walked back inside the door to the station, "He hopes that you will make it back for the next trip this summer. He says that all of you will need to be careful."

The steam engine's whistle blew loudly as the old train arrived. It wouldn't be here long. As the passengers got on the train, I had to ask Mary one thing, "I feel that I know you from some place, but where?" She only answered as she climbed on the steps to the train, "Perhaps we both will find out on our next trip to The Land of the Eagle Feathers."

Chapter VI
The Secret Passages Are Delivered:
What Did They Say?

I watched the old train pull out of the station. I had misgivings about some of the people in the group. Antonio was the one who I trusted the least. He obviously was hiding something. It didn't matter. I needed him to decipher the text of the book. I went over and got on my white horse. I took one last look at the train. It was out of my hands now. I turned my horse toward the mountains and headed home.

The group had settled down in the old passenger car. They didn't say much to each other. The beautiful scenery of the mountains was a sight to behold. Everything had a different color of green to it. The leaves of the trees were full of rich green colors that contrasted with the white rock cliffs. Thoughts of home filled their minds.

Rose was looking forward to New Orleans. She missed the party atmosphere, especially the rich spicy food. Her friends would wonder where she had been for so long. She had told them that she would be gone for a few weeks. It had been six weeks since she had seen her friends. She started to make up a story about where she had been to satisfy her inquisitive friends. A good lie always has some truth in it. Why not tell them she had met a younger man, and that they had spent several wonderful wild weeks together? That's a story anyone would like to believe.

She looked at Nick and thought, "Why not make that story true in the future." He certainly was well equipped for the long hot nights of New Orleans. Maybe, she should have sampled some of his charms. Nick smiled at Rose. Rose could feel his animal lust for her. He was very good at hiding it. She enjoyed feeling it. It was a feeling that touched her. It made her feel young, like a teenaged girl full of hormones, wanting to be wild and free. I better watch myself, she thought. This young stud is getting to me. Another part of her brain was saying, why not?

Moses and Lo Ming sat together. They were communicating as usual. Lo Ming told Moses that she would be going back to San Francisco to attend to her business. She needed to visit her family. Moses asked her if she was going to tell anyone about him. Lo Ming replied that her family and business associates were not people she shared her personal life with. They were very protective of her. Moses could see the thoughts in her mind of other men who they had driven off if they thought she could be hurt in any way. Moses told her that he understood. He knew that things were going to change in the future for them. He had ways to change people's minds that only his people knew. He had to go back to Australia to do the same thing she needed to do.

June planned to spend the next few weeks researching at various libraries, museums, and other historical sites around North Carolina. There had to be more information about The Land of the Eagle Feathers. Whether it was mentioned in symbols, legends or myths, she would find out more. She couldn't wait to visit her tribe on the great prairie.

The picture of the young brave was still on her mind. Her heart told her that they would be together again. She couldn't wait. She would ask the Great Tribal Elder and Medicine Man about him. At least, she didn't have to worry about making up a story about being gone so long. Her friends and tribal members knew she was doing research for a paper on lost tribes. She often was gone for weeks at a time. Her only worry was that one of the Elders would see through her.

Nick was wondering what he should do for the next few weeks. He loved living out of doors. He liked being alone. Thoughts of the past times in the lonely desert were inviting. He could go somewhere else to pass the time. Why not visit New Orleans? He dismissed that idea quickly. Don't mess up a good thing, he thought. He had a bad habit of that in the past.

That old Indian motorcycle he had popped into his thoughts. A long ride in the desert on his beloved cycle would do him wonders. He needed to get back to his roots anyway. Even though he had just completed one journey, the sacred places and painted rocks of the desert were beckoning him to come. He needed to hone his skills more. A few good lessons taught by his grandfather and his grandmother could be helpful in the future. He loved his grandmother. She was the only one who could tame his demons. His grandfather knew of the old ways. He was fun to be around. Sometimes, his grandfather could be a bit too serious.

Mary was thinking of what her next move would be. She had plenty of money and time before she needed to go back to college in Maine to teach. Her specialty was holistic medicine. She had some misgivings about returning to The Land of the Eagle Feathers.

Her father and stepmother had insisted on her going on this trip. What happened next just reinforced her need to find more about John and The Land of the Eagle Feathers. The train was starting to go into a tunnel. The dark background created a reflection of her face on the train window. What she saw in that reflection surprised her. She got up from her seat and immediately went to the bathroom. She looked in the mirror.

She could not believe what was staring back at her. Her hair was completely free of any gray. The bags and wrinkles under her eyes were gone. The mirror was like a fairytale. It was saying back to her that she was the fairest in the land. This time it meant that she looked almost fifteen years younger. Hurrying back to the passenger car, she decided to take a good look at the others. She had taken a picture of all of them before they had started down the trail at the bar-b-que. By comparing the picture to them now, she knew she had to go back. Everyone looked to be several years younger. Could they have found something that was a myth: The Fountain of Youth? It didn't matter what her father and stepmother wanted her to do. She would go to Houston to attend the corporate meeting. Then she would go back to Maine to prepare for the journey back.

Antonio was apprehensive about his trip back to Houston. The business he had to attend to was dangerous. He had to be very careful. One person who he did want to see was the love of his life, Angela.

Her dark long hair and warm dark tanned body drove him mad. He would do anything for her. She had seemly cast a spell over him. He was addicted to her. He couldn't get enough of her. Without her and her approval of him, he would be nothing.

He remembered when he had gotten the invitation to go on the expedition to The Land of the Eagle Feathers. He had told Angela that he had the possibility to go on an expedition to a land he only had heard about in legends. It didn't surprise him that Angela thought the expedition was a great idea. When she had suggested that he take a leave from his work and go on this trip, he knew he had them. She used the excuse that her business associates were interested in what he would find. He knew better. Her business associates even put up money to fund his trip and paid him a handsome retainer to encourage him to go. Her business associates were known to be ruthless. He didn't care. His plan was working.

The only thing on his mind was seeing her again. He needed to get his fix, and it was her. The rest could wait for later. He wouldn't tell her everything. ***The Book of Spring*** would be one thing he wouldn't tell anyone. It would be his ace in the hole. He remembered what John had said. There are dark forces that would stop at nothing to get knowledge of The Land of the Eagle Feathers.

The encouragement of Angela and her company for him to go on the expedition was starting to make sense. They wanted this land very badly. This gave him an advantage. He only had to play everyone against each other. If he played it right, he could double cross everyone, including his bosses who had sent him here. He could have it all and Angela. He could become the most powerful man in the world. That thought could corrupt anyone.

The train pulled into the station. It was time for everyone to go their separate ways. Moses gave Lo Ming a big hug and smile. Everyone else hugged and said good-bye until next time. As they walked away from the train station to the bus station, they all turned to look at the train one last time. To their amazement, the train and tracks were nowhere to be seen. They saw the old man with an old dog. Each one wondered how they got here. They thought they had left them at the Eagle Train Station.

They asked the old man with his dog sitting in a rocking chair where the train station had gone. He told them that they must be crazy. "There hasn't been a train station here for 50 years. Once in a while, the local train museum down the road has "Railroad Days." They have an old steam train. It never leaves there. There are no tracks for it. This year, just before summer, they will be having the event to raise money. You're welcome to come back for it." They told him, "Don't worry, we will."

Antonio was heading back to Houston. He called Angela from a diner. She arranged for a company car to pick him up. After waiting about four hours at the diner, a black limousine pulled up. The limo driver was a big dark man in his late twenties. The driver stood out because of his black suit, white shirt and black tie. Being bald and having a scar that ran down his right cheek told you that he wasn't any one to mess with.

The driver knew who Antonio was as soon as he saw him. The driver quickly gathered up Antonio's belongings and put them in the trunk. Trying to be considerate, Antonio asked him if he needed something to eat. The only answer he got was that Angela told him to get him back to Houston as quickly as possible. They had no time to waste. The way he said it made it sound like you had better not be late or you would be sorry. Antonio got in the limo. He never spoke to the limo driver during the long trip.

Mary noticed that her car was covered with dirt and dust. Since it had been there for several weeks, this was to be expected. She was almost surprised to see that it was still in the lot where she had parked it. You would have expected that it would have been impounded.

The old man with the dog told her that they were used to people being gone for weeks in the mountains. They just waited for them to return. Most of the people did, but once in while some didn't. He pointed to some old cars on the opposite side of the lot. "If they don't come back, we use them in the local parades and festivals. Isn't that 1956 Chevy a beautiful piece of work? When I was a kid, everyone wanted one of those. That 1950 old black Rolls Royce is my favorite. I don't know why that lady never came back to get it. I saw a picture of her once. She looked somewhat like you. We looked for years but couldn't find any relative of hers to take it. Oh! I forgot I've got a picture of her in my pocket. Take a look!" he said.

Mary glanced at the picture more to please the old man than to look. What she saw took her breath away. The lady looked like her real mother in pictures that she had seen. It could have been an identical twin, but she had no other sisters. They had told her that her mom had died years ago. She had no memories about most of her past, just bits and pieces. It didn't matter. The woman would have to be in her nineties by now. "What was her name?" Mary quickly asked. The old man petted his old dog and smiled, "Nobody knows." Before she could ask anything more, the old man and dog had turned and walked down the street. Mary started to follow him but thought better of it. The drive to Houston was a long one.

June; Rose; Moses; Lo Ming and Nick were waiting at the nearby bus station for the local bus to pick them up. A large white passenger van pulled up in front of them. June noticed that the front license plate had a picture of an eagle on it. A young Native American woman was driving. She got out. Going up to them, she said that John had chartered the van for them. It was her job to take them to the nearest airport and to see them off safely. They thought that was great. Who wanted to ride in an old bus anyway? Without hesitating, they got their stuff and loaded on to the bus. They were happy to be on their way back home. The van had bag lunches for them to eat, and a small bar for drinks.

The bright streetlights of Houston were shining as the limo pulled in front of the best hotel in town. They called it Triple Tree. The limo driver stopped at the front door. The porters in their bright red uniforms ran out to get the luggage and escort Antonio to his room. The room that Angela had booked him was the Penthouse Suite. Antonio thought that this was how to live. Before opening the door, the head porter told Antonio that they had orders to not go into the room. They would take his luggage to the secure storage room for him to get tomorrow. Angela told them to tell him that everything that he would need tonight was already in the suite. All he had to do was just step in and enjoy. That's just what Antonio did.

The lighting in the suite had been dimmed. There were some nice slow and mellow music playing in the background. The smell of food was in the air. Room service must have brought him some food. He was hungry. The limo driver never stopped for them to eat. He just drove like he was on a mission. Antonio turned the corner to go into the main room of the suite. He expected to see what room service had left him. What he saw was better than food. Angela was standing there, holding a glass of red wine for him. It was what she was wearing that made his heart race. She was more beautiful than he remembered. Without thinking, he held his breath and took a long lingering look. The porter was right. He didn't need anything. He had all he could handle and more.

Angela's eyes glowed red. His love made her dark spirit stronger. She would drain as much energy of his spirit as she could. That way she could control him more and more. Antonio felt weak. It must have been the long trip. He only wanted to sleep. Angela led him to the bedroom. Angela, totally satisfied in so many ways, knew this. She whispered in his ear that it was okay for him to sleep. He would need to rest. He had a meeting with her associates tomorrow evening. He smiled at her. He took another glimpse at her and drifted off to sleep. She got up, took a shower and left. She was pleased with herself and her plans.

As he stirred from his sleep, Antonio was disappointed when he realized Angela was gone. He found a note on her pillow that said she would see him at dinner tonight at 7 p.m. He was to wear the black pinstriped suit that she had left in the closet. Looking in the closet, Antonio was pleased to see that she had forgotten nothing. Besides the suit, there was a white shirt, black tie with small silver stars, black belt and black dress shoes. The dresser was filled with underwear, socks and other items.

After ordering lunch, Antonio took a long, hot, steamy shower. Wearing the black robe from the bathroom, he ate his lunch. He called the front desk and had his luggage brought up. He wasn't surprised to see that someone had gone through his clothes and other items. They had been incredibly careful. He was used to his luggage being searched. He had left items in certain ways that allowed him to notice if anything had been disturbed. He smiled as he picked up his jacket that he had apparently tossed on the floor last night. Angela had not found *The Book of Spring* that he had carefully sewn into the back of the inside of his jacket.   After all, the best place to hide something is in plain sight.

The next thing Antonio did was search the suite for electronic bugs. He found three bugs. He didn't try disabling any of them. He would use them to his advantage. He studied their locations and located blind spots in the suite that they didn't cover.

He would use the local city museum to study the book to translate it. His friend Rico was the superintendent and would let him use whatever he needed to translate the manuscript. All he had to do was to tell Rico that he was writing a best seller about ancient history and romance. Rico wouldn't resist it if he told him that the main character was based on Rico's loves and lovers. Rico was too vain not to give him the backroom space.

The business meeting that he was to give his report about The Land of the Eagle Feathers was being held at the company where Angela was part owner. He had no choice. He had to tell them something because they had paid him well to go on the expedition. Angela had told him that her company had a corporate meeting room where only the best Houston chefs would serve dinner to their clients.

Dressed in the clothes that Angela had furnished him, Antonio arrived 30 minutes early. He hoped that he could talk to some of her associates before the dinner meeting started. Antonio had a game plan. He would talk in enough detail to interest them but not tell everything he knew. It was his understanding that this company's business was in oil and other fossil fuels. They did have some holdings in precious metals and gems. The Company's name was A, D and S Holding, Inc. He told Angela he could guess what the A stood for but not D and S. She only laughed and said D could mean the Devil or just David. She never did say what S stood for.

Antonio was impressed with the company's building. It towered over Houston. Its large glass panels that covered the building were tinted in gold paint. This gave people the idea that this company had money and power. Antonio could feel the sense of power and knew they had deep resources. A lovely, young conservatively dressed secretary met Antonio at the front desk. He laughed to himself as he noticed she was checking him out. So as not to be rude, he made it obvious that he was checking her out.

The young lady escorted him to the elevator and guided him to the meeting room. One thing for sure, she did have that sexy librarian look down. She did have good looking long legs. As they went into the meeting room, Antonio saw Angela, standing by the ceiling to floor windows. The secretary winked at Angela as if in approval of her choice of companions. Angela smiled back and introduced Antonio to everyone in the room.

There were more associates than Antonio expected. Counting Angela, there were 13. Their ages ranged from seventies to the mid- thirties. All races and genders were present. Most appeared older with their white or graying hair. They were all very polished in their manners and small talk. Angela stood by him while she introduced everyone to him. Everything seemed to be going well. Angela told him that he would speak after they ate. He should relax. This was to be very informal. The only thing that Antonio noticed about Angela's associates was their eyes. Their eyes seem to be searching for something.

The food was five-star. After dessert, Angela introduced Antonio again. Antonio gave a convincing recap of the trip. He was an excellent speaker. Angela asked for questions. An older gentleman who sat at the very end of the big wooden conference table asked Antonio if he had seen anything of value, such as precious metals or gems. Antonio stated, "Yes, I had seen what I thought were very priceless gems. I brought some along tonight."

Antonio loved to make a statement. In a quick movement of his right hand, he produced a black bag. He ripped open the black bag, causing diamonds and gems to spill onto the table in front of him. The dark tabletop was covered with the gems that he had taken in the tunnel from The Land of the Eagle Feathers. He passed them around the room.

One of the associates, a white-haired woman in her sixties, examined the stones and pronounced that they appeared to be quite rare and valuable. This caused a great buzz of talk in the room. Antonio knew he had these people in the palms of his hands. They would back his adventures. He would get the funds and power he would need. He could play everyone against the middle. He had done this before, and he was good at it.

One of the women, who appeared to be a leader spoke to him. "Are you going back to this land that you described?

We want to know more. We have an interest in obtaining this land. We need to know more."

Antonio stated, "I was thinking of going back at the first of summer to learn more. I will need funds to cover my lost income. I am currently writing a novel." They all just laughed, and one said, "My boy, name your price, and we will cover it." Antonio gave them a price and then some. He boldly stated, "I also want Angela for myself as let's say a personal assistant." They laughed again and said you always had her. You must let her speak for herself. Angela smiled, "I know you do, and I accept your offer. You may get more than you bargained for with me."

Antonio noticed a dark-haired man, sitting in the shadows in the back of the room. This must be David. There was a woman sitting with him. Antonio couldn't see the woman clearly. He wondered who she was. As he glanced at them through the corner of his eye, he saw something that he couldn't believe. He couldn't see her completely, but he could see her ankles. On one ankle was a tattoo of a butterfly. There was only one person he knew who had butterfly tattoos. It had to be Mary. Rose said there were two scorpions in their group. He smiled. He had found the other scorpion. He would keep this a secret. It would be to his advantage. It would make things more difficult. Angela asked him why he was smiling. Antonio replied that he was enjoying himself.

Antonio left the corporate meeting shortly after his presentation. Angela handed him an envelope as she escorted him to the conference room's door. She told him that she would be needing to stay. She would not be able to see him for a while. She needed to go on a business trip.

Antonio was disappointed. He wanted to her to come with him tonight. He got on the elevator. Being alone would give him a chance to start deciphering *The Book of Spring*. He couldn't risk doing that in the apartment that

Angela provided him. It was a little late, but he could go to the Museum of Natural History and do that there. It wasn't too far of a walk from the Hotel.

They had arranged for a car to drop him off at his hotel. It didn't take him long to change clothes. He took the book and his writing materials. Taking the service elevator, he slipped out the service entrance of the hotel. The five blocks to the museum didn't take too long. Soon he arrived at the back entrance to the museum. His friend, Rico, had given him the pass codes to the alarm system. Antonio laughed at the need to have the codes, but he had to have a reason if he was caught inside at this late hour. He would have broken the codes in a few minutes, regardless.

He made sure to locate the night security guard before going to the basement office that Rico had set up for him. He told the security guard that Rico needed for him to finish the book he was writing as soon as possible. He told him that was why he was here, working so late. The night watchman laughed. He told Antonio that he knew about the novel that Antonio was writing. It seems that Rico was enormously proud that the book was based on him. Rico had told everyone about the novel that Antonio was writing.

Antonio settled down in his basement office in front of his old typewriter. He didn't trust using a computer because someone could hack it and get the transcripts of the book. He liked using the old typewriter. It was trustworthy. Nobody could get any information from it. It made him feel like an old-time novelist writing a mystery novel. Taking out a sheet of paper, he put it in the typewriter.

The first important poem or information would go the Lo Ming. His other employer had told him that she was key to finding the most important book of all: ***The Book of Winter.***

He smiled as he started deciphering the book. Currently, he had two employers that he was working for in this adventure. If ***The Book of Winter*** was that powerful, he would find a way to keep it for himself. As he read the first passage of ***The Book of Spring,*** he started changing his mind. The passage was in poetry form. It seemed to be directed right at him.

Many Moons Ago

Hey Yi, Hey Yi, Hey Yi, Yo
There is a land where spirits go
Ruled by Mother Earth and Father Sky
Only they know the reasons why

Many moons ago, they chose you
You will lead The Chosen Ones thru
You will be the only one to understand
The secrets of this land

It is in the stones in dirt
Hidden and picked by Mother Earth
She will send you the secret words
Carried by the song of the birds

All things have a reason
All things have a season
All things are a part of the other
All creatures are a sister or brother

It was written that you will come
Your face was in the moon and sun
It was written many moons ago
Hey Yi, Hey Yi, Hey Yi, Yo

After reading this passage, Antonio felt confused. He had always prided himself on not becoming involved emotionally with others. He liked the people who he went with to The Land of the Eagle Feathers. For the first time, he had reservations about double crossing them. Was what he had experienced in The Land of the Eagle Feathers starting to influence him? He was wondering why The Elders knew so much about him. Did they see something in him that he didn't? Once he had been a true believer in the good of mankind. He had become the opposite. The years of missions had changed him. He had seen too much death and destruction. Was The Land of the Eagle Feathers changing him?

One thing that Antonio couldn't figure out was how to get the passages to the other members of his group. He found out how to do this in an unusual way. When he worked the first night on the book, he went back to the hotel to get some sleep. He had a vivid dream that night. In the dream, there was a young woman riding a painted Indian pony. He dreamed that he was walking outside the museum late at night when this young woman on horseback rode up to him. She asked him in an ancient language to come at midnight to a spot in the park across from the museum near a great oak tree whenever he had a passage to give to one of his group.

He could summon her by pointing at the Southern Star with whatever book he was working on. She told him that she only needed the name of the person. She would find them and deliver them the passage. In his dream, she would ride off into the park and disappear.

Antonio understood the meaning of the dream. In many American Indian cultures, it is believed that dreams have great significance. A dream could convey messages from

147

the great spirits. This dream was so vivid that he was sure it was a message that he would have to follow.

One day, he hoped that he could follow his dreams. It is believed that a person could detach their soul, and their soul could move anywhere while they were dreaming. Perhaps, with some assistance from one of group, he could learn to do that very thing. If anyone would know how to do that, it would be one of the women in his group. Presently, he would do as the dream instructed him to do.

He followed what the dream instructed when he finished the first passage. He left the museum a few minutes before midnight. It was a clear night. The stars were very bright. It is almost impossible for you to see stars in the middle of a city at night because the bright lights of the city usually block out the lights from the stars. Antonio realized this was a sign to demonstrate the power of the dream. When he reached the spot in the park, he took out *The Book of Spring* and pointed it toward the Southern Star. Behind him, he heard a woman's voice. The woman told him to turn around. He turned around. He saw a young woman on a painted pony. She was unbelievably beautiful with braided black hair and copper skin. He noted her dress was red buckskins with leggings. She rode up to him. She reached out for the brown envelope he had in his hands. He handed it to her. The envelope had Lo Ming's name on it. Taking the envelope, she nodded her head and rode behind some trees in the park and disappeared. This was the way he handled every envelope from that point on. Antonio knew not to reason why, but to only to do what he was asked.

Antonio had been working tirelessly for two weeks, deciphering the passages from *The Book of Spring.* Rico didn't bother him too much. To convince Rico that he was working on a novel, Antonio would write several pages using stories that Rico told him about himself. That seemed to please Rico. He gave several pages to Rico to read every day.

He had finished the last of the pages of **The Book of Spring.** Antonio had studied the pages he deciphered very carefully. It had taken him several days of almost nonstop work to figure out the book's secrets. After studying several passages carefully, he found there were subtle clues that pointed to which poems were important and which poems were just put there to confuse or mislead.

Deciphering the passages took all of Antonio's knowledge of ancient languages. He was glad that he had once worked as a decoder for several agencies like the C.I.A. and Russian Intelligence. This helped him unlock the code that told him which poems were important. He was proud that he had the knowledge to break the code. Only a few people in the world could have done this. Perhaps, as the Council had said, he was the only one who could have done this job. The Great Spirits of The Land of the Eagle Feathers were indeed knowledgeable.

What Antonio didn't know about was the meeting that Angela had with David after the corporate meeting he had attended. Angela had waited for the corporate meeting to end before approaching David, the company's CEO. She had to be diplomatic. David was a very difficult person to confront. After the last corporate person left, David asked Angela to come to his office to discuss some business matters.

As they walked down the long hallway to his office, Angela made sure to walk in front of David to give him a good view of her assets. They had once been close, but that ended many years ago when he met Benita, his current wife. Angela did know that David did love looking at beautiful women. Angela opened the door to David's office. David followed her and asked her to take a seat near his large walnut desk. There was only one small office lamp lit. Angela never cared for David's office. She felt it was too dark, and the furnishings gave it a cold atmosphere. A large painting of himself, riding a black horse, covered the wall behind him.

David sat down behind his desk. "I can see that something is bothering you," he said. Angela tried her best to be calm. She was too upset to be diplomatic. "Why did you have those men attack the group leaving the passageway to The Land of the Eagle Feathers?' she said in a sarcastic tone. David had the look of someone that had been caught off guard. "What do you mean? I didn't have anyone there, but you and your men assigned to this mission," he replied to her. By the angry look on David's face, she realized that David was telling her the truth. She knew him well enough to recognize when he did sometimes tell the truth.

David leaned back in his leather office chair that looked more like a throne than one you would expect in a corporate office. He ran his hands through his long black hair. Angela knew he was thinking of a response. Before long, David leaned forward. He stared at Angela, searching her eyes for the truth. Angela never liked it when David would look at you eye to eye. It made it almost impossible to hide anything from him. His eyes told her he was mad and upset. This was not going as smoothly as Angela would have liked.

"This is not good, Angela. It means that someone else is interested in The Land of the Eagle Feathers. We have spent too many years on trying to obtain the powers of that land for me to do anything that would be so foolish. We both know that we need everyone who accompanied that guide to stay alive. We cannot get the information we need to obtain *The Book of Winter* without them," David emphasized each word as he spoke.

"How do we know if it is just one group trying to get into the land?" Angela asked.

David answered her question, "You are probably right. I can think of several people who would be ungodly interested in obtaining both the riches of the land and its power. I don't worry too much about the ones who want the riches. They are not that powerful. It is the ones who have other mystical powers who worry me more. They won't stop until they obtain the powers that we seek. Those powers are a prize that anyone would want."

"What do you want me to do?" asked Angela.

"You must protect Antonio at all costs. He is the key to our success. You watch him closely. We don't trust him, but we need him. I know you will do whatever you need to keep him happy and safe," David laughed. Then David got very serious. "We don't know much about the other members of Antonio's group. I have a feeling that they were selected for two reasons. One is that they can take care of themselves, and the other is that they have special powers. I will send some of my best operatives to check on their safety. I doubt if they will need any assistance. You take a few days off before seeing Antonio. Let him work on his so-called novel. Then give him a call. As they say: absence makes a heart grow fonder."

Chapter VII
Nobody is Safe:
Where Can We Hide?

Lo Ming returned home to San Francisco. Her business partner picked her up from the airport. Van Lo Sing was about fifty-five years old with gray hair. He was extremely physically fit for his age. Years of martial arts practice and mystical arts instruction kept him that way. Wondering where she had been had worried him. She was supposed to be gone for only a few weeks, not several weeks. The first thing he did notice about her was that she looked at least ten years younger. She did smile more and wasn't so cynical about things. When he asked her about her trip, all he got were very vague answers. He suspected that there was more about her trip than she was telling. He didn't press for more information. That was her business.

Her business, which was down by the docks, had the best spring season ever. Even the most expensive items were selling well. Lo Ming didn't seem that interested in the bottom line. That was unusual for Lo Ming. The bottom line was one aspect of her business that she watched closely. Van Lo Sing didn't mind for he was extremely glad to have her back. He missed their sparring matches. He missed their studies of the mystical arts. She was special. Her powers were greater than anyone he had taught.

Lo Ming told him that she would be going back on another trip in a couple of weeks. Van Lo protested that he needed her here to help him with the business. All Lo Ming said was she had some sort of unfinished work to complete. She appreciated his loyalty and was especially impressed with how well he had managed the business.

She wanted to give him most of the profits. He deserved to become a full partner with her if he wanted. Van Lo thanked her. He said that wasn't necessary. She insisted. She told him that for the next two weeks they would need to spar and study like her life would depend on it. Van Lo was curious. He would do as she wanted. There was no arguing with Lo Ming. The extra money would give him the ability to gain more knowledge. He could obtain more of the secret mystical books from Tibet. He would enjoy making Lo Ming wish that she never suggested to him to train her so hard.

It was an early bright spring morning when a messenger rang her doorbell. She opened her door to discover a young beautiful woman holding a large brown envelope. She was dressed in a short American Native Indian buckskin dress. She asked if Lo Ming was here. Lo Ming told her that she was Lo Ming. The young lady smiled, "Antonio said I should give this envelope to an Asian lady who was both mysterious and lovely." Lo Ming smiled as she took the envelope.

Lo Ming told the young lady to wait. She would give her a tip. The young lady laughed and told her that Antonio had already tipped her. She showed Lo Ming a yellow diamond that Antonio had taken from the secret passage in the mountains. Lo Ming told the young lady that she must be someone special for him to give her that for a tip. The young woman didn't reply to her. She gave Lo Ming a bow, turned and left the house. Lo Ming watched the young lady leave. The young woman mounted her Painted Indian pony. She rode toward the brush on the lower part of the hill in front of her house. As the horse entered the brush, they both seemed to disappear.

Lo Ming opened the envelope as soon as she was inside her house. It was a page with a note on it from Antonio. It told her that this was for her eyes only. The envelope

contained only one page. This page was typewritten which
she thought was unusual.   She knew that Antonio was
very smart to do so.   That meant she had the only copy of
the passage.

The Spirit Lives On and On and On

Some say, it's always been
When you feel the touch of the wind
You feel the touch of one who's gone
The Spirit lives on and on and on

Riding the stars in the sky
Flying so low, flying so high
Hiding in the leaves of the tree
Flying so close, flying so free

Singing these songs of an ancient race
Touching your body, touching your face
Playing in the spray of a fountain
Flying to the valley, flying to the mountain

Telling the stories of those left behind
Visiting your world, visiting your mind
Dreams coming in the still of the night
Flying to the left, flying to the right

Visiting the land of those who know
Touching your mind, touching your soul
Only known to the minds that understand
Flying to the mountain, flying to the land

Rose was glad to be back in New Orleans. She went
straight to her favorite restaurant, The Black Widow.
Cajun food was something she had missed. She ordered
almost everything on the menu. Her friend, Wanda, the

waitress/cook, was glad that Rose was here. Wanda thought that the trip had done Rose wonders. Rose looked relaxed and somewhat younger.

Wanda noticed that Rose was deep in thought. "What is the matter?" she asked. Rose replied, "It's about a younger man who I met on my journey into the mountains." Wanda knew it had to be a man. Every woman can tell when a woman has fallen for one. She questioned Rose about everything that had happened. Rose replied that she was somewhat troubled about having a relationship with a much younger man. When Rose showed her a picture of Nick, Wanda whistled. She said, "Now honey, if you don't want him, I would be happy to take that handsome young man off your hands." Rose told her that that wouldn't be necessary. She had plans for him herself.

The next morning, Rose went to the bank to get more money for her needs. When she got there, she got out her safety deposit box. She noticed that it felt heavier this time than the last time she had it out. Opening it, she closed it quickly. She opened it again. There must be a mistake. The box was full. Inside it was a large green bag.

Taking the green bag, she tore it open. It was full of hundred-dollar bills. The amount in the bag came to exactly $50,000. A note was attached. It stated that one of her clients wanted to give her some of his business profits. He had asked her for advice about what to do with his business. Rose had read her cards and done other things to assist him. The client stated that he had become successful because of her advice. She was receiving this out of his gratitude. "Have a good life," it said. "There is more where this came from. If you need anything, all you need to do is ask."

Rose asked the teller how anyone had gotten into her bank deposit box. The dark-haired female teller replied that a handsome gentleman had stopped in to put something into her box. He had a note signed in her handwriting indicating that he could leave something in her box. The note was even notarized. Rose was puzzled but who could argue. If she said anything, who would believe her? Nobody drops by and puts $50,000 in your bank deposit box.

Rose asked the teller to describe the gentleman. The teller said he was average in height. It was how he was dressed that caught her eye. He was not dressed like a local. He dressed well. It was the off-white hat he carried. It looked like an old cavalry hat. It had a figure seven on the crown. He said something about the fact that he owed you for saving his life.

A smile crossed Rose's lips, she knew exactly who he was and why. She immediately left the bank taking the money. She was going to pay off what little she owed. She didn't worry about missing her business appointments because only getting back to the Land of the Eagle Feathers mattered to her.

When Rose got back to her home, she saw a young Native American woman standing on her porch. She asked the young woman what she wanted? The woman replied that she was here to deliver her an envelope. She handed a brown envelope to Rose. "You came far to give this to me. Let me fix you some tea or coffee." The young woman replied, "That will not be necessary. I need to get back." With that said, the young woman turned and walked down to the street in front of Rose's house. Rose watched as the young women whistled three times. A painted pony came out of the wooded swamp across the street. The young woman mounted her painted pony. She waved good-bye to Rose. Rose watched as she turned her pony, and at full gallop rode her pony into the wooded swamp. Rose worried about them for a few seconds. That swamp contained quicksand and other wild animals. Rose smiled.

She knew that the young woman and her pony would be all right. Spirits have a way of taking care of their own.

The envelope had only her name on it. She intuitively knew who had sent it. Tearing it open, it contained one page. A note was attached to the page. It was from Antonio. It said that this page is for you to study, decipher and memorize.

The Spirits are Always Watching You

See the star shining bright
It's an Indian brave riding in the night
See the tree swaying in the wind
It's a message the spirits send

It may be hard to understand
Spirits live in an unknown land
No matter what you do
The spirits are always watching you

They come at day or night
They come if you're wrong or right
They have no form or shape
From them, there is no escape

There's nowhere you can run
The spirits know what you've done
There's nowhere for you to hide
The spirits are by your side

When you've done wrong, they'll know
You'll see an unknown glow
So be careful what you do
The spirits are always watching you

On the Northern prairie, June watched from the hill above the Indian village. There was a young Indian woman on a Painted pony riding up the hill to her. The young woman stopped in front of her. She said to her in June's native language that a friend had asked her to deliver this. The young woman handed her a brown envelope. Before she could say anything, she turned her pony and rode over the hill behind her. June started to tell the young woman that she was going the wrong way. The young woman yelled back that she knew where she was going. June had just received her correspondence from Antonio. The text was in poetry form. She carefully looked at the passage he had sent her.

The Wisdom in *The Book of Spring*

Mother Earth and Father Sky
We come to ask you why
Spring is the season for rebirth
We are all children of Mother Earth

Watch the river flowing South
Look for orange backed trout
Hunt for the split oaken bough
Listen for the gray wolf's howl

The pink moon rising in the sky
Points to where it may lie
The wisdom of the ages is there
Hidden in the den of the bear

The wind will whisper your name
Nothing will ever be the same
Everything old will seem new
Everything false will seem true

It is now and has always been
Listen to the songs of the wind
The voices of the birds will bring
The wisdom of *The Book of Spring*

It would be a test for her to locate the hidden meanings of the passage.

After a while, she showed some of the deciphered text to the Elders of her tribe. They found them to be quite unusual. They were both excited and worried. The Great Elder would only say that there were wise meanings to the text, but you must be very careful. He had seen this type of text many years, long ago. There once was a young warrior who had discovered a text like these. He had shown them to him. The Great Elder could not decipher their meaning. The young warrior decided to go on a vision quest to find their meanings.

This young warrior was one of the greatest warriors of our tribe. He was brave and wise for his years. Many warriors of our tribe were surprised that he did not return from his quest. The Great Elder tried to contact the Great Spirit. The Great Spirit gave him no reply to his whereabouts.

The Great Elder stated to her, "You must go to find out more. I will teach you everything the Elders know. You must learn more about how to use your powers. I can foresee that you will be going on a great journey. You will need all your powers to survive this journey to come home to us."

Mary decided to attend a business meeting in Houston, Texas before going back to her home in Maine. Her father had a company there. She wanted to talk to her father. Mary believed that her stepmother was running the company.

Mary had taken a consulting job with her father's company. She thought that it might be a way to get closer to her stepmother. Maybe, she would be able to use it to get back in good graces with her father. Mary always felt that she was never good enough for him. He was a hard businessman. This time, she would show him.

Nick had finally gotten home. Home for him was his grandfather and grandmother. The New Mexico desert was beautiful this time of year with the cactus blooming. His grandmother greeted him with a hug as he got off his old Indian motorcycle. She was a small stout woman. Her dark red face showed the years of living in the hot dusty desert. She was dressed in the traditional Indian clothing of her tribe. She told him that she would be making his favorite native dishes for the evening meal. As she went into the house, she said something to his grandfather as he came out of the adobe house to greet Nick.

His grandfather could tell that something was different about Nick. Nick's eyes had a little bit of glimmer in them. Nick's grandmother had seen it. She had whispered to him that she knew that Nick had a girlfriend. Nick noticed that his grandfather had a smile on his face. That was not the usual expression for his grandfather.

His grandfather asked Nick how long he was going to stay this time. Nick replied for just a few weeks. He had to go back to be somewhere before the first days of summer. His grandfather asked him what he wanted to do in the next few weeks. Nick surprised him by saying, "I want to learn about the old ways. I will need to learn as much as possible about the great medicine that our people have passed down through the years." His grandfather asked him why. Nick said that he was going on a great journey of discovery. To survive this journey, he had to learn as much as possible. His grandfather only said a few words, "We will begin tomorrow at first light."

About a week after Nick had arrived at his grandparents, a young woman on an Indian pony rode up to the adobe house. His grandmother greeted her. She could tell that the young woman's ancestry was from ancient times. Nick's grandmother knew such things. She had not seen a woman with those dark features and high cheek bones for many years. The young woman was friendly but was in a hurry. She gave Nick's grandmother a large envelope and asked her to give it to him. Nick's grandmother asked her to stay for dinner. The young woman said, "I have other deliveries to make."

Nick's grandmother walked the young woman back to her white painted pony. It was grazing in some grass near the old road in front of the house. As the young woman mounted her pony, Nick's grandmother said to the young woman in an ancient language to have a safe journey. The young woman replied to her in the same language an ancient Indian saying, "May you have many happy moons and circles of the sun ahead of you." The young woman turned her pony toward the old dusty road. The wind started to blow, causing a great cloud of dust. After the dust cloud settled to the earth, there was no sign of the young woman or her pony. This didn't surprise Nick's grandmother.

Nick's grandmother was not happy. She knew who had sent this young woman. It had to be the one called Antonio. She had taught Antonio many years before the ancient language that the young woman spoke. Antonio had said he was a professor of languages. She knew better than believe him. The great spirits of the desert had told her to teach him anyway. Who was she to argue with the great spirits? If her grandson was working with Antonio, he could be in great danger.

Nick and his grandfather came back from the desert caves that night. His grandmother told them of the young woman that had delivered a large envelope for Nick. She gave it to Nick. Nick took it to his room and opened it. It contained a note and a sheet of paper. The note was from Antonio that said for him to study the passage. He must find the clues. He could not let anyone see it unless they could be trusted. Nick looked at the passage and read it.

It Comes at Night

The sun is starting to set
I'm feeling things I can't forget
They get stronger with the twilight
I know it comes at night

The darkness is starting to appear
The visions are starting to become clear
It's a feeling I can't fight
I know it comes at night

The silence of the dark surrounds me
There's something here I can't see
I can't resist or try as I might
I know it comes at night

I see its vision, and we are together
It touches me with an eagle feather
It makes everything seem so right
I know it comes at night

I see the first break of day
I know it'll have to go away
It'll ride the eagle away in flight
I know it comes at night

Later that night under the desert's full moon, Nick's grandparents were sitting outside talking. "You know what this means," said his grandmother. "Yes, I do. It means the legend is true," replied his grandfather. "The spirits have told me in a dream that our grandson is a great warrior. He has won many battles in the old countries in a far eastern land, but his soul has wounds," his grandmother stated looking at the full moon. "We must teach him everything we know this year. He is special. He has a path that he must follow. Let us hope that it will be enough. We will begin his lessons tomorrow," his grandfather replied as he took his wife's hand in his. They decided to sit a little bit longer and enjoy the desert's songs and sights.

The old house in the southern Maine woods was small and comfortable. It had been raining for several days. It was midmorning. Mary had just arrived back from Houston, Texas about two days before. She loved listening to the rain on the old slate roof. Sitting in the old library, she researched for any information she could find about any land called Eagle Feathers. In her hand was a very old book on mysterious lands. It mentioned Indian legends. She found a small passage that told of an ancient land believed to exist in the green mountains of the eastern United States. This land was called The Land of the Eagle Feathers. The only thing the passage said was that many people had tried to find this land, because of the riches that it contained.

It is believed that the people who lived in this land had access to powerful knowledge. This knowledge could make anyone all powerful. The passage stated that many men had tried to discover this land. It appears that most of them were never heard from again. They seemed to disappear.

Mary noticed that the rain had stopped. She decided to go outside to her flower and herb garden. She was on her knees weeding the garden when she heard a horse snorting. Turning her head toward the sound, she was startled to observe a young Native American woman standing behind her.

"I didn't mean to scare you," the young woman laughed. Mary jumped up immediately to face her. "Don't be alarmed. I am here to deliver an envelope from a friend of yours," the young woman said to her. Mary wiped her dirty hands on her old brown apron to clean them. She took the brown envelope from the young lady's hands. Mary knew who it would be from before reading the note inside. Mary asked the young woman about her dress. "I love your dark red buckskin dress and leggings. Are you attending the Native American Indian festival in town?"

The young woman replied, "No, I would like to attend. I hope you don't mind my painted pony grazing on some of your wonderful green grass. I need to get along to deliver some more envelopes." Mary watched as the young woman mounted her painted pony. The young woman rode into the forest behind her home. She seemed to disappear as soon as the pony entered the forest. There was one thing disturbing about that. There was no horse trail she knew of in that forest.

Mary took the envelope into the house. She sat down in the library at her study desk and opened it. Inside was a note from Antonio that told her to read and study it. Taking the sheet that the note was attached to, she read it and started to decipher any meaning it had for her.

Hidden in Your Mind

Look to the eyes of Father Sky
Wait for the sound of the eagle's cry
Listen to the voice of the wind
That tell you secrets the elders send

Watch for signs from Mother Earth
Listen for the sounds of birth
Wait for the sounds from a bird's nest
That tell you secrets while you rest

North is South, and South is North
Watch for the deer to go forth
Wait for brother wolf to howl
That tell you when the animals bow

Look for the old oak tree
Wait for what you will see
Listen to the leaves that roar
That tell you how to open the door

Look at everything you saw
Watch and listen to it all
Wait for images of a circle
That tell you of nature's miracle

Then only can you know
You're within a stone's throw
Then only will you find
The secrets that are hidden in your mind

    The Australian Outback was not as hot this time of year.
It was very dry. In Australia, it was fall. Moses had
decided to take a short walk-about to clear his head. He

needed to think about the whole experience that he had in his journey to The Land of the Eagle Feathers. He had hiked at least one hundred miles from civilization or any person. He had chosen the most barren land he could find for this walk-about. He liked the challenge of survival in this harsh land. Most of all, he loved being alone with his animal friends.

He felt it before he saw it. Looking to the west, he saw a small dust cloud rising from the earth. That could mean only someone on horseback coming fast. It would take someone about an hour to reach his location. He decided to sit in the shade of a large boulder and wait to see if the person would be riding by him. This interested him because only the most experienced person could survive out here, especially with a horse. Moses leaned against the boulder taking his Aussie hat to cover his eyes. He would take advantage of this time to take a short nap.

After about an hour, Moses sensed that the rider was near. He didn't move from his position. The rider's pony had told him that they had come in peace. The painted pony stopped in front of him. A female voice said to him, "I have an envelope to give you, Moses." Moses uncovered his face. He was a little surprised to see a young Native American woman on a painted pony with a brown envelope in her hand.

"How did you find me?" Moses asked.

"It was not that hard. You are skilled in covering your tracks. I did enjoy tracking you. It did cost me a little extra time to reach you. Now, take this envelope. I need to leave," said the impatient young lady.

Taking the brown envelope from her hand, he noted how she was dressed. Her buckskin leggings and dress protected her dark copper skin from the sun. The one thing that stood out was the American white cowboy hat on her head. "I notice you are wondering about the hat on my head. A friend of mine told me that I would need it to protect myself from the sun. I think it makes my dark, black hair look good. Have a good day, Moses."

The young woman turned her painted pony back toward the east. Before Moses could tell her that it would be closer for her to keep going west, the wind started blowing, causing a cloud of dust. When the dust cleared, the young woman and pony had disappeared. Moses just smiled. This was a good place to camp for today. He had some reading to do. He sat back down, opened the envelope, and started reading the sheet of paper inside studying it. It was written in the form of a poem.

The Great Spirit's Land

In the times of the old
There are secrets the spirits hold
A few remain who know the story
Of times of honor and glory

Listen to what the winds say
Listen to the music of the trees' sway
Listen to the echo of the ancient flute
Listen to the message in the Owl's hoot

Look to the direction of the skies
Look to the eagle that flies
Look to the symbols on the rock
Look to yourself to open the lock

Your ears will let you hear the winds
Your ears will hear what the tree sends
Your eyes will see where to go
Your eyes will see what you should know

Oh, Great Father in the sky
Oh, Great Creator up so high
Give him the wisdom to understand
How to enter the Great Spirit's Land

It was about midnight when Antonio arrived at the city park. He went to an old oak tree near the wooded area of the park. He waited for the young woman and her painted pony to appear. At midnight, the old church bell struck 12 times from across the street. A cold wind started to blow, moving the branches of the old oak tree back and forth. Behind him he heard a woman's voice calling his name.

Antonio turned. The young woman mounted on her painted pony was there. "I know that you have been concerned about the passages that you have sent. The Great Council is pleased that you sent the right ones to each member of your group. I delivered the last one yesterday." Antonio nodded to the young woman.

The young woman smiled. "The Great Council members are pleased that you figured out which passages to send. They realized that you used your knowledge of astrology to match each passage with each person. The Great Council wondered if you knew the secret. You will be pleased that each member of your group is deciphering the passages as I speak. You were worried that they would not be able to understand their meaning. You underestimated their expertise. Do not worry. They will have the right answers at the right time. It is written. It is their heritage that allows for that. They have many special skills, and that is just one of them."

The young woman's face became serious. "You always had faith in both astrology and the mystical arts, even though this caused problems for you. It seems your religious superiors did not believe in those things."

The young woman laughed. "You have come far. You still have far to go. We hope you survive your many journeys. We will be watching you. May you choose the right path." The young woman rode her pony past Antonio and disappeared into the trees. Antonio watched her go. He was relieved, but he did not know why. He felt that he needed to see Angela. He would need Angela more than ever. Somehow, she was a key to finding the last book. At least that was what the last passage of *The Book of Spring* told him.

Angela was busy at her downtown office. She had just returned from two weeks off. She was planning the next move to take over The Land of the Eagle Feathers. She had worked for several years with David, the CEO of their company. She never trusted him. She smiled as she thought about that factor in their relationship. They once had been close, but that was only a matter of convenience for each.

Angela had been confident that she could control her position in the company. Until, unexpectedly, David announced that he was getting married to Benita. Benita was his second wife. It didn't take Angela long to realize that her time with the company could become short.

David had a habit of removing loose ends. Angela was one because she knew what had happened to his first wife. Angela was directly involved in a plot to eliminate his first wife. Angela had done a lot of dirty work for David over the years. If David only knew that Angela did not always follow his orders to the letter, David would have killed her many years ago.

Angela's thoughts returned to Antonio. He was her ticket out of this bad situation. Antonio was her soulmate. He was as unscrupulous as she was. Angela could sense that she should never trust him. That was why they were so good together. She liked dealing with him. He was exciting and intriguing to be around. They had met briefly many years ago, but she had broken off their relationship. Now that Antonio was here, she could use his talents to turn the tables on David.

Over the years, Angela had come to realize that there were other forces and people behind David. These forces were evil. Evil never bothered Angela. These people were different. These people were much more ruthless and powerful than any she had ever dealt with. Analyzing her situation, she had to get out. To protect herself, she had to get something more powerful than they were. *The Book of Winter* would do just that.

It had been several days since she been with Antonio. She had done what David had asked. She had not seen Antonio. She called Antonio. Angela asked if Antonio had missed her. Antonio told her that he was trying to finish his novel. He had certainly missed her for several reasons. She knew why Antonio had missed her.

Angela knew that he was lying about that excuse about the novel. Antonio was playing everyone against the middle like she was. She knew men. She asked him to come over to her apartment for dinner. He would come. It was the after-dinner activities that he could not resist.

It was a hot day in the Outback. Moses had studied the passage that Antonio had sent him. He memorized it. He lit a match and burned it. He could sense that the weather was changing. The animals were restless and taking shelter. That meant the rains were coming. In the desert, that was both good and bad. The desert needed rain, but the flash floods were extremely dangerous.

It wasn't the rain that bothered Moses. There were people coming. They were coming for him. He was told in a dream to beware. It was his grandfather in the dream who communicated to him about these men.

It seems that several men had been asking about him in the nearest town. That town was over a hundred miles away. His grandfather told him that Old Cap, an old enemy of Moses, had agreed to track him for these men for a fee. Moses knew that Old Cap would be able to find him because Old Cap was considered one of the great Aborigine trackers. He never blamed Old Cap for being his enemy. Like many friendships, a beautiful woman can come between the best of friends. Moses cursed himself. It was his fault anyway. No matter how much he tried, Old Cap never forgave him.

Moses broke camp. He would head deeper into the desert. It would be a few days before the storm would hit. Old Cap would be able to deal with the desert. The men whom he was guiding would not be able to.

Moses would enjoy the next few days. He wondered if Old Cap was still as good as he once was at tracking. He hoped so. Moses would lead them to a perfect spot for an ambush. It would not be Moses who would ambush them. Mother nature would decide their fate. Like most Aborigines, Moses believed that humans and nature were equal. He believed that the humans became or changed into the features of land and that mountains, rivers, and other significant land features had the spirituality of man.

Lo Ming had been studying the passage from Antonio. She used her knowledge of the ancient myths of Asia and other cultures to finally gain the meaning of the passage. After she was satisfied that she had extracted all the passage's meaning, she burned the paper it was printed on.

High in the hills above the ocean bay, the morning sun was coming through the east bedroom window of Lo Ming's mansion. Slowly, she rose into a sitting position. Her body hurt from the workouts with Van Lo Sing. There wasn't a muscle that wasn't sore. This was only a small price to pay for the hours of ancient combat teaching Van

Lo had given her. Van Lo had pushed her to her limit of endurance. The training sessions had honed her fighting skills.

Van Lo had taught her other aspects of the ancient arts as well. He was a master mystic of the Asian mystical arts. He taught her these skills to fight the "Dark Ones." Lo Ming had asked him how he knew about the "Dark Ones." He told her that now was not the time to discuss that. He did tell her to be extremely careful. The "Dark Ones" were very dangerous.

Lo Ming took a hot shower to loosen her sore tight muscles. As she put on her silk bathrobe, she noticed that the large mirror in the bathroom that was covered with moisture had writing on it in Chinese. It was a mystical message from Van Lo. It said that her life was in danger. Two men had been asking about her in Chinatown. They wanted to know where she lived. They must have found out. They were last seen this morning driving toward her mansion. She should be very careful. He was coming as fast as he could.

Lo Ming heard a loud cry of an eagle outside. She looked out the bathroom window. All she could see was a black sedan parked on the street below. She noticed two large Asian men, dressed in black suits. They were getting out of the black sedan. Lo Ming wasted no time in running into her bedroom. She grabbed her fighting stick that she always kept by her bedside.

The cut of their hair and the tattoos on their arms told her that these men were assassins. Someone had hired the best assassins from Japan. Lo Ming didn't have time to change. She would have to fight in her robe, but that didn't matter. Her robe was loose enough for her to move quickly. She quietly moved downstairs. She would need room to fight these men. She picked the great room to wait for them.

She would find out if Van Lo Sing's training would give her the edge she needed to survive.

Moses had been running for about two hours. He did not try to conceal his tracks. In about six miles, he would be at a dry riverbed. Moses would lead Old Cap and his guests down the dry riverbed to a small canyon. Here would be a good place to ambush them. Unless Old Cap figured out what he was doing, Moses' plan would work. He thought it would take them two days to reach the canyon. It would be late in the day, so they would probably make camp for the night. The storm should arrive upstream about 11 o'clock. The canyon would flood about midnight.

Moses would let the Rainbow Serpent decide their fate. The Rainbow Serpent is the God of Water in the Outback. The sign of the Rainbow Serpent is a large rainbow. It is said that wherever a rainbow touches the ground, the Rainbow serpent finds a waterhole in the desert. If someone breaks the laws of the desert, the Rainbow Serpent will deal with them as it feels necessary.

Antonio had just received a phone call from Angela. He was exhausted from the days and late nights that he had worked on the manuscripts. It was one thing to work on *The Book of Spring,* but another to write a fake novel to please Rico. Antonio was starting to think that maybe he would publish the novel about Rico someday. After all, it was a romantic novel. These were selling well these days. Antonio couldn't wait to see Angela tonight. He would cook an Italian dinner for her with some excellent Italian wine.

Angela had picked out a very short tight black dress that accented her best physical features. When Antonio opened his apartment's door, he had to stop and stare. Angela smiled and asked Antonio if he could stop staring and let her into his apartment. Antonio replied to her that she was more beautiful than ever. Angela told him if dinner was half as good as it smells, the food would be delicious.

Lo Ming waited for the two men to break in before doing anything. She would surprise them. She would be in the hallway closet between the front room and kitchen. One of the men rang the front doorbell. The other man broke into the back of the house, breaking down the patio door to the kitchen. The man in the back of the house slowly crept toward the front door. As he moved into the hallway toward the front past the closet door, Lo Ming carefully opened the closet door. With the intruder now having his back to her, she swung the fighting stick and caught the man in the back of the head. He fell to the floor with a loud thud. The man at the front door had forced open the lock and charged at her. Before she could recover, the attacker had knocked her down. They both fell to the floor, knocking Lo Ming's fighting stick down the hall. Lo Ming jumped up quickly into a fighting stance. Lo Ming was amazed to see that the large man had done the same. This man was a skillful fighter. He had been trained well. Without her fighting stick, Lo Ming would be at a distinct disadvantage in this fight. Luckily for her, the first man didn't get up. Lo Ming worried that if the man recovered, she would have a very difficult time in winning this battle.

Lo Ming faced the man in front of her. The man had on a black mask, but his eyes told her he was not wanting to fight her. In the world of combat martial arts, Lo Ming was known for her fighting ability. Lo Ming waited for the man to make the first move. She would use his momentum against him. As the man lunged at her, she grabbed his arm and threw him over her head. This gave her a chance to reach her fighting stick. Even though the man landed on his feet, he couldn't react fast enough to avoid Lo Ming's fighting stick. In two swift blows, Lo Ming finished the man. He fell unconscious by the other man on the floor.

Lo Ming heard another man's voice coming inside the front door. Van Lo was at the door with two of his men. "I guess you don't need any help," he said.

Lo Ming answered, "You warned me. That gave me the advantage."

"They look like they come from Japan by the tattoos on their arms. Someone paid a lot of money to hire these men," Van Lo replied.

"What do you want me to do with them?" asked Van Lo.

"Put them in their car and take them to the docks. Put them on a freighter to Japan with a note saying: I won't be so kind the next time," stated Lo Ming.

Van Lo motioned to his men to take the two men. After his men had done as requested, Van Lo looked at Lo Ming. "It appears that the someone knows about you. Don't worry, these men were here only to warn you to stop what you are doing. They will come to kill you the next time."

Lo Ming looked straight into Van Lo's eyes. "It seems you know more about this than I thought."

Van Lo replied back, "Yes, my child. More than I will ever tell you. I will give you some advice about this journey you are on: Be very careful. Many great warriors have died over that land. I will teach you as much as I can to protect you on your journey. Fix us some breakfast so we can continue your training. I don't want you to ask me any more questions. Since you have already had your fighting lesson today, we will concentrate on the mystical side of things."

Van Lo became serious. "There is one thing that bothers me. Someone you know must have betrayed you. These men would never have known about you unless someone had told them about you. Don't trust anyone. Wealth and power can corrupt. I hope that you have someone on your journey that will have your back." Lo Ming knew it must have been the woman who had been with Antonio in the snowstorm. Hopefully, it wasn't Antonio.

Lo Ming quickly replied, "Don't worry. I do."

Old Cap looked down at the sandy ground. This was too easy. He knew that Moses was too good to leave so many signs to follow. Old Cap was certain that Moses knew that he was being followed. These men had made too many inquiries about Moses in town. Someone would tell Moses' grandfather about strangers asking questions about Moses. Old Cap knew that Moses' grandfather was a great medicine man. He had ways to get a message to Moses. Judging by the amount of signs Moses was leaving behind, Moses knew he was being followed. That didn't set well with Old Cap. He would not tell these men that Moses knew. Old Cap had a score to settle. These men could help him settle that score.

With the speed that Moses was traveling, they would probably catch up with Moses in about two days. Old Cap looked at the few clouds in the sky. He listened carefully. He sensed that the animals were restless. He smiled. He knew what Moses was up to by the direction he was taking them.

Moses picked up the pace. The rocks and sand made walking difficult. He enjoyed thinking that the men behind him would suffer from the ordeal of the heat and sheer physical exertion of dealing with the desert. He did have one worry. Old Cap would know that he was leading them into a trap. He had made his trail too obvious for Old Cap not to know. Old Cap may have been a fool in love at one time, but he was not a fool when it came to the Outback. Old Cap was like him: a survivor.

Angela was sleeping with Antonio's arms around her. Antonio always wondered what Angela's true race make up was. He knew that she was bi-racial but could not put a finger on exactly which two. Her exotic look and features were startling beautiful. No man nor woman wouldn't be attracted to her.

Old Cap was surprised that the four men were doing so well in the desert. He thought that these men would be showing more signs of fatigue by now. This was the third day of hiking in the Outback. The men wore black uniforms like ones you would see on special forces in the army. They were armed with semi-automatic rifles and pistols. Their leader didn't talk much. When he gave commands to the others, they jumped at his instructions. These men were professionals. Old Cap soon realized that these men were on a mission, and it was not just to talk to Moses. He sensed that they were going to kill Moses if they ever got him in their gunsights. He didn't have any trouble about them killing Moses, but he began to worry about what they would do to him after that. Old Cap had a plan for that. He would just melt into the desert when the shooting began. These men were skillful, but they were no match for his skills in this wasteland. They would never find him in this desert. They probably would never find their way back.

Moses had set up camp for the night. He would lead the men behind him into the riverbed of a remote canyon tomorrow. He would take an around about way. Night would be falling about the time they would enter the canyon. He knew Old Cap would set up camp about that time. He would soon know if Old Cap wanted him dead. He could deal with the men with Old Cap, but Old Cap was another thing.

As Moses settled down to get some sleep, he gazed at the sky overhead. The bright stars sparkled. His thoughts turned to the journey to The Land of the Eagle Feathers. He had a special feeling wash over him when he thought of that faraway land.

His grandfather had told him that even though he was born in Australia in the Outback, he belonged to a different land. He was special. One day, he would find that land. It was a land that chose you. Once he found that land named after a great bird, he would never be able to live without it. He would become part of it. It was his destiny. He would find there what no man could find elsewhere.

Just before closing his eyes to sleep, Moses saw it. A moving rainbow coming up from the South. It slithered like a large, bright, colorful serpent. He would soon know if his destiny would be fulfilled. The Rainbow Serpent would show him. Moses turned over and went to sleep.

Old Cap was watching the sky. He had told the men that they were very close to finding Moses. They would camp tomorrow night by a canyon. He told them that Moses liked to go to that canyon to meditate. It would be easy to catch him there early the next morning. Moses would not be expecting them. As he bedded down for the night, he didn't expect what he saw moving toward the canyon. Instantly, he knew that his part in this was not of his choosing. It was destiny. The gods and spirits were in control. What was going to happen next was up to them.

As he had planned, Moses led the group behind him to the canyon. He took a place in the rocks, high above the riverbed at the entrance to the canyon. As it was getting dark, Old Cap and the men arrived at the canyon's entrance. Moses could hear Old Cap give orders to camp here for the night. The leader of men didn't like the idea of camping in an old dry riverbed. Old Cap reassured the leader that there was no problem. There was no sign of rain. It would be safe. Moses knew that Old Cap was lying to the men he was guiding. Old Cap was too good not to know that it was going to rain about midnight. Old Cap would never set up camp in a dry riverbed.

The leader of the men had posted two of his men on guard. He wasn't taking any chances that Moses could escape from the canyon. A few minutes before midnight, some water started trickling down the riverbed. The water began filling a large empty pool by their camp in the riverbed. The large full moon, along with their campfire, provided good lighting to see. The leader of the men went over to Old Cap and roughly grabbed him out of his blankets. The leader knew that Old Cap had tricked him and his men. He put a gun to Old Cap's head and yelled for Moses to come out or he would kill Old Cap. As this was going on, all the men got their weapons out and were ready to shoot anything that moved.

Moses sensed it was time to meet the men. He slowly walked out of the shadows behind the men. "I have been waiting for you. Let Old Cap go. He did as you wished. He led you to me," Moses yelled at the leader. The men and their leader turned toward Moses. The leader motioned Moses to come toward him. Everyone noticed that Moses only had a whip tied to his waist and a large knife in his belt as weapons.

The leader replied to Moses, "You are making this too easy. Why lead us way out here? I knew Old Cap was in this with you. I could even track you with the signs you were leaving behind."

Moses looked at Old Cap. Old Cap was sweating profusely. The leader still had his hand on Old Cap with a gun pointed at his head. The leader asked Moses how he thought he was going to take down him and three of his best men with only a whip and a knife. Moses smiled back at him. Moses replied that that was easy. I have spirits and gods on my side. You have only your guns.

"Moses, you must have been out here too long for me to believe something like that. I think I will just shoot Old Cap and then you right now," said the leader. Before he could pull the trigger of the gun, Moses swiftly pulled out his whip and knocked the gun from the leader's hands. In almost the same instant, a large colorful serpent rose up from the large pool of water in the riverbed. Everyone froze and looked at the giant colorful serpent. Before the men could react, several large eagles swooped of the dark sky and attacked the men. The eagles' talons pierced their hands, forcing them to drop their weapons.

The leader yelled at Moses to make the eagles stop. Moses said that he did not control the eagles. He would ask them to stop if the leader agreed to leave this land and not come back. There were two eagles with their talons in the leader's hands. In pain, the leader yelled back, "I will never come back here again with my men to this land. I will never harm you. That is a promise of honor among warriors." That appeared to signal to the eagles to stop. They flew away into the night. The Rainbow Serpent looked at the men with its bright eyes and fanged mouth wide open.

"Leave here now. Take only your knives for protection. Tell this story to your superiors. As one warrior to another, I will allow you to go in peace. Remember, every breath you take is a gift from the great spirits. Leave before the Rainbow Serpent decides differently," Moses spoke in a spiritual way that commanded respect. The leader signaled to the others to follow him into the dark night.

The Rainbow Serpent looked at Moses and Old Cap. Moses could swear that the Rainbow Serpent had a smile on its face. It did not say anything but only moved on to the next waterhole. Old Cap looked at Moses. "I guess it was our destiny," Old Cap said. "Who am I to question what just happened?"

Moses answered back to Old Cap, "In life, sometimes you must believe in your destiny. I trust that you and I are now over."

"Yes, we are. You know that I married her several years ago. We have many children and grandchildren. I guided these men here to try to save you. My wife told me that you told her, she should marry me. I felt that I owed you that much. When I saw the Rainbow Serpent last night, I knew we had nothing to worry about. Good luck to you, Moses. We have both our destinies to fulfill. I will be going now. I need to get back to my wife and family."

Moses watched Old Cap pick up his bedroll and disappear into the night. A roar of thunder clapped above him. Instinctively, he looked toward the sky. He could see the storm clouds in the distance. There were shapes forming in the clouds. A vision was forming before his very eyes. A man smiled down on him with the Red Woman beside him. There were scenes of bright green mountains and valleys. He had recognized the man at once. It was his father standing by the Red Woman. They were both in The Land of the Eagle Feathers watching him. Moses raised both his arms above his head. He pointed toward the sky. He said a warrior's prayer out loud to salute them. They both nodded. Then the vision disappeared in a flash of lightning.

Moses knew his destiny. His destiny was in a mystical land and a beautiful Asian woman waiting for his return. Before he would go back to them, he would visit the sacred places in the Outback. He had to pay his respects to the great spirits of this land. He would also visit his grandparents to honor them. He knew that when he visited his mother, he had many questions to ask her.

The heat was rising in the New Mexico desert. The southern wind was dry. Dust clouds were starting to form on the horizon. Nick couldn't see the far mountains to the

North. He was glad that he was at the mouth of a large cavern. His grandfather had been teaching him the ancient ways of his mystic tribe called "The Others." He told Nick that one day he would tell him the history of his tribe, but that was for another time.

Nick had gotten the impression that his grandfather was not too happy that Nick had decided to go on the journey to The Land of the Eagle Feathers. His grandfather said that many great warriors had tried to save the land from people who would destroy it for its wealth and power. His grandfather was not so sure that anyone should possess the immense power that was rumored to be hidden in The Land of the Eagle Feathers. When his grandfather asked him questions about who was involved with him on this quest, Nick would not give his grandfather an answer. Nick told his grandfather that it was better for him not to know. It would be safer for his grandfather not to know.

Nick's grandfather stood beside Nick as they watched the western sky turn bright red from the dust. Nick's grandfather didn't like what he saw in the dust clouds. "Those clouds are an omen," he explained. "You must be very careful. There are many dark powerful people who will want to stop you. Some want the power for themselves, but others do not want anyone to have them. You and your friends are in great danger. The clouds are a sign that you need to go back at once. Get your Indian Motorcycle and get packed and leave while you still can. I must deal with some evil people who are coming."

Within an hour, Nick was on the old back road to the nearest city. His grandfather insisted that he leave at once. Nick argued that he should stay, but his grandfather resisted. It would take Nick about 15 hours of hard riding for him to get to town. This road was dusty and very windy. He had to slow up for the curves and steep inclines. As he rounded one of the many curves, he had to hit his brakes. Ahead of him was a wrecked car turned upside down across the road. It was burning from a small fire in the engine compartment. Nick quickly got off his cycle to run over to investigate if anyone was hurt.

Nick observed that the black sedan had hit a boulder on the left side of the road to cause it to roll over. As he crawled on his stomach to peer into the driver's side of the sedan, he saw a young woman unconscious still attached to her seat belt, hanging upside down. Nick knew that he had to act fast. He took a rock and smashed out the driver's side window. Reaching as far as he could into the car, he unfastened the woman's seatbelt and pulled her out of the car to safety.

When he had her about 50 feet from the car, it exploded into a red fireball. Nick landed on top of her. It took Nick a few seconds to recover from the blast. Slowly, he rolled off the young woman. He wasted no time and started to examine her for injuries. The blond headed woman opened her green eyes and asked him what was he doing? He replied to her that he was trying to examine her for injuries. She told him to stop. She could check herself. Nick was surprised that the woman did not seem too grateful for his help. Soon, he would find out why.

The woman stood up. She was dressed in a black leather outfit. She rebuttoned her V necked leather top that Nick had unbuttoned when he was examining her for injuries. "I hope you got a good look," she sarcastically said to him. She was now standing next to Nick. "I'm sorry, I should be thanking you for saving me," she said. Nick was beginning to think something was wrong with this. The woman appeared not to be hurt at all. In the back of his mind, he was having a flash back to Iraq. He knew this woman from long ago. He was about to say something when everything went black. She had done her job. She had distracted him long enough to let her cohort knock him out.

June had finished packing her bags. She was leaving to start the long journey back to meet John and the other members of the group. She would take a little side trip to the sacred mountain on her way back. She saddled her horse and packed the old mule with her supplies and belongings. It was just getting light as she rode out. The sacred mountain was about twenty miles away. It would take her at least a day and half to get there. She was looking forward to having a few days to herself. She would return her horse and mule to a small town about two days away from the sacred mountain. She had arranged for her tribe to pick them up at the tribe's stable. It was a beautiful day for a ride across the green prairie. There was a chill in the air, but that was fine with June. It made her feel alive.

A council meeting had been called by the Great Elder in The Land of the Eagle Feathers. Seated in front of them was Night Panther. Night Panther was angry. "I do not agree with the Council. My people feel that your decision to allow John and the others to try to find *The Book of Winter* not a wise one. It could mean destruction of everything we have fought for, for many moons. You need to stop this before it is too late," he stated with much emotion.

The Great Elder looked down at the seated Night Panther replying, "We know your objections but cannot see any other way to save this land and its people. There are too many forces wanting this land. We can barely keep them out now. We are grateful for the sacrifice of your people. You may think that you are able to stop them. We know better. Your band has suffered greatly. You are not as strong as you once were. The last great battle cost you many warriors. If it hadn't been for John and his warriors,

184

we would have lost this land. We want to save this land.
We will take this risk. It is too important. This land is the
last of its kind. It is special and sacred. We have made our
decision. Now go back and tell your tribe."

Night Panther stood up. He looked at the Council
members. "My people would rather see this land
destroyed if it meant that nobody could ever get their
hands on the powers that *The Book of Winter* contain. I
will take my warriors and stop John and members of his
group. You can not stop me. My tribe has the powers to
leave this land. I know that we will not be able to return.
It will be the price we will pay."

The Red Woman stood up to reply to Night Panther. "It
is written in the stars that there will be strife among us. It
is said that what happens in the future will be determined
by who wins. Remember, if you leave, we are the only
ones who can let you come back." Night Panther gave his
answer by turning his back to the Council. He proudly
walked out of the meeting.

After the Council meeting, Red Woman summoned One
Feather. When One Feather arrived, she spoke to him. "I
know that you are in love with the one called June. If you
want to save her, you will have to go to her. Night Panther
and his tribe have decided to stop her and the others from
returning." One Feather replied, "How can I get there in
time?" The Red Woman stated to him, "There is a way.
You have a special gift from the spirits. You can send
your spirit anywhere. Your physical body will remain
here. You are what is known as a Spirit Warrior. Come, I
will teach you how."

June reached the sacred mountain about midday. The
weather was warmer than she expected. She had dressed
in a white leather dress with beads. The colorful beads
depicted symbols of the stars and moon. She pastured her
horse and mule at the base of the mountain. There was

plenty of newly green grass starting to grow in the warm weather. Taking her medicine bag and some provisions, along with a blanket, she commenced her climb to the top of the mountain.

June had found a faint trail that she followed toward the mountain's peak. About halfway up the mountain, she noticed a very faint moccasin footprint beside the trail. Someone had taken great care in not leaving a trail behind them. It would have to be someone very skilled in native ways. June thought that maybe she should stop and go back. She might be disturbing another native in their religious ceremonies.

After giving that some deep thought, she decided to go on to the top. She would use her great skills of tracking to keep from being seen. If there was anyone on the top still there, she would wait until they left by hiding among the great boulders on the mountaintop.

June reached the summit of the mountain at twilight. She had taken time to survey the area around the top of the mountain. There appeared to be nobody around. Satisfied that she was alone, she walked over to the sacred stone table located in the middle of the mountaintop. She took out of her medicine bag several objects. Painstakingly, she placed her objects in a circle in the middle of the stone table. Then she took out some red and yellow powder and drew circles around them. When she finished, she took out a long leather string. She attached the string to each object until all were finally attached with the single string. She held a hawk feather in both of her hands. Saying an old Indian prayer, she raised her arms toward the setting sun. She pointed the hawk feathers toward the sunset in the west.

The stars and moon were soon bright in the sky. Turning her arms to the east, she said another old prayer. She lowered her aching arms. A voice behind her startled her.

It was a man's voice. It was dark now. She tried to locate the source of the voice. The voice told her that she should stop her quest for the sacred books. She spoke back to the invisible man to say that she would not stop. A puff of red smoke rose from the other side of the stone table. When the smoke cleared, an old Indian Medicine man appeared. In her tribal language, the Medicine man spoke to her again.

"You must stop this quest with your friends to find the ancient texts. Only dark evil will happen if you do. Their magic and powers are too great for anyone to have. If you do not stop, we will be forced to stop you. We will not hesitate to destroy you," the Medicine Man commanded.

June spoke back to him and selected her words with care, "I have heard of such, but we have no choice but to find them. Evil dark forces will overrun the sacred lands if we do not find them."

"We think not. We will work to stop anyone from trying to get the books," he replied.

As if to show her his powers, he raised his hands. A great gust of wind hit her in her chest, knocking her down toward the edge of the mountain cliff. Before she would go over the cliff side, she jumped to her feet. Pointing both of her hawk feathers toward him, she shot a bright yellow lightning bolt back at him. Waving his hands toward the sky, he deflected the lightning bolt. Before he could do anything else, a spirit appeared. June recognized the Spirit Warrior at once. It was her brave standing between them. "I am One Feather," the spirit said. "You must leave."

The Medicine Man realized the woman before him must be a great Medicine Woman. He could fight her, but he could not fight them both. He decided to vanish. A red puff of smoke covered him. He vanished into it.

June heard his voice one last time, "Stop, your quest for the books or all of you will have the same fate as your parents." June yelled at the Medicine Man as he vanished, "I could not if I wanted to stop. Only the great spirits can stop us. I have already performed a sacred ritual that binds my group together until the quest is over." She heard the Medicine man reply, "Then, we have no choice but to destroy every one of you."

June ran toward One Feather. He raised his hand to motion her to stop. "While I am a spirit, you cannot touch me. The Red Woman sent me to help you. We will meet again soon." One Feather faded into the sky. June smiled. She now knew her brave's name.

Chapter VIII
The Danger Continues
Who Are the Scorpions?

Nick's head hurt. He tried to get up, but soon realized that he was tied down. His arms and legs were tied to stakes. No matter how hard he tried, he couldn't get up. It was dark now. He could barely make out two people standing by his cycle about 100 yards away. He watched as they went through his cycle's saddle bags. They seemed to be searching them for something. They threw the contents of the bags over the ground. The two figures were now walking back toward him. He knew that this was not going to be a friendly meeting.

As the two figures came closer, Nick could make out that one of them was the female that he had tried to save from the car wreck. Nick had been in this situation once before several years ago in Iraq. Several enemy soldiers had tied him up the same way to try to lure his troops into a trap. He was lucky. An American sniper must have observed his predicament. The sniper must have been a great marksman. He cut both of his arm restraints with two shots. This allowed Nick to untie himself and crawl back to his squad to safety.

He asked his men who fired the two shots. They did not know. There were no American snipers in this sector. It was several days later when a forward observer told him what he saw. A man, using an old frontier rifle, had fired those shots to free him. He noted that the old rifle made a lot of smoke. The only other thing that puzzled him was that the man had on an off white colored old cavalry hat. He thought the man must have been from one of the First Cavalry units. Sometimes, they liked to wear those hats.

Nick snapped out of his train of thought. Here he was in a New Mexico desert many miles from anyone who could help him. His mind was racing to think of some way to escape. His grandfather had taught him some spells and secret ways. He could use one of them to save himself. As the woman in the black leather approached him, he thought of a plan. He just hoped that he would be able to summon them.

The woman in leather was right in front of Nick. "I know you were going to say you know me. It's been a long time. You were in bad shape when I happened to see you at that bar on the post. We had a good time for a few weeks. You never came back after that last mission. Some said that you were dead. Some said that you wished you were dead. You know there are legends about you back there in that mess of sand and desert. You know what they called you? They called you the Killing Machine. Nobody could ever stop you once you started. You were more like a machine than a human. The legend goes that a ghost dressed in an old cavalry hat finally stopped you and took you away."

"You know me. I work for the highest bidder. They hired me to locate you and eliminate you because of your unique skills. I think it would be a waste to kill someone who has the skills that you possess. I only want the papers that Antonio has sent you. Nothing more. We can say that you got away."

"Why do you want those papers? I destroyed them days ago," Nick replied. "That's too bad for you, Nick. My associate and I will just have to get you to tell us what were in the papers. You can do this the easy way or the hard way. You will tell us. My associate here is an expert at getting the truth out of a person. Now what will it be?"

It was dark with only a large campfire near them for light. Nick saw that there were red hot iron rods sticking in the fire. The large man, as if he knew Nick was not going to talk, walked over and picked up one of the iron rods. The woman walked over to Nick and tore open his shirt, exposing his muscular chest.

"Too bad, we must burn such a great body to get the information we want," as she ran her fingers down his chest. She looked at the large man and told him to go back to the cycle and look for the papers. He was not to come back until she called for him. "I have a better way to get the information out of him," she wickedly smiled.

The blond woman motioned to the large man to leave. The large man smiled. He knew that Nick was no match for this woman. He turned and left. In a couple of minutes, he returned with a warm blanket. He tossed it at the young woman. He told her to not take too long. They had to leave before sunup. The woman smiled back, saying, "This could take a while."

After the man left, the blond woman took out a long sharp knife from her belt. She told Nick that he had better relax. The blond woman took a hold of her hair and pulled off the blond wig she was wearing. Under the wig was her long auburn hair tied in a bun. Nick thought that destiny has a way of intervening in your life when you least expect it. Twice it had, just like in Iraq.

Here she was, Shanna, his girlfriend from High School. You don't forget your first love. It is always special. He had missed that touch. Shanna moved her hands up and down his chest.

She was the wild girl in his High School. Both Shanna and Nick were the kids who never quite fit in with the other students. It was a different time. They were young and free. They had been like kindred spirits together. He remembered their first date. Her hair had the scent of cinnamon. It was a night that he would not ever forget. He had missed her so much.

She knelt and kissed him. He returned her kiss back. She had used the kiss to drug him with a pill she had placed in his mouth with her tongue. He swallowed it before he knew what had happened. He didn't care. For the last two years, he dreamed of seeing her again. He was captivated by the memories of a love lost long ago.

Nick was beside himself. His memories of their love flooded his mind. Shanna said, "I will let you go after I am through. I took this assignment just to touch you and hold you once more. I could never get enough of you."

He was again that young wild boy in the sand dunes of the beach before her. She was the wild young woman who couldn't get enough of him. He could hear the waves of the ocean on the shore. She took the knife and cut his ropes.

Shanna held Nick in her arms for several minutes. The drug had done its work. She cursed herself. She still had feelings for him. She never planned to kill him. But what was she to do now? Her associate would kill him. She had to have some information to give to the people who hired her, or they would kill her.

Her associate was coming back from their pickup truck parked by Nick's motorcycle. She took the blanket and covered Nick with it. Then she re-tied his hands and feet to the stakes. She only tied them very loosely. Nick would easily be able to release himself from the stakes later.

Her associate arrived and said he had found something. It was the letterhead of a Professor in Maine called Mary ----. The people who hired them wanted to know who the female professor on Nick's journey to The Land of the Eagle feathers was. They knew everyone except for her. Shanna now had the information she wanted. Her associate asked her what she had gotten. She lied and said that she has gotten that much out of Nick.

Satisfied that they wouldn't need Nick anymore, her associate took out his knife to cut Nick's throat. That's what they were paid for, and that's what he was going to do. They were not to leave any loose ends. Nick was a loose end.

As he turned to walk toward Nick's body, Shanna took her knife out. She told her partner to stop where he was at and turn around. The man did as she told him. She never trusted her associate, and he didn't trust her. As he turned around, he started to throw his knife at her. The last thing he saw was Shanna's knife sticking out of his chest as he fell to the ground.

Now, I have no loose ends, she thought. I will tell them that my associate got careless, and Nick killed him. Then Nick escaped. Having the name of the last person would be enough for her employers. She looked at Nick one more time. A tear dropped into the sand by her feet as she turned to leave him. "We will meet again," she said out loud. "It is our destiny. Only the spirits know the paths for us to follow."

A couple of hours later Nick awoke. He still had his hands tied to the stakes, but they were no trouble for him. Shanna was gone. Her associate was lying face down in the sand before him. In one of his hands, there was an envelope with Mary's address on it. He knew that Shanna had this information and would give it to her employers. He also knew that Shanna had left it for him to find.

His thoughts turned to Shanna. He couldn't help but remember the hurt he felt long ago. One day, she left a note for him at their spot on the deserted beach near San Diego. It only said that she needed to explore the world. She had to do that herself. He was hurt and lost. His pain had been so great that he decided to join the army. His grandparents had tried to persuade him to go to college, but he wasn't the college type. He thought the army would give him release. He had wondered what had happened to her.

After he spent time in the army hospital, he tried to find her. Nobody had claimed to have seen her. In fact, there was no evidence that she was ever in Iraq. There could be only one explanation for that. She was a contract CIA operative. After he received a phone call that said his inquiries about her could put her life in danger, he stopped looking for her. His eyes teared remembering how hard that was.

The pain in his heart began again. He couldn't help himself. He needed to see her. As he dried his tears, he did have one thought that helped his heartbreak. The Great Spirits had brought them together. He prayed that the Great Spirits would bring them together again.

Nick went over to his motorcycle. The man had damaged it too much for him to fix it. On the ground beside his cycle was a note from Shanna on top of some clothes. The note said, "I hope that the clothes fit you. Stay safe."

Nick looked at the sky with a tear in his eye as he made the sound of a bird call. High in the sky overhead a buzzard appeared. It flew down beside him. He told the buzzard to go and get his grandfather to help him. The buzzard nodded at him and flew away. He would wait in the shade of a boulder for his grandfather to come.

Rose was setting down in her shop in New Orleans. It had been a rough day. She was upset. On the small wooden table in front of her was her small crystal ball. Rose was as much upset with herself as she was with what she had seen a few minutes before in the crystal ball. She knew she shouldn't use her powers to spy on others, but she couldn't help it. Something told her that Nick was in trouble. Fearful that he was in danger, she had used her crystal ball to find him. Witnessing the episode of what had happened with Nick in the New Mexico desert alarmed her. She knew she had no right to be upset with him about the strange woman. It was she who kept Nick at a distance. She was confused about what she saw. The woman could have hurt or even killed Nick but didn't. In fact, the strange woman had saved Nick. Now she realized that she had competition for Nick's affections. Rose still was confused about her feelings toward Nick.

Rose had known better than to use her crystal ball to locate Nick. It is said that you cannot use your powers for your own gain. Since she felt that she was in love with Nick, why was she able to see Nick at all? Was she really in love with Nick or did Nick remind her of her first great love? Something was wrong. She would have to find out about that later.

One thing that she did see that worried her more than Nick's love life, was that the woman knew about Mary. Surely, she would report back to her employers about her. Rose knew that the mysterious woman had to protect herself. Rose would use her crystal ball one more time today. She had to locate Mary and try to warn her about being in possible danger. This would take her a little while. Rose only hoped that she could locate Mary in time.

For Rose to locate Mary, she would have to use her crystal ball in a different way. She would have to ask the crystal ball to start from where she had seen Mary last. The crystal ball started showing Mary leaving the train station. She had gotten into her car to start her journey home. Rose was surprised to see that Mary's car was heading west instead of north toward Maine.

The next scene that the crystal ball revealed was Mary talking to an older man. He said to Mary, "Welcome back to Houston from your trip to The Land of the Eagle Feathers. Did your trip go well?" Mary was seated next to him in the shadows of a large conference room. Mary replied, "Nothing that I couldn't handle, father." It seemed that they were watching a man give a presentation to a small group of people. Rose studied the man in the background. It didn't take her long to recognize the man. It was Antonio. He was talking about his trip to The Land of the Eagle Feathers. The group was very interested in the trip, especially when Antonio opened the bag of gems.

Mary was still talking to her father. "I know that you want The Land of the Eagle Feathers. I see that your plan with Antonio is working. He does not know that I am involved with your company. I plan to keep it that way."

Mary's father looked at her and said, "You have done well. You need to be careful…" Before he could finish, he noticed Antonio looking at them. "You better go before he recognizes you. That would ruin our plans. Take the exit door behind us." Mary got up and left quickly. The next scene was her arriving in her hometown in Maine. Rose could see the town's name on a road sign.

At least, one thing was clear to Rose. She had found the other scorpion. It didn't matter to Rose about whose side Mary was on. Rose knew that Mary had some good in her. The only thing that did matter was it would take every one of our group to get the books.

The crystal ball flashed other images. It appeared that there were several groups who were trying to obtain The Land of the Eagle Feathers for themselves. Rose asked the crystal ball to show her the groups who were the most dangerous. The crystal ball flashed an image of three groups. It did seem to point out one group more than the others. From what she could decipher from the images, this group didn't want anyone to have such power in their hands. They wanted to stop Rose's group from finding any of the books. They must have been the ones who tried to kill Antonio. They had only to kill any one of them and they would be successful.   They may be the ones who hired Shanna. The crystal ball flashed an image of the leader of this group in a forest watching Mary's house. Rose had to warn Mary.

Rose did not see the old man who had entered her shop. She had been concentrating on her crystal ball. She looked up from her desk and her heart sank. An old man with white hair was standing before her. He had on a black three-piece suit with a black cape that was lined with red velvet. His black fedora with a white band was in his hand. Rose knew she was in danger. There was only one man in the whole world who wanted her dead and hated her that much.   He was standing five feet in front of her.

Zorn smiled down at her. "I see you have been busy. The word in our world is that you have been traveling to far places." Rose replied, "I did not know that I was that interesting or famous to have people following my movements." Zorn replied, "Only you wish."

Zorn was here to kill her. She looked for a weapon to use on him. "Do not worry. I am not here to kill you. I just want some of your time to talk about old times," Zorn hissed at her. "I have wanted you dead for a long time, but that would have been too easy. I want you to suffer. Killing you would relieve your pain.   That just wouldn't do. I have a surprise for you." Rose looked at the old man, "You tried to kill me once, but instead you killed your son. Zan loved me so much, but you did not want him to marry me. Your evil killed him, not me."

The smile turned to a frown on Zorn's face. "I am here to tell you something. I had to see your face when I did. You will not like what I am going to tell you. Zan is alive. He is not dead. You only thought he was. I had him taken to a land that only a few people know about."

Rose did not know what to say. Was Zorn doing this to torture her? This news was double-edged. He was alive was wonderful news, but he was being held somewhere. "I do not believe you. You are lying!" she yelled at him. "Let me touch your crystal ball. I will momentarily take the spell off that keeps him hidden from you," Zorn stated. Cautiously, Rose moved back from her desk. Zorn walked over to her desk. Taking his right index finger, he touched the crystal ball with it. Her crystal ball turned gray. As the gray faded away, an image appeared. It was Zan in a meadow surrounded by mountains. He was picking flowers. She could hear him saying something. It sounded like he said to the flowers, "I miss my beautiful Rose. She was as pretty as you." There were tears in his eyes as he took the flowers and tossed them into the air where they turned into colorful songbirds and flew away.

"You will never find him. He cannot escape. He is in a place called The Land of Nightmares. Nobody has ever escaped from there. You see, I got my revenge from both of you. You will never see each other again. For as long as both of you live, I will get the satisfaction of knowing that. No, I won't kill you. I will enjoy the pain that you feel knowing that." Rose grabbed some of her crystals from a table behind her to throw at Zorn. Before she could turn to throw them, her world turned black. As she was falling unconscious to the floor, she could hear Zorn say, "Have a good nightmare."

It was morning when Rose woke up on her office floor. Zorn was gone. Yesterday seemed like a nightmare. She tried to clear her mind and concentrate on what had happened. It took her some time to get enough strength to get off the floor to reach the chair at her desk. On the desk was a painting she had done a few days before. It was a mountain range with a golden sunset. She almost fell off her chair as she looked closer at the painting. It couldn't be! Closing her eyes, she tried to remember in detail the image of Zan in the meadow. There were mountains in the distance. They had a gold color to them. There were several large birds flying around them. She knew where Zan was or at least close to where he was. She had to get back to The Land of the Eagle Feathers.

Her crystal ball flashed on the desk in front of her. A picture appeared. It was Mary being carried by a man into the emergency entrance of a hospital. A trail of blood from Mary was on the concrete. Then, it hit her. No, she had to go to see Mary. She had just realized that she needed to go to Maine. She only hoped it wouldn't be too late.

The spring day was warm for Maine. Mary was in her rose garden, attending to rose plants. Judging by the morning sun, Mary guessed it was about 10 o'clock. Some tea and sweet breads for her morning break sounded good for Mary. Getting up from her bent over position was not so easy. She had been working since 7 a.m. Her back was getting stiff. She stretched her back as she straightened up. As she was stretching, something caught her eye, moving in the woods behind her house. Maybe, it was a deer or some other wild animal. There were many other animals in these woods. Giving it little thought, she went into the house through the outside kitchen door.

Shanna had reached a small desert town. It had a few stores. Cell phones didn't work very well in this area. She tried to use hers but couldn't get a signal. As she drove down Main Street, she saw a rundown café across from the post office. Since she was hungry, it made sense to stop and get something to eat. They might have a pay phone there. Only some out of way place like this would have a payphone.

She stopped her red pick-up truck in front of the café. Getting out, she headed into the café. She asked the waitress behind the counter if they had a phone she could use. The waitress nodded and pointed toward the phone located close to the restrooms in back of the café. Shanna told the waitress that the call would be long distance. The old waitress smiled at her and told her just to reverse the charges. Shanna wanted to tell her that nobody did that anymore but decided to try it anyway.

Shanna located the phone in a hallway between the two restroom doors. It was an old black rotary phone with the white dial. She thought that these phones have been out of use for several years. She decided to look at the phonebook attached to the phone cord. The phonebook looked new. She caught her breath when she noticed the date on the book. It was dated 1961. The hair on the back of her neck told her that she could be in trouble. Looking out of the front picture window, she realized that this town was out of place. Everything looked new, but the style of the buildings was more like an old 1960's movie set.

Shanna was about to pick up the phone to dial when the phone started ringing. She decided to step back. She would let someone answer it. She sat down at a table just down the hallway from the phone. After about six rings, a young man ran down the hall. He picked up the receiver to answer. A flash of light lit up the hallway. When Shanna eyes adjusted back to the darkness after the flash of light, she looked back at the phone. The young man was gone. Shanna didn't wait. She ran for her pickup. This town was a town you didn't want to be in too long.

As she opened the driver's door to her pickup, a large man dressed like he was a sheriff grabbed her door. Shanna didn't care if the man was the sheriff. In one movement, she turned and kicked the man in the face, knocking him down. The sheriff hit the ground. He started to draw his pistol, but Shanna kicked his gun hand and knocked it away. The sheriff yelled at her to stop. Shanna quickly opened the driver's side door and jumped in, starting the pickup in one fluid motion. She put the pickup into gear. Pulling out of the parking place, she pressed all the way down on the gas pedal. Smoke and her tire squeals could be heard down the block.

It was only about 600 yards to the edge of town. Behind her were two sheriff's patrol cars. They caught up with her about 100 yards before the town's limit sign. Wasting no time, she turned her steering wheel to the right and hit the patrol car near the driver's side front tire. This caused the patrol car to crash into a gas station. A loud explosion and fireball erupted as the car hit the two fuel pumps in front of the station. The patrol car on her left tried to bump her car. She countered by hitting her brakes. The patrol car missed her pick up but was now in front of her. Pressing the gas pedal to the floor, she hit the back side of the patrol car sending it past the city limits sign. As the patrol car ran pass the city limits sign, the car burst into flames and vanished before her. She finally took a deep breath. She was relieved that she had made it out of town as her pickup raced by the city limits sign.

Looking back in her rearview mirror, she watched the town slowly disappear into the sands of the desert. She had been lucky. She should had known better. There are legends about old desert towns like this located in rural areas. If you do anything like answer a phone; eat; or stay in a hotel, you can never leave. The sheriff was trying to stop her from leaving, but luckily for her, she was too good for him.

In the back of her mind, she knew that this town had been set up as a trap for her. It would take someone or a group immensely powerful to produce such a town. Whoever was behind this was now wanting her dead or worse. After about two miles out of town, she had a cell signal strong enough to call. She didn't pull over to make the call, because she wanted to put as much distance as possible between her and the town.

After she made two phone calls, she decided it was be
time to disappear. The first call was to pay back a debt to
someone who had saved her life in another desert. Now, it
was paid in full. She also told him that she called her
anonymous employer. John wasn't too happy that she
gave Mary's name to them. He did know she had no other
choice. She had to give them something to protect herself
and Nick. Whoever her employers were would be very
dangerous. John asked Shanna if she had heard through
the grapevine that others were interested in The Land of
the Eagle Feathers. Shanna had replied to him in one
simple word: yes.

Shanna smiled as she drove. She liked speed. Having a
chance to see Nick again was a real bonus. John had used
her services before on several occasions. He would call on
her again. She would have done this job for free if she
knew Nick was involved. She was puzzled. Who was this
older woman, Rose? She caught a fleeting glimpse of
Rose in Nick's mind when they were making love. Rose
must be very special to him. She pulled out the yellow
diamond from her pocket. John had paid her well. She
would go off the grid for the next few weeks. There was a
spa in South America that was beckoning her.

Mary heated up the water in her teapot. She used
propane for heating and cooking in her cottage. She
poured the boiling water into her teacup. She liked Lady
Grey tea. The day was getting warmer. She walked
outside and sat down on a cement bench in her rose
garden. Looking back into the woods, she thought she saw
something moving through the brush. As she watched the
woods, a creature moved out of the dark woods. It was a
huge grizzly bear. It crossed the road behind her cottage.
She watched as it turned to run straight for her. Its mouth
was open, showing its teeth. The large bear would be on
her within seconds. It was running at amazing speed.

She knew it was no use to run. Mary picked up the sharp hoe in front of her. At least, she would give it a fight. The bear was about 10 yards from her. She raised her hoe, but she knew it would be useless. The large grizzly hit her, knocking her down on the grass. The bear stood straight up right in front of her. It raised its right paw with its sharp claws out to strike her. As it started to swing its paw, she heard a loud bang. The bear disappeared into a large cloud of smoke before her. The only thing in front of her was a small gold ball at her feet. Turning toward the sound of the gunshot, she could see a white horse with a rider, coming out of the thick underbrush of the woods opposite her cottage.

Antonio was in the museum. He was writing some more pages of what he called the "Great Rico" novel. It was late at night. Angela had left town to visit some of her friends. For some reason, the old museum seemed spooky. The old wooden floors creaked more tonight. Antonio usually didn't let the old museum get to him. Some of the employees had told him ghost stories about the old museum. He never let the stories bother him. Tonight seemed different from nights he had spent here before.

Antonio froze. He could hear footsteps of two or more people, walking above him by the creaks of the wooden floor. Antonio looked around to try to find a weapon. He could take on two thugs without a weapon, but four would be a stretch, even with his skills. On his desk was a sharp pencil that would have to do. Turning out the lights, he left on the computer's motor to give some light to see. He heard two people get into the elevator on the right side of the room. He heard someone open the stairway's doors to the basement. These men were smart. They knew that he couldn't cover both sides of the basement at once.

Mary heard the door open behind her. Two men in black masks stood behind her. She realized that the bear was just a creature conjured up to distract her. Picking up the hoe, she decided to use it to defend herself. It would take the rider some time to reach them. She didn't worry about him. She recognized him immediately. She told the men that she had been waiting for them. Both men had large curved knives in their two hands. They were here to kill her.

The men moved toward her. Mary struck the man on her left with the blunt end of the hoe. She used the sharp head of the hoe to block the knives of the second man. The first man recovered. He jumped up from the ground, swinging his knives at Mary.

Mary soon realized that she would have been able to take on one of these men, but these men were professional assassins. Their graceful movements were smooth and deadly. She kept moving back before blocking their thrusts. She needed help. Lucky for her, there was a wall behind her which kept anyone from getting behind her. The first man made his move while the other swung his knives at her. She blocked the second one's knives, but it was too late to block the other man's knives. A biting sting in her left side let her know that the first man had cut her. Using the sharp blade of the hoe, she cut the first man on his brow. He staggered back with blood running down his face.

Blood was starting to drip down her side. Getting weaker by the second, she was no match for the professional assassins. The other large man stabbed at her. She was too weak to move quickly enough to stop him. As the blade was about to strike at her heart, a man came down on top of him. Mary turned her attention toward the other man. Using the last of her strength, she swung her hoe, knocking the two knives out of his hands. She followed this move with a sweeping movement of the blunt end of the hoe. She hit him on the head, knocking him out. Everything was turning black. The last thing she faintly observed was a man fighting the second assassin as she slowly fell to the ground unconscious.

Antonio felt the presence of the Old South American Tribal Priest before he could see him in the dark room. A dark red glow of two eyes like two embers of fire appeared in the middle of the room close to his computer table. The four men had reached the basement office. With two skilled mercenaries on the only exits, it would be very difficult for Antonio to escape. Antonio realized that combat was no option with a powerful Priest and four skilled fighters.

The Old Tribal Priest was dressed in a black robe trimmed in gold with a black cloak. He was hard to see with the only light being the computer screen. "I know that you are here, Antonio," the Priest announced. "Please come out and talk to me. My men will not hurt you unless I say for them to."

Antonio stood up saying, "I know your voice, Kamir. Why are you interested in me?"

Kamir answered, "I want to conquer The Land of the Eagle Feathers."

"You are just as greedy as the last time I dealt with you in South America. As I remember, you lost that battle," replied Antonio.

"That was then. I am not here seeking your help. I am here to stop you from deciphering the books. You see, I don't want you to find that powerful book that you and your friends are seeking," Kamir replied.

"Everyone wants that book. Why are you so different?" asked Antonio.

"You see without the book; the Elders of The Land of the Eagle Feathers will be defenseless against my people. They will also be defenseless against the Dark Ones," Kamir answered.

"I take it that your plan is to stop us. You will let every group that wants a piece of The Land of the Eagle Feathers fight it out. Then it will be easy for your group to take the land. You don't want the power. You want to get rid of the competition so that you cannot only conquer The Land of the Eagle Feathers but conquer the other worlds as well," Antonio stated back.

"Antonio be smart. You were once one of us. Come back to your people. We will gladly welcome you. You are a legend. I know that you are powerful," Kamir answered him.

Antonio's eyes glowed with anger. He forcefully spoke to Kamir, "The Elders of the Land of the Eagle Feathers are wise. I will not let you destroy them. Our ancient South American Indian tribe was once something to be proud of. We respected the ways of The Land of the Eagle Feathers. We lost our way. We turned to the evil that all men have inside them. Now you use your great powers for evil, not for good. You have no right to The Land of the Eagle Feathers."

Kamir laughed as he answered Antonio, "What they say is true. Perhaps, it's the Italian blood in you that has changed you, or do you want the power for yourself? I don't believe everything you say. Your past says another thing. Antonio, there are others besides our group that want to stop you. Who is to say who is right? The Land of the Eagle Feathers is a sacred land, we could do so much more with it. The Elders only want to keep things a paradise for all who seek it righteously. Don't be so naïve."

Antonio looked back at Kamir. Antonio's great ancestral blood was boiling within him. He wouldn't let Kamir have his way. An ancient wand appeared in Antonio's hand. In one swift motion, he shot a flash of lightning at the spirit. Kamir laughed as he blocked the lightning bolt.

"I have your answer then. I will leave you with my men. We will meet again," Kamir stated as he vanished.

Antonio's wand was knocked from his hand. One of the men had thrown a knife and hit it. Antonio said to himself, "This is going to be a long night." In his mind, he heard a voice speaking to him. The female voice said to him, "It's time to have some fun." The voice was Angela's. She was somewhere in the room with them. Antonio's mind answered back, "Yes, we will."

I ran over to Mary. Her side was bleeding badly. She was losing too much blood. I took my handkerchief from around my neck and pressed it hard against her wound. A voice spoke behind me. "Why are you trying to save her? a man's voice in the ancient language of The Land of the Eagle Feathers asked. I turned my head to see an Indian dressed as a medicine man, standing behind me. I recognized my old friend at once. He was called Night Panther because he was silent and deadly in battle. "This woman is the daughter of one of your most dangerous enemies!" he exclaimed.

He saw the puzzled look on my face. "I see that you don't know who she is. That surprises me, John. I thought you could feel a closeness to her. Her evil father must have put a spell on her. I come to warn you. My group will never let you or the others obtain **The Book of Winter**. It is too dangerous for anyone to have. Even if it means the destruction of The Land of the Eagle Feathers, nobody should obtain the power that book contains. You will soon have to decide where you stand on this. Once you find out about Mary and her father, you may want to change sides. We feel that the Elders are wrong about obtaining the book. Join us. We once fought together as brothers. You died in my arms. You don't owe the Elders anything for bringing you back. I will leave you now. Save this woman if you must. Remember, everything is not as it seems, my blood brother. I will take my fellow braves with me. Don't go into the house!" With that said, a puff of smoke covered us. After it cleared, they were gone.

I had my hands full trying to save Mary. I picked her up and put her on my horse and raced to the nearest town. There was an explosion behind us. Mary's house was full of flames.

David was not happy when he heard the news. Angela had called him as soon as the fight was over. She was standing in the restroom cleaning off her face that was covered with blood. "You mean there is a group from South America that is trying to stop them from obtaining *The Book of Winter*," he replied back to Angela. "Yes, it appears so. I can't talk any longer because Antonio is coming," she replied as she clicked off her phone. She didn't tell David the other things that she had overheard between Antonio and Kamir.

David was upset. What if they know about my daughter? He immediately called for his butler. He told him to get his private jet ready. They would be leaving within the hour for Maine.

The sunlight was shining into the hospital room's window. Mary was starting to regain consciousness. There was a dark figure standing over her. She thought she must be dreaming as her eyes adjusted to the bright room. "What happened to you?" David asked. Mary replied weakly, "Some men tried to kill me. I don't know why. Judging by where I am, they almost succeeded. The only thing I do remember about one of them is that he had a tattoo of a Panther on his arm."

"I'm glad that they didn't succeed," her father softly whispered back to her. For the first time, Mary saw her father very upset. Mary wondered if her father was upset that she had almost died before helping him obtain the book, or if he really cared about her. She chose not to believe he really cared. "Is the man who saved me here? I didn't get a good look at him. Everything was just a blur."

David shook his head. "You get some rest. I told them to give you the best care. It appears whoever attacked you is long gone. That's what my men reported to me. I must leave to attend to some unsettled business. Please be careful, we need you to continue to help us obtain the book." Mary thought she saw something different about her father. There was a small tear in his left eye. She knew that it couldn't be. Sleep was beckoning her.

David was deep in thought as he boarded his jet back to Houston. He had seen the Panther tattoo before. It belonged to a small group of warriors from The Land of the Eagle Feathers. He had fought them long ago. They were cunning and very dangerous. He was confused. Why would they attack Mary? She was supposed to be helping the Elders obtain *The Book of Winter*. It could only mean one thing. Night Panther's group didn't want anyone to obtain the book.

He had heard that some of the people in The Land of the Eagle Feathers did not want the book found. This was not good news for him. He had two major groups trying to stop anyone from getting their hands on the *Book of Winter*. Things were getting out of his control. He would have to rethink his plans. This would mean that he would have to meet with John, his greatest enemy.

The closeness of Angela felt so good to Antonio. His bedroom was dark. His body hurt all over. If it hadn't been for Angela's assistance, he would probably not be alive. In his early days, he would have been able to beat them. Maybe, it was that he had not fully recovered from his wounds from the journey into The Land of the Eagle Feathers. As his eyes adjusted to the darkness, he could see the cuts and bruises on Angela's body. As if paying homage to her, he started kissing each one. "It is going to take you some time to kiss each one," Angela said without opening her eyes. "I'm not in any hurry," Antonio passionately whispered in her ear.

Rose arrived shortly at the hospital after David had left. She went directly to Mary's room. Mary was sleeping. Rose was relieved that Mary seemed to be recovering from her wounds. She went over to Mary's bed and took Mary's hand into hers. Rose could feel everything in Mary's body. She could feel that Mary had a long way to go before she would be able to travel.

Taking out a yellow Jasper gemstone from her pocket, she grasped it as tightly as she could. Rose said an ancient spell. Yellow is the color that corresponds with the solar-plexus chakra. Mary had one of the strongest solar-plexus chakras ever known. She placed the yellow Jasper over Mary's heart. Mary's body jerked wildly for a few moments. Rose had been holding Mary's hand. She removed her hand from Mary. She felt very weak. She sat down in a chair beside Mary's bed. In just a few seconds, Rose fell asleep.

Lo Ming felt the warmth of the red turquoise stone in her pocket. She took it out of her pants' pocket. It was glowing. John had given each one of them a red turquoise stone. He said that when it started glowing, they must return to the Eagle Train Station on the seventh day from the day the glowing started. A worried look came over her face. Something had to be wrong. They were not scheduled to be back for two weeks. She needed to get her business in order. She would meet with Van Lo Sing to tell him that she would be leaving in a few days. There was one good thing about this. She would be seeing Moses soon.

David watched the moon rising from his penthouse office. The city lights were starting to switch on, one block at a time. The city council had used a light sensor for each section of the city. The lights came on much like the pattern of a quilt blanket coming together, one piece at a time. David's mind was unsettled. The past several hours had made his task much more difficult. The attack on his daughter and Antonio demonstrated to him that there were others after what he wanted to obtain. He could feel the forces being disturbed.

David had never been close to his daughter. Her mother had sheltered her from him. After her mother had been declared dead, he married Benita. Benita was much like him. She was cold and ruthless. He liked that about Benita. She was a match for him in every way. The challenge was to stay one step ahead of her ambitions. He knew that if she ever got the best of him, she would kill him and take his place. He always enjoyed playing with fire. She was exciting and very passionate about everything. It gave their lovemaking an added dimension with each one trying to best the other.

He felt her coming before she arrived. The lights on each floor below had gone out, one by one. He smiled as the door opened. She came into the dark room. It wasn't Benita. It was his superior: Raven. Benita must have told her about him flying to Maine to see his daughter. He was waiting for Raven to arrive. Raven always dressed in a tight black silk pantsuit with a black cape trimmed in red. He knew that this was not going to be a cordial meeting. She was beautiful with a hint of exotic danger about her. Most men would die to have her, and many did just that: die.

Raven and David went back many years. He had known her before she became his boss. He despised her. She had risen in the organization, taking the job he wanted. Raven was as evil as they came. Anyone that had crossed her was dead. David did know one thing. Raven wanted *The Book of Winter* for personal reasons. There was a legend about

The Book of Winter. It is believed that the book has the power to unite dead lovers. He knew that Raven would kill John after they obtained the book. John was the one who had killed Raven's lover. Perhaps he could use this to eliminate both of them.

Raven settled down in the darkest part of the room on one of his black leather chairs. David had lit a candle before she came into the room. Raven would suck the electricity out of any room. She was that powerful. David waited for Raven to speak. You never spoke before she spoke to you.

"I see that our plans have some unexpected problems," Raven said.

"Nothing, I can't handle," David replied.

"We are not so sure. We have been very patient with you. Your results have been better than the others before you, but only a little better," she sarcastically stated.

Before he could speak, Raven interrupted him. "It appears there are other groups who want the book, and some that don't want anyone to possess it. This complicates matters. Remember, we must get that book. We must have it. The group that John leads must be protected until they get the book. Then we can take it from them. In the wrong hands, nobody is safe. Do you understand? This is the last time I will come." As she finished, the candle blew out. There was complete darkness in the room.

David could feel her leave in the darkness of his office even though the office door didn't open or close. He had the information that he wanted. By not mentioning anything about conquering The Land of the Eagle Feathers, he knew that his superiors were worried about something else. There was something out there more dangerous than them. ***The Book of Winter*** was his only hope to survive. They would eliminate him sooner or later. That's what he would do.

His superiors were known as The Omen. With the book and The Land of the Eagle Feathers, they could control everything. They also could conquer whoever was as strong or stronger than them. He didn't care. With the book, I could have it all. There would be no power that could stop me. John was the key. Without him, his group would be lost. Whether he liked it or not, he needed John for his plan. He decided he must risk talking to John. Maybe, he could persuade him to come over to his side. After all, they both had the same weakness: his daughter, Mary.

Angela was getting dressed. Antonio was captivated by her beauty. He had known that she had been spying on him for several months. They had a past together many years before in Italy. He had been assigned by his superiors to watch her. He laughed to himself when he remembered that he had once been a priest. He should have known that the sins of the flesh would be too much for him to resist. He had been defrocked. The church told him that didn't matter to them. They needed someone like Antonio. They needed someone that would check on problems confronting the church. He was a secret that only a few of the highest members of the church knew about. His superiors assigned him to investigate ancient mystical groups. This could very dangerous. Not only was he assigned to investigate these groups, the church would sometimes order him to eliminate them. He didn't mind that part too much.

There were times that his missions required the use of special powers. In fact, that's how the church found him. He had been a magician in Europe for several years. His skill had caught the eye of a mysterious man who was a high-ranking priest for the Pope. Many years ago, there was time that you could be burned at the stake for performing magic. Many people thought that magic was the black arts. Magic was evil. His superiors knew better. It was his ability with languages that made him so valuable for them.

Everyone has secrets. When he found out that he was really working for a secret society called The Council of Religions, he quit. Some said he quit because of other reasons. He knew the real reason. His last mission for them resulted in the death of someone very close to him. There was no need for them to kill his friend. Iham was not a terrorist. He was just a Muslim Cleric. He wouldn't hurt anyone. That's when he became a mercenary. He rebelled against everything. His reputation became known as a man who would do anything for money. A man of great talent, but one that liked women, luxury, gambling, and adventure. He became a man who could not be totally trusted. That's what attracted him so much to Angela. She was so much like him.

As Angela was looking in the mirror in the bedroom, she asked Antonio, "Are we going to continue this charade?" Antonio was not caught by surprise by her question. He knew that she had been reporting back to David that he had been deciphering the manuscript. How much she told David was the only question that he wanted the answer to.

"You know that it will take the rest of the year to obtain *The Book of Winter*," he answered. "That's when we will have what we want. I know that power is what turns you on."

"Not only power but being rich doesn't hurt either. Let's hope that your former associates from South America don't stop you. It was very smart of you to trick David into providing you safety. He knows that to get his hands on the book he needs to keep you safe. Then, it's everyone for themselves," she laughed. That's when Antonio grabbed her by the arm and pulled her back into bed with him.

As Antonio pulled Angela into his arms, he knew that he wasn't the same man as before since his trip to The Land of the Eagle Feathers. That land was more than a land of great resources and power. It was a living, breathing land that could reach into your soul and change you. He was starting to have his doubts about his plans with Angela. Maybe it had to do with John's blood being part of him. He knew better than that. Maybe it was what he had been looking for all his life. He shook these thoughts out of his mind. The soft warm body of Angela broke his thoughts. He noticed the red turquoise stone glowing in his pants' pocket on the floor. He would be going there soon. For some unknown reason, he couldn't wait to get there.

Mary slowly opened her eyes. The room was dark. She could see that it was night through the hospital window. She noticed a female figure in the chair by her hospital bed. As her eyes focused on the woman, she started to recognize who she was. Mary could tell by the woman's breathing that the woman was asleep. The woman's necklace of precious gemstones was shining in the dark. There was only one person who Mary knew who wore such a necklace. The woman had to be Rose. Mary reached out her arm and touched Rose's arm with her hand. Rose woke up immediately.

Mary asked Rose why she was here. Rose only stated back that she knew Mary needed her. Rose took out a small crystal ball from her pocket. "I saw it in this that you were in the hospital in bad shape and came as fast as I could," she told Mary. Mary asked Rose if she had seen who had brought her to the hospital. Rose replied to her that she didn't know who it was. Mary looked at Rose and studied her expression. She could sense that Rose knew more than what she was telling her. Mary didn't pursue that matter. She would wait to talk about that later.

The hospital room door opened. A woman dressed in white walked into the room. She told Mary that she was lucky to be alive. If that man had not got her to the hospital when he did, she would probably not be alive. Whoever he was had done a remarkable job of stopping her from bleeding to death. Mary asked her what he looked like. The surgeon said that the emergency room staff was shocked that he had brought her in by horseback. He left before they had a chance to talk to him. It was like he had disappeared into thin air. Before Mary could ask any more questions, the surgeon began examining her wounds.

The surgeon's face had the look of someone very puzzled. "I operated on you three days ago, and what I see now is impossible. The wounds are almost healed completely," she exclaimed.

Mary smiled at Rose while replying to the surgeon, "I always heal quickly. When can I get out of here?"

Judging by the healing of her wounds, the surgeon told her that probably in the next two days. Mary told her that would be fine. She needed to go on a trip in about a week. The surgeon left the room still puzzled about her patient's quick recovery. Rose knew why Mary said that she needed to go on a trip because Rose's red turquoise stone was glowing in Rose's blouse pocket. Mary looked into Rose's eyes as she said, "Thank you, Rose for healing me. By the way you look, it must have been extremely hard on you." Rose replied, "It was for selfish reasons because we need you for our journey back to The Land of the Eagle Feathers."

Mary could sense that there was something else bothering Rose. She could feel that Rose was upset. Rose picked up on Mary's concern. She tried to hide her feelings from her. Rose was upset. Zan was still alive. How could she face Nick? She was still in love with Zan. She had feelings for both men. She was anxious about what would happen. She would find the answers in The Land of the Eagle Feathers.

The morning sky in the Outback was bright red. Moses didn't like what he saw. There was going to be a storm. The dark clouds were forming in the west above the mountain ranges. Lightning was flashing between mountain peaks. He turned around on his daily jog, heading back to the old ranch house. There was smoke coming out of the chimney pipe on top of the roof. The smoke was going down. This meant that the storm would be that more intense. He would need to close all the shutters on the windows as soon as possible. First, he would need to see who came to visit him way out here. As he stepped up to the top of the porch that ran around the length of the house, he saw a woman cooking in the kitchen through the front window. His mother must be here. He was pleasantly surprised to see her.

Being as silent as possible, he approached the front door. His mother yelled at him to take off his running boots. He swore to himself. Even though he could sneak up on a wild dog in the Outback, he could never do that to his mother. She must have a sixth sense or something. By the door, there was a bucket of well-water, a rag, soap, a towel, and clean short pants. He stripped off his clothes and began cleaning up for breakfast.

He knew why his mother had only left him short pants and no shirt to wear. It was her way to see if he was staying in shape. She was very strict about that. She had always stayed in top physical condition. She was famous throughout the world as one of the best martial arts fighters. It didn't matter if you were a man or woman, she would beat you. She didn't just beat you. She would embarrass you. She had never been beaten in a martial arts match. There was only one time that she had fought to a draw. The referees stopped the match before they would have killed each other.

He had stepped into the kitchen after washing up. Two water buffalo steaks were cooking on the woodstove in a large cast iron frying pan. The aroma of the oriental seasonings and steak cooking filled the air. The aroma brought back memories of his childhood with his father and mother. It was a happy time for them. His mother turned around from the woodstove to face him. She was satisfied with what she had seen. Moses was in great shape. He had trimmed down to fighting weight. His shoulder muscles were big and tight. His dark chest had strong pectoral muscles. His stomach was more like a twelve pack instead of a six pact. His arms and legs were strong with large bulging muscles. "Well, I see you are trying to stay in shape Moses," she said.

That was about the best compliment he ever got from his mother. He smiled as he looked at his mother. She was in great shape. She was tall for a female with Chinese descent. Wearing only a tank top and shorts, he could tell that she was training for a match. She must have been training intensely to be in such physical condition.

She told him to sit down at the table and dished his meal up for him. Somehow, she could make him feel like a little boy. He asked her if she was going to have some more exhibition matches. She replied to him that she might need to because she had heard he had a girlfriend. She might need to fight her to see if his girlfriend is good enough for him. He told his mother that his girlfriend was an excellent martial arts fighter. She had better watch out. She is one of the best fighters he had ever seen.

"We will see about that!" his mother answered back to Moses.

"You are not serious about fighting her," Moses replied.

"What is your girlfriend's name?" asked his mother.

"Her name is Lo Ming Sing," answered Moses.

"I know her," said his mother.

Moses was taken aback by his mother's answer. How did she know anything about Lo Ming or even had ever met her? It hit Moses like a water buffalo. Lo Ming was a match fighter who gave exhibitions. He had dismissed the fact that Lo Ming could have been the fighter who his mother had not beaten. He thought Lo Ming just had the same name as the fighter his mother didn't beat.

"Yes, Moses. Your Lo Ming is the same fighter who I never beat. I have vowed to beat her. I will be going to San Francisco with you. I need to settle this match once and for all. We can't have your future wife being better than your mother."

"You can't be serious, mother. Your match with Lo Ming is the stuff of legends. It lasted over two hours. I even heard about it here in the Outback. I never saw it myself. They say that you two would have killed each other if they hadn't stopped the exhibition match. I can't have each of you fight each other. I could lose the two most important people in my life. I forbid it."

Moses' mother could not help but laugh at Moses. Her smile could calm the most savage beast. It took a few moments for Moses to realize that his mother was playing with him. She did have a good sense of humor. "I got the answer to my question of whether you love her or not. I am especially proud that you love me as much as her. Come over here and give your mother a big hug." Moses jumped up from his chair and did just that. He knew that his mother and Lo Ming would probably have that match sometime in the future. They were too proud not to want to know who is the best.

It was early afternoon when the storm hit. Moses had closed all the shutters in the front of the house. The wind was howling, and they could hear the rain hitting the roof. His mother had made some strong English tea. They sat in the kitchen, looking out the back windows. They watched the rain come down in torrents. The back windows were not facing the wind. His mother noticed that there was a red turquoise stone that was glowing by the kitchen sink. Moses had not noticed the glowing turquoise, but he did notice a frown forming on his mother's face. "What is bothering you?" he asked. His mother visually upset, could only point to the stone. "I know what that means," she replied.

Before he could say anything, his mother told him that only an old friend of hers ever used a red turquoise as a signal. "There is word in my mystic circles that my friend had formed another group to find a sacred object. I also heard that you were in that group. I know what was rumored is true. Many people have died looking for that sacred book. Now you know why I am here."

"Are you afraid that I might die looking for it?" Moses answered.

"Yes, I am. The word in my circles is that there are many groups wanting to stop you or get the book for themselves. Your odds are getting more insurmountable each day. It's bad that you have to contend with the Dark Ones, but I hear the other groups are just as bad," she spoke softly.

"How do you know so much?" he asked.

With tears flowing down her face, she answered, "Because the last time John tried to get the book, your father died. I thought that John had died as well, but the Elders must have saved him."

A window to Moses' mind opened before him. He remembered the last time he saw his father and mother leave this house together. He had been a little boy. He had not paid much attention to the man who had visited his parents on the porch the day before they had left. He could visualize the man more clearly now. His mind was replaying the memory like a film in slow motion. The man had ridden in on a white horse. He had on a cavalry hat with the number seven. The man was John.

Moses' face got red in anger. How could his mother have hidden such a fact from him? She had told him that his father had died in an accident. His mother had lied to him for so many years. Moses got up from his chair. He went into his bedroom and started packing. His mother yelled at him to forgive her. His answer back was that he would not deal with her or John until after the sacred book was found. That was only due to Lo Ming and the others needing his help. They were committed to the mission. After Moses had finished packing, he went into the kitchen to confront his mother. He found the kitchen door open to the outside. The storm was still raging. He yelled for his mother but got no answer. She was gone.

The sun in the west was setting by the time Nick's grandfather arrived in his old gray Jeep to pick him up. Nick had a worried look on his face. His grandfather asked him what had happened. Nick filled his grandfather in on the events of the last several days. They could not find any identification on the man who tried to kill Nick. His grandfather suggested to Nick that they bury the man in the graveyard by the deserted old mining town a few miles away.

After they got back to his grandfather's home, Nick stayed to himself. He didn't talk much to his grandmother. His grandmother could sense that Nick was upset about something he had done in the desert. One night, his grandmother decided to have a talk with him. She chose to sit on the back porch with him. She had told his grandfather that she would handle whatever was bothering Nick. Nick's grandfather agreed and went to bed early that night.

Nick was looking at the stars in the night's sky when his grandmother handed Nick something to drink. He asked what the drink was. She told him it was an ancient potion that makes it easier to discuss what was bothering him. At first, he didn't drink it. After his grandmother kept insisting, he finally gave in and drank it.

His grandmother was right. Nick's anxiety was giving way to a feeling of peace. His mind seemed to float into a sea of calm. His grandmother asked him what was troubling him so deeply. He explained that he had a girlfriend who was much older than he was. She was a gypsy and could see in her crystal ball what he was doing.

His grandmother asked him what he did that would make her upset at him. Nick explained what had happened in the desert with Shanna. He explained that he had once loved Shanna. He could feel that Rose knew what he had done. He couldn't face Rose. He would have to soon, because he was due back next week to continue his journey with her.

His grandmother looked at him and told him that he had to be truthful to Rose and tell her what had happened. After all, it was Rose who would have to choose her path. "Everyone has a first love. Are you sure that Rose does not have a first love? I saw it in the stars last night. You both have questions to be answered. You both will have to deal with your first love. It is written in the stars that love can triumph over anything. You can only wait and see what happens. Only the spirits know. Be patient, my grandson," she said. She felt that things will work out, but it will be difficult. Nick fell asleep. His grandmother covered him with one of her quilts. She smiled. She could feel the spirits talking to her.

The next morning Nick woke up. He went into the house. He was hungry and wanted some breakfast. He saw that they had packed his belongings. They were by the front door. Nick's grandfather told him that they knew that he must leave today. Nick asked how they knew. Nick's grandfather told him that the red turquoise stone was glowing. Nick started to say something, but his grandmother interrupted him. She told him that they had fixed breakfast and to sit down and eat it with them.

He was about to ask his Grandfather for a ride to town. His Grandfather knew what he was going to ask. His grandfather told him to take his old Indian Motorcycle to continue his journey. It would be a gift from them. As he was leaving, they both shouted, "May the spirits be with you."

The bright moonlight gave June enough light to make her way down the sacred mountain. She would sleep the night at the base of the mountain. She made a bed of soft green grass with a blanket over it. Looking at the sky, she watched the stars. Several meteors lit up the sky. The cold prairie wind was starting to blow. It would be a cold night. Her thoughts wandered to One Feather in The Land of the Eagle Feathers. It would have been nice to have him here to keep her warm. It won't be long until I see him again, she whispered to herself. Her eye caught the red turquoise stone glowing in her backpack. She smiled, "No, it won't be long before I feel his strong arms around me."

Everyone was going back to the train station at the foot of the mountains. They were thinking about what had happened to them during their time away from The Land of the Eagle Feathers. Did everyone have similar experiences? They would be curious to find out. One thing that they did know was these last few weeks had changed them. The reasons for starting the journey months before had changed. They had many different reasons for returning. For some, the reason was the find something or someone who had been missing in their lives. Others were to seek knowledge. Some had to deal with their past. Even revenge was a reason for one. For whatever reasons they had, they knew there was danger involved. They knew that many people were interested in The Land of the Eagle Feathers. They didn't care about that. They had personal reasons to return. It seemed that the destiny of The Land of the Eagle Feathers was intertwined with their own destiny. Whatever happens to The Land of the Eagle Feathers would affect them forever.

Chapter IX
Who Returns:
How Will We Know Who to Trust?

It was about midnight when the last of their group arrived at the old café at the base of the mountain. The old man with his hound dog was sitting in the chair on the front porch. He looked up and saw Nick. Nick was the last one to arrive. The old man told Nick that he was getting worried that Nick wasn't going to show as he spit his tobacco into the spittoon. Nick just smiled at the old man and petted his old hound dog. When he turned to go into the café, he swore that he could see a faint smile on the old man's face. There was a big table in the middle of the room full of food and drink. Nick threw his backpack on the floor close to a nearby table. "Was that you on the motorcycle?" asked Moses. Nick nodded yes as he grabbed a plate and filled it high with food. Everyone was busy eating. Nick noted that nobody was talking. It appeared that they were waiting for someone to break the silence.

The front door to the café opened. The old conductor dressed in his black uniform told everyone to get their luggage and gear. The train would be leaving shortly. It wasn't long before everyone was seated in the passenger car. Moses sat by Lo Ming with Nick and Rose across from them. June and Mary were seated with Antonio across from them. Antonio broke the silence.

"Mary, tell us what happened to you?" he asked her. Mary replied to him, "What do you mean?" "It doesn't take a genius to observe that you have been hurt in an accident or something. You are pale and walk with a slight limp," he answered her question. Before she could answer back, the train whistle blew. The old steam engine moved, shaking every car as it proceeded to start up the old tracks toward the Eagle Train Station. Nobody said anything for several minutes. They looked at each other. Rose knew that every one of them had a story to tell about what had happened to them this Spring. She had seen some of it in her crystal ball. She would let them decide if they would tell each other.

Lo Ming could sense that something was bothering Moses. He was staring into the passenger window. Finally, she said to the others that she had something to tell them. She told them about the men that tried to assassinate her. She told them that she did not kill them. She sent them back to tell whoever sent them that she wouldn't be so nice next time. Her revelations seemed to wake Moses out of his thoughts. Moses asked her why didn't she tell him about that? He decided to tell everyone what the group of murderers had tried to do to him.

Everyone decided to tell their stories about what happened to them since they last met. Rose smiled as each one told what had happened to them. She knew that many of them had left some things out of their narratives on purpose. Mary was one of the last to tell her story. She was the only one who almost died from her experience. After she told the story about Rose coming to Maine to heal her, the others knew instantly that Rose knew more than all of them together. They asked her why didn't she tell them about what she observed in her crystal ball? She answered because she couldn't interfere directly in events while they are happening; only afterwards when she used her crystal ball. She helped Mary only after her event happened. The rest of you did well by yourselves. We need everyone here to finish what we have started.

Antonio was uneasy about the revelation about Rose being able to spy on them. What if Rose knew about Angela or David? At first, he was worried, but then he relaxed. He had used some of his ancient knowledge to block anyone from using devices to spy on him. He knew Rose would recognize that something was preventing her from spying on him. Antonio decided to tell his story to them. He told them only about people trying to persuade him to stop looking for the book. He did tell the group that the people were from South America, and they were very powerful. They were very dangerous. He knew that because he had had a run in with them many years ago.

Everyone became silent. They knew that what they thought was going to be a difficult task of finding the books had become that much more dangerous. They had at least two groups trying to stop them and perhaps many more trying to find the books for themselves. Rose, being the oldest one of the group, told them that their first concern were the groups trying to stop them. The other groups, trying to get the remaining books for themselves, would not try to harm them until they got the most important book: ***The Book of Winter***. At that time, those groups would descend on them like locusts.

The old steam locomotive pulled into the train station. The white- haired conductor shouted for everyone to disembark from the train. He helped them get their gear on the platform. The conductor boarded the train. Before the old train pulled out, he looked at them as if this would be the last time seeing them. "It has been nice meeting you all. I hope to see you again. It would be sad if you end up like the others before you. Good luck, you will need it," he yelled as the train pulled out of the station.

June was the first to notice that something was wrong. Strong winds from the west were blowing dust and dirt into the air. There were no people in the street. The town looked completely deserted. The buildings were in disrepair like nobody had been here for years. The town looked like a ghost town in the American West. Doors and windows were missing or broken. Dust clouds were blowing down the streets. The only sound was the wind, blowing the doors open and shut. June sensed them before they came. She shouted for everyone to get down on the floor of the platform. As everyone fell or jumped flat on to the wooden platform floor, at least 20 arrows whistled by them, embedding themselves into the side of the old station. Nobody had to tell them what to do next. They picked up their belongings and ran into the old station.

They assembled in the station. June told them not to worry about being attacked. This was just a warning. Night Panther's people were giving them one last chance to back out. If they were to leave now, they could. If they go on with John, there would be no more warnings.

Antonio looked at the group around him. He told them it was one thing to fight groups who did not know this terrain. It is much more difficult to fight an enemy who has the advantage of the knowledge of the terrain and land. This is what makes Night Panther's people so dangerous.

Mary's face was red with anger. She told them that did not matter to her. They had tried to kill her. She had a reason to go on. She had a score to settle. This surprised the others. They had not ever seen this side of Mary before. Moses looked at everyone saying, "I have many reasons to go on, too. I know everyone here has their own reasons to finish this journey. Let's stop wasting time and get our gear on. John is waiting by the corral.

I was waiting by the corral for the group. They should have been here by now. I could sense Night Panther's people leaving the area. He wouldn't risk a fight in this old town. My group would have the advantage fighting here. The dust storm was getting worse by the minute. I could see only a few feet in front of me. A man dressed in black was standing a few feet away. I knew he was there. I was waiting for him to show. He had his hand up in a

228

sign that he wanted to talk. I would let him talk. Then I would decide if I would kill him. He had been one of my greatest enemies.

"I won't kill you, David, until you have your say," I shouted above the wind. David slowly walked closer until he was only a couple of feet away from me. "I have not come to fight, but to thank you," he said.
This caught me off-guard. I quickly replied, "Why?"

"I am surprised you don't know! You saved my daughter's life in Maine a few weeks ago. I never thought I would owe you anything. We have been fighting each other for more years than I care to count. It appears that there are many others who either want the books or want to stop us from getting them." David almost choked on every word

I knew about competing groups, but I was trying to sort out my thoughts about Mary. This couldn't have been the Mary who I knew. She had been the love of my life, but she was dead. She had died in childbirth.

"I know that you have trouble believing me. It is true. I tricked you into thinking that she was dead. I have used my powers to wipe her mind clean of you. I also used my powers to disguise her by changing her appearance. It was part of my plan to get the books. She doesn't remember anything about you. My second wife saw to that problem. If you tell Mary, the shock will kill her. You have your son to think about. Mary thinks he died in childbirth," David stated with a smile.

I started to reach for my knife. I could see Angela standing behind him with an old flint lock pistol in her hands aimed at my heart. I should have realized that David never went anywhere without his trusted bodyguard: Angela. Angela and I were once partners long ago before we became mortal enemies. It had something to do with

David's first wife. David was right. He was holding the high cards. Everything was changing before my eyes.

I had some cards to play myself. Shanna walked out from some trees behind me. "Now, I know why you wanted me here," she said. She had my Hawken rifle pointed at Angela. David smiled. He knew that we were in a standoff. He had underestimated his enemy. "So, what do you suggest?" I answered his question, "If everything you say is true, then we will need each other. You cannot get the books without us. I suggest that we have a truce for now. There are too many people or spirits trying to stop my group from getting the books. It is difficult to say this, but we need each other. I need your assistance in fighting the groups trying to stop me, and you need me to obtain the books. After I obtain the last most powerful book, it's every man for himself," I stated back to him.

David smiled back at me saying, "It will be a pleasure killing you a second time. The Elders can't bring you back again. I am as shocked as you are now knowing that Mary is still alive when I found out you were alive. You are a hard man to kill, John. To be sure that we don't go back on our word, you know what we must do?" I agreed with him. Afterwards, David and Angela moved back into the dust storm and disappeared.

The wind was dying down. The dust was settling to the ground as Antonio and the others emerged from the old train station. They changed into their traveling clothes. Carrying their weapons and gear, they started toward the corral. Sitting in front of the old delivery stables was the old man and his dog. The old man motioned for them to come into the stable. They stepped into the old delivery stables finding that their horses had been saddled. It was daybreak.

Their supplies for the journey back to The Land of the Eagle Feathers were already packed in the boxes to be put on the mules. Moses and Nick picked up the boxes with the supplies and put them on the mules, along with the gear that they had brought. The old man told them to keep their weapons with them. They might need them. The old man walked out of the stable's door with his old hound dog following him. Lo Ming wanted to ask the old man a question. She went outside to talk to him. When she got outside into the bright morning sunlight, the old man and his dog were nowhere to be found.

Moses asked Lo Ming to get her horse. When she came back inside the stable, Moses asked her what she said to the old man. Lo Ming said that he had just vanished with his dog. He wasn't there. The others noted what she said but gathered their horses. Moses and Nick took charge of the mules with their horses. Everyone walked their horses to the corral. They saw John under the old oak tree on a tree stump waiting for them to arrive. They were all surprised to see a young woman sitting by John.

I looked up to see them coming down toward me with their horses and gear. Morning Star had just arrived before them with breakfast. I introduced Shanna to the group as a friend who was coming with us. On an old wooden table, Morning Star had placed warm food for everyone to eat. I told them to eat up. There would be some special quests arriving soon. I thought that Nick was going to choke on his food when Shanna sat down beside him and Rose. I could tell that Rose was not happy that Shanna was here.

The bright morning light was starting to fade away. Dark clouds were covering the blue sky. Some flashes of lightning jumped from cloud to cloud without hitting the ground. The sound of thunder could be heard in the distance. Everyone had finished their breakfast. They sat on the ground in a semi-circle talking. The horses and mules were tied to the corral fence. Something was making them nervous.

A bright flash of lightning blinded everyone for a moment. As our eyes started to focus, we could see the Elders of The Land of the Eagle Feathers before us. They were standing several yards in front of us. In one motion, they sat down on the ground cross legged. Only the oldest Elder remained standing. The Elders are only allowed out of The Land of Eagle the Feathers once a year. This day was the day. That is why they chose to come. It was the day of the solar eclipse. It was the only day that The Elders could leave The Land of the Eagle Feathers.

The Elder started addressing the group. "I, being the Grand Elder, am here today to honor you. The other Elders and the Red Woman are witnesses to this ceremony. We have observed your trials and actions. You have proven yourselves to be great warriors.

Warriors must possess several traits. The first is to be brave; to face impossible odds and to fight for others, whether you can be victorious or not. You know that you face many forces greater than anything you have seen before. You know your chances of survival are not good, but you came anyway.

The second trait is sacrifice. All of you could have remained home, but you didn't. You came back, not out of selfishness, but out of something greater. You may not have realized it. Your hearts have changed. You are beginning to see that you must sacrifice for others to find your true soul. You will have many sacrifices in the journeys that lay in front of you. We see what many of you do not.

The third trait is that a warrior must protect all the members of their tribe. It does not matter how they personally feel about the individual members of their tribe.

You have proven that you care for each other. Each of you has risked your life for other members of your group.

The fourth trait is that a warrior must respect each other's beliefs. Each of you has your own religion and beliefs, but you do not question or disrespect those who don't have the same as yours.

The fifth trait is that warriors recognize that there are forces greater than themselves. Your experiences in The Land of the Eagle Feather have shown you that. To overcome those powerful forces, you have learned to work together. A warrior is much more powerful with other warriors. A warrior needs the power of the whole tribe to confront those forces.

You are not perfect. Mankind is not perfect. Many of you have demons inside. Warriors are not perfect. They rise and fall throughout their lives. It is like the flight of the Eagle into the sky above as it rises from the earth filled with the lowest of mankind to the heavens with the great spirits.

The Land of the Eagle Feathers is in danger of vanishing. We are observing the slow decline in our land and spirit. Some of our tribe disagree with our decision to find the books. Night Panther and his followers are now able to move in and out of our land without any difficulty. We cannot stop them. That makes your quest more difficult. They feel that the power the books contain will corrupt our ways. We disagree with them. The only way to save this land from the evil forces that wish to possess it is to obtain the sacred forces of the universe. We did not make this decision lightly.

Many warriors have tried to find the books to obtain *The Book of Winter*, but they have failed. You are our last chance. You are not perfect. That is why we feel that you can succeed. Not being perfect is what will make you succeed where others have failed. You bring knowledge from every part of the world. Only by working together will you succeed.

The Old Elder sat down. The Red Woman rose to speak. "We, the Elders of The Land of the Eagle Feathers have observed you. We find that you possess what many others did not. Our servant, John, has finally found what we could not. He has brought before us a group of humans who possess what is needed. We have seen it in the stars. It is written there for all to see. We do what is written in the times of legends long ago. Your group will be forever called: **The Keepers of the Yawi.** The spirits have spoken to us. The rest of the story has not been written. It will be written in your deeds. You have the fate of The Land of the Eagle Feathers and the universe in your hands."

The Red Woman waved her hand. Each member of the group felt a burning on the outside of their hand. A tattoo appeared. The tattoo was an eagle feather. "This Eagle Feather tattoo is the symbol that you are one of **The Keepers of the Yawi**. May the great spirits be with you."

As she finished, a flash of lightning blinded us followed by darkness. The sun was covered with a dark cloud. There was complete silence. Everyone held their breath. They could feel an evil presence near. A cold wind started to blow the darkness away.

Two dark, cloud like figures appeared before everyone. A force seemed to hold everyone. The two figures floated above, about ten feet in the air. Each figure had red eyes. They moved toward John. Picking him up, they laughed at the Elders and Red Woman. One of them said, "We have been watching you. Without John, you will never obtain ***The Book of Winter***. It is only a matter of time before we control everything." The creatures took John with them and vanished into the forest.

The Red Woman stood before everyone. "This is what we feared. We have no name for those things. To give them a name is to give them more power. We call them the creatures without names: The Unspeakables. They are one of the reasons you must get the book. I agree with them. We need John."

"I can get him back," said a voice behind the horses by the corral. A man walked from behind the horses. He was dressed in a black suit. A woman dressed in black leather was standing by him. The Red Woman stared at him. "I am the only one who can because I possess forces that can match theirs. I have one trait that you don't have." Before he could finish, the Red Woman interrupted him and finished the sentence, "You are evil enough to match them."

Mary was startled to see her father standing there before them. How did the Red Woman know him? Mary stood up and said, "How do you know him?"

The Red Woman looked at Mary as only a mother does when she is trying not to hurt her child. "He is the leader of the Dark Ones. He has been trying to conquer The Land of the Eagle Feathers for many years. David is very powerful. I know him very well. He cannot be trusted, but it takes evil to fight evil."

David looked at the Red Woman. "Tell her the truth. Tell her why you know me," he demanded. Antonio was puzzled. All this time, he had thought that David didn't know about his part in the group. For David to come out and blow his cover, there had to be a major reason for him to be here. As David and the woman in black came close, Antonio turned pale. The woman beside David was Angela. Antonio was upset. Did David know about Angela and his plans? Was Angela playing him or David? What he did sense was that he was in great danger. He would have to play David and Angela to survive this. That didn't matter for now, Antonio couldn't wait to hear what the Red Woman would answer.

The Red Woman looked at the Great Elder before answering David. The Elder nodded for her to answer David. "Mary and your group should know the truth. I am sorry that you must learn this from me. I am your mother. I will tell you the rest of the story later. At this time, I can only tell you that we need to have David's help."

David demanded again, "Tell her the rest. Tell her about her child, our grandson." The Red Woman looked directly at Mary. "You have a child. He is with me. I raised him. David did not let you know that he is alive. I protected him from David. His father thought you were dead. Until John brought you here, I thought so too. I was able to see through the spell that David had put on you. One day, I was going to tell you, but the risk was too great. I know that David has too much to lose if something happens to The Land of the Eagle Feathers. Remember, he is evil. He wants only one thing: power."

Mary couldn't believe what she was hearing. Everyone was in shock. Their only thoughts were about what just happened.

David broke the silence. "I don't care about all this. I want to get the books. I want the power the books contain. You need to get the books for yourselves to stop me. Without John, nobody will get the books. I am the only one capable of getting John back. You have no choice but to let me lead your Keepers of the Yawi to get John. You see, John and I made a pact to work together to obtain the books. I didn't know that he would trick me into saving him and the books. I signed a pact in blood to work with him until we obtain all the books. I have no choice but to honor it. John must have known that this might happen."

Rose smiled to herself. She had told John that he was in danger. She had seen it in her crystal ball. Rose knew more than any one of them. They didn't know about Rose's past.

Before the Red Woman could speak, the Great Elder arose saying, "It is written that a man in black will save the leader of The Keepers of the Yawi. What you say is true. It is up to The Keepers of the Yawi to follow you until you recover John."

The Great Elder said, "Every one of you is linked to The Land of the Eagle Feathers in some way. That is why John chose you. Your destiny was determined long ago. John knew this. He kept many things from you. In the days ahead, you will find out for yourselves why each of you were chosen. He was wise to gather you together. All of you must make that choice for yourselves. We are finished here." The Council faded before their eyes and vanished.

Everyone looked at each other. They were confused and unsure about the events that took place. Moses looked at David. Moses didn't like what he saw. Why should they entrust their lives to an enemy? Mary was not the person they thought she was. Was Mary working for her father to obtain the Books? Was Mary an innocent person who her father was using? Lo Ming was thinking the same things. Lo Ming never totally trusted Mary. She could sense that Mary was hiding something. If Mary was working for her father, was she playing them all along?

Rose looked at David. She told him that they needed to discuss whether they should follow him. Rose could feel that the group was starting to unravel. She knew more about this than anyone did. Her mother and father had told her before she began this journey that she would become part of a group of people who could save The Land of the Eagle Feathers and maybe the world from evil forces. They told her that Rose must keep the group together. This group would be called **The Keepers of the Yawi.** They would be the only ones who could deal with the many forces who were wanting to obtain the Books or keep them from the Books.

Rose's mother was a powerful Voodoo Priestess, and her father was a powerful Wizard. They had told her she was special. Her mother told her that they knew the day she was born that she had a quest or mission to fulfill. Her mother knew about such things.

After David and Angela left to go back to the station house, the group started their meeting. It was unusual for Nick to say much, but he was the first to speak.

"It appears that we have a bigger problem than we thought. None of us are what we have presented to each other. We all have secrets that we have kept from one another for many reasons. We have different reasons for being here. We have a tough decision to make. Do we stay together? Can we work together and trust each other to have our backs? I was in the Army. If we cannot trust each other, we will surely die. If we do trust each other, we have a chance to save John and The Land of the Eagle Feathers and perhaps the world from evil."

June spoke from her heart, "I know that we have a bond. We have fought together. We have saved each other when danger was near. We have chosen to be together and not run away from our past. I don't care who or why everyone is here. We are not perfect. I do know one thing. John would have given his life for any one of us. We, as warriors, must honor him and go after him. He is a true warrior. We are true warriors. That is sacred to my tribe. I know it is sacred to yours."

Antonio looked at the group. He could only tell them that what June said was true. He would have to go. John gave him life. He is John's blood brother because John gave him his blood to save him. He told them that he didn't care what they did. He had no choice.

Lo Ming agreed with June. Being a warrior, she must honor the traditions of her ancestors. She would go. To do anything else would be a disgrace. Moses agreed with her. These were the same traditions of his tribe as well.

Everyone looked at Mary. She had a very confused look on her face. She knew that the people before her had many reasons not to trust her. Carefully, she chose her words. "I know that I am probably the one person who you have the most reasons to not trust. Like you, I did not know about some of the things said today. Yes, I hid many things from you. I was working for my father, but I did not know that he was the leader of The Dark Ones. I only thought my father was a ruthless man who wanted power. I did not know that The Red Woman was my mother. I can only say that I have more reasons to continue this journey than most of you. There is one thing more that makes me want to go. I have a son who I have never seen. I was saved by John in Maine. Rose told me. I owe him just like you. I also need to find out who I really am. I am going. I don't trust my father. He is a very hard man. He is ruthless. He will be very difficult to follow, but he has a blood contract. He will follow that contract. When it ends, he will be very dangerous. We must all remember that."

Rose chose her words carefully, "I know more than anyone of the importance of us staying together. If anyone of our group is killed or quits, we will die. It is as simple as that. My parents told me that we must be united. My job is to keep us together. I warn every one of you that I will do whatever is needed to do that. We have a sacred mission to fulfill. I intend to do just that or die trying. I think that it is settled. It is written in the stars. We are **The Keepers of the Yawi**."

June offered some of her tribe's wisdom. She knew that everyone was worried about following David. She told them a Native Indian legend about birds. She was told this by a wise medicine man. She said, "It is said that each bird has two wings. Without having two wings, it cannot fly. The two wings are opposites. By working together, the wings make it possible for the bird to fly. The bird can only complete its journey by the wings working together. Even though we are the opposite of David, we need David to reach the end of our journey. We will have to put aside our differences. We need him. He will be the other wing to ours. It has been said that we must remember that the right wing and left wing belong to the same bird. Without David, we are like a bird with a broken wing that cannot fly."

The old man and his dog watched as **The Keepers of the Yawi** led by David with Angela by his side started up the trail toward The Land of the Eagle Feathers. He knew that the group had no choice but to follow a man who they couldn't trust. They had to be very apprehensive about following him. They wouldn't know where to start to find John. They had no choice because David did.

The old man looked at his old hound dog and said, "I wish them luck. They will need it to survive with so many against them. I can't wait to see what happens with Shanna and Angela going with them." The old hound dog barked. "Yes, I know that we might have to help them. I am surprised about Angela being here. David must not know who Angela's father is," he replied to the dog.

The old man smiled. He knew that it was written in the stars. Their journeys had just begun. There were three more books to obtain. Each book will give clues where to find the next book. Each book was one more season: *The Book of Summer, The Book of Fall,* and finally*, The Book of Winter.* Years from now, people would sit by the campfires and tell the legends about The Keepers of the Yawi. Each legend will be greater than the last. The Keepers of the Yawi had finished their first journey. The last sunset of spring had come and gone. They were riding into the sunrise to begin their next journey. The old man decided to write their first journey down for future generations. He would call it: ***The Land of the Eagle Feathers: The Book of Spring.***

As the sun rose and The Keepers of the Yawi disappeared into the forest, they were beginning their next journey. He hoped that he would be able to write about the next one. ***The Land of the Eagle Feathers: The Book of Summer***. Only time would tell if that story would be told. The sunrise was bright red. He knew what that meant. It wasn't a good sign. He told his old dog that they had better get their supplies and his horses.

The old man got up from his rocking chair on the porch of the train station. His old dog barked at him. He laughed at his old friend. He lifted his arms and pointed at the doors to the stable. The old stable doors slowly opened. Out of the stable came a beautiful black stallion with a silver trimmed saddle. Following him were two pack mules loaded with supplies. The old dog grinned back at the old man. The old man reached down and petted his dog. "We know about the group in front of us. They just think we are two old characters. Won't they be surprised when they find out who we really are?

About the Authors:

Joe G. Morin was born and raised on a small rural farm. He currently lives in East Tennessee where he taught Adult Education for several years. His ancestors came from Tennessee, Kentucky, and Virginia. His current publications on Amazon.com are *Why Men Have Problems with Women and An Angel in the Kitchen.* He loves to tell stories. He is from a family of story tellers. He would listen to his Grandfather tell his stories about being a rural schoolteacher and farmer for hours. You may contact him at joegmorin@gmail.com

Jo Ann Bullard was born in East Tennessee. Having been a professional entertainer, she traveled all over the world. There is no place like East Tennessee. She lives and writes in the foothills of the Smoky Mountains. Her ancestors were Cherokee, Blackfoot and Scotch-Irish. Her current publications on Amazon.com are *The Problems with Men, and Angel in the Kitchen.* She has written several articles for professional publications. She is currently working on a volume of song lyrics. You may visit her at ja2bullard@gmail.com

Book Cover designed by Dar Albert of Wicked Smart Designs.

www.ingramcontent.com/pod-product-compliance
Lightning Source LLC
Chambersburg PA
CBHW070604130626
46556CB00001B/266